VOW OF DECEPTION

MINISTRY OF CURIOSITIES, BOOK #9

C.J. ARCHER

C.J. ARCHER

CHAPTER 1

HERTFORDSHIRE, SUMMER 1890

rakingham House could have stepped out of a Gothic novel with its arched windows, abundance of turrets, and a vine creeping up one of the stone walls. If it weren't for the lake sparkling in the sunshine, and the lush green lawn, it would have looked grim. The house reminded me of Lichfield Towers but on a much larger scale.

"So this is Freak House," Gus said, tipping his head back to squint up at the gabled roof.

"Don't call it that to Mr. Langley's face," I warned, fixing a smile in place for the benefit of the approaching footmen. "We don't want to upset our host."

Seth held out his hand to assist Alice from the hack that had driven us from the station. "Not before we get information, anyway."

"Seth!" I hissed.

He merely shrugged and turned a beaming smile upon Alice. She was too busy blinking owlishly at the handsome couple framed by the arch of the massive doorway to notice. The gentleman's dark good looks and impressive height certainly drew my gaze at first, but it was the woman's abundance of curly red hair that demanded more attention. That and her lovely blue eyes. They brightened when she smiled. So this was Mr. and Mrs. Langley, the couple Lincoln had met in Paris before he met me. Apparently Jack Langley was a fire starter and knew about demons and portals that led to other realms. Indeed, a portal was said to exist on the Frakingham grounds.

"Welcome to Freak House," Hannah Langley said, taking her husband's arm.

Gus tossed a smug look my way.

Lincoln shook Mr. Langley's hand and bowed before Mrs. Langley. We exchanged introductions and insisted on calling one another by first names. It wasn't at all what I expected from the residents of such a grand country manor. Although I hadn't truly known what to expect. Lincoln had met most of my questions about the character of the Langleys with blank looks. He'd merely noted that Jack Langley had an investigative mind but could be overprotective of his wife. And apparently Hannah Langley had a courageous streak. Lincoln wasn't one for noticing whether a person was easy to talk to, kind, or amusing.

"We don't stand on formality here," Hannah said as we headed inside. Her husband walked alongside her, his hand on her lower back.

"Nor do we at Lichfield Towers," Seth said. "We all prefer it that way. Except for my mother. If it were up to her, I'd be head of the household and everyone else would be at my beck and call."

"Actually Lady Vickers would prefer it if *she* were head of the household," Lincoln said with a straight face. I knew he was joking, of course, and Seth and Gus seemed to know it too, but Alice and the Langleys gave tight smiles. Lincoln really ought to learn to laugh or wink when he made a joke.

"You mean she's not?" I said. "Someone really should inform her."

Hannah laughed, turning her eyes even bluer. "The footmen will take your luggage up to your rooms. Would you like some time to yourselves before we take tea in the drawing room?"

"No," Alice said at the same time that I said, "Yes, thank you."

She and I exchanged glances. "Just a few minutes," I assured her.

She was eager to learn as much as she could about herself from the Langleys. I hoped they had something to tell her. Alice had been restless of late. While usually composed and poised, I often found her at the piano giving the poor keys a pounding. She'd jumped at the offer to meet the Langleys after Lincoln received Jack's invitation last week. Two months ago, Jack had refused. I wondered why he'd changed his mind.

"May I show you to your room, ladies?" Hannah said, indicating the stairs.

We headed up the stone staircase, our footsteps deadened by the red carpet. The landing spread both left and right before more stairs ascended up and up. It would have been a cold entrance to the house if not for the summer sun streaming through the arched windows reaching high up the wall.

The men went one way, led by a footman, and we went the other with Hannah. Jack remained downstairs, talking quietly to the butler.

"I'm so glad you could come," Hannah said, lifting her skirts just enough so she didn't trip on them. Her gown was a lovely forest green and cream that complemented her hair and showed off her neat figure. "I think we can learn a lot from one another."

"What changed Mr. Langley's mind?" I asked. "I mean, he wasn't all that keen to meet us. Lincoln gave up requesting an audience some time ago."

"*I* happened."

"I don't understand," Alice said.

"Jack's worried that talking about the supernatural with people we don't know will invite danger to Frakingham. We've had quite our fair share of supernatural problems and we don't wish for any more, and we have a baby to protect now. But I knew Mr. Fitzroy—Lincoln—could be trusted when we met him in Paris. I convinced Jack to change his mind." Hannah smirked. "Sometimes husbands need to be reminded that their wives are not always delicate flowers. We don't all faint at the sight of paranormal activity."

"Quite true," I said. "Although I think Lincoln knows that about me. Seth, on the other hand…"

Alice stiffened. "Why are you looking at me, Charlie?"

"I…er…no reason."

We arrived at the room Alice and I were to share for the night. Hannah made sure the maids had set it up and the footmen had deposited our luggage before leaving us to change out of our traveling clothes into something prettier. Hannah had offered the use of a maid, since we'd not brought one, but we declined.

"What do you think of this house?" I asked Alice as I removed my jacket.

"It's quite forbidding on the outside, but I like it." She unpinned her hat and carefully placed the pin on the dressing table. "The abbey ruins down by the lake give it quite a spine-tingling feel, though."

"I thought the ruins added to the charm. Imagine being here in the midst of a storm with lightning cracking over the roof and black clouds closing in. What a commanding sight that must be. I can see why the locals call it Freak House." At her silence, I glanced up from my cuff buttons to see her staring at me.

"You have an appreciation for the dramatic," she said.

"It must be because I raise the dead. Although this place does tend to make one think of dark, stormy nights."

"And Lichfield doesn't?"

"Of course not. Lichfield is quite homely if one doesn't venture down into the dungeon."

She laughed. "Or the tower prison."

"It's not a prison anymore," I shot back. "Not until we capture something or someone worth imprisoning, that is. Now, stop disparaging my home and help me with this gown. It does up at the back."

Alice's cool, nimble fingers quickly had me out of the bodice. I put on my pale blue dress with the white trim and waist sash. Alice changed into a yellow gown embroidered with orange flowers. It was quite the thing this summer according to the latest edition of *The Young Ladies Journal*. Alice had brought it to Hertfordshire with her, after having it made last year before being sent to the School for Wayward Girls in Yorkshire. She was always ahead when it came to fashion. I, however, didn't care a whit for it. Sometimes I dreamed of leaving the house dressed in my training outfit of loose trousers and man's shirt. The sensation I would create was as much of a lure as the comfort.

We finished dressing and tugged on the bell pull. A moment later, a maid arrived to escort us to the drawing room. We passed through a maze of rooms and traversed staircases and galleries lined with gilt-framed paintings. I half expected the eyes of the men and women depicted in the gloomy portraits to follow me.

A flash of movement up the stairwell had me pausing mid-step. I caught sight of a very tall man with dark hair receding into a widow's peak. From his deathly pale face, I'd say he was a ghost that hadn't yet crossed to his afterlife, but the figure was gone from sight before I could get a proper look. Alice did not react.

The maid directed us into the drawing room, a large airy space filled with sturdy furniture and thick brocade curtains. Delicate china had been set out along with sandwiches and cake. The others stood upon our entry, and Hannah welcomed us. Jack asked the maid to leave and shut the door behind her. Alice twitched at the click of the latch.

Seth took her hand and directed her to sit with him on the sofa. He smiled gently and spoke quietly to her, as one would an elderly aunt. She nodded at whatever he said and seemed to buck up, although her fingers wouldn't stay still in her lap.

I sat on one of the other sofas and Lincoln joined me. "Have you noticed any hidden passages from your room?" he whispered.

I stared at him. "Honestly, Lincoln, only you would ask a question like that. No, I haven't found one."

"But you'll look?"

"Why? Planning to visit my room tonight and ravish me?"

"Only you would ask a question like that," he quipped.

I smiled and he smiled back—sort of. "You'd better behave yourself or the resident ghost might report you to the master of the house," I said.

"Ghost?" Gus echoed, proving we weren't being as quiet as we thought.

"What ghost?" Jack asked.

Hannah paused in pouring the tea and glanced at Gus. "There are no ghosts here. Cara and Emily have assured us."

"Mediums?" Lincoln asked.

Hannah nodded and continued pouring the tea. "And good friends, although we don't see them as often as we'd like. They live in London. Jack?"

She didn't have to say anything further. Jack seemed to know that she wanted him to hand out the teacups.

"Who thinks they saw a ghost?" he asked Gus.

Gus took great interest in the Oriental decorations on his teacup. "I must have misheard."

"I did," I piped up.

I felt rather than heard Lincoln groan beside me.

"You're a medium?" Hannah asked. Apparently mediums were so common to her that it didn't even warrant a glance in my direction.

"I'm a necromancer."

That got more of a reaction. She set down the teapot and studied me intently. Her husband handed me a cup and saucer but did not let it go immediately as he too eyed me.

Seth gave a slight shake of his head, warning me not to say too much. But Lincoln said nothing. He was leaving it up to me to tell the Langleys whatever I wanted about myself. I wondered what self-control it cost him to remain quiet.

"It's all right," I said. "I promise not to raise any bodies while I'm here."

Jack released the saucer. "We appreciate it."

"Anyway, it may not have been a ghost." I described the man I'd seen on the stairs.

"That's Mr. Bollard, Jack's uncle's friend," Hannah said. "He can seem rather ghostly at first but he's quite the gentle giant. And alive."

"Will we meet Mr. Langley, your uncle?" Lincoln asked.

"I doubt it," Jack said, taking a seat near his wife. "He doesn't like visitors."

"I hear he's brilliant. I'd like to discuss his pathology research."

"It's complicated, and he doesn't like explaining his theories and experiments to laymen. I'm sorry, but that's just the way he is."

I spoke up before Lincoln said something cutting. "He wouldn't have to explain much to Lincoln. He was tutored by a physician when he was younger and has quite a thorough knowledge of all medical and scientific things."

"That may be so," Jack said. "But my uncle prefers not to meet strangers. He has a low tolerance for people he doesn't know well. I hope you understand."

"Oh, I do," I muttered, keeping my gaze averted from Lincoln.

Alice cleared her throat and dropped her teacup heavily onto the saucer. "To the matter at hand," she began crisply. "Tell us what you know about portals, Jack. Lincoln says you have one here that leads to the demon realm."

"Perhaps we should discuss that after tea," Seth said quickly. "We ought to get to know one another first."

Alice didn't seem to care about manners or the proper order of things. It was most unlike her. But I did understand. We'd come all this way to Hertfordshire so she could learn more about herself. Idle chit chat didn't interest her. I knew it didn't interest Lincoln either.

"It's all right," Hannah said, passing the plate of cakes to me. "We don't mind discussing it now. The only problem is, where to start?"

"Start with the portal," Lincoln said. "Where is it?"

"Down by the abbey ruins." Jack told us about the ancient abbey that had once stood on the site. The abbots had been guardians of the portal and of the book of spells in their possession. When the abbey was destroyed, only one page was saved—the page that told how to open and close the portal.

"What's beyond the portal?" Seth asked.

"Wonderland," Alice murmured.

Everyone looked at her. "What is Wonderland?" Hannah asked.

Alice shook her head. "It's a place. I...I'm not entirely sure where."

"Another realm?" Jack asked. But Alice had no answer for him. "It's likely," he went on. "There are many realms, apparently, although I suspect the shape shifting one is closest, as they appear to be the most common supernaturals here. The portal is our doorway to those realms."

"May we see the portal?" Gus asked.

"There's nothing to see," Jack said. "It looks quite normal until it's opened. And no, I won't open it for you."

"Where's the page with the spell kept?" Lincoln asked.

"Somewhere no one can find it. We're the guardians now, along with our friends."

"Is it wise for others to know about it?"

"I trust them," Jack said icily.

Lincoln's eyes narrowed ever so slightly. "You can trust me, too."

"Not yet."

"Tell us about the ministry," Hannah cut in before an argument erupted. "It's a secret organization, is it not?"

"Not all that secret," Gus said. "You'd be surprised how many know about us."

Seth told them about the ministry's function and some of the supernatural problems we'd faced in recent times. He told them about the records of supernatural bloodlines that we kept and how the committee had acted as guardians through the centuries when the ministry lay dormant.

"So you have people you trust too," Jack said to Lincoln.

"I only trust Charlie," Lincoln said flatly.

"And us." Seth waited for Lincoln to agree. When he didn't, he added, "He does trust Gus and me, he just doesn't like admitting it. He considers it a weakness."

Lincoln shot him a flinty glare. "Have you traveled to any of the realms through the portal, Langley?"

Jack nodded. "Just one. It was much like our world. A friend of ours is somewhat more knowledgeable about other realms than we are, however."

"Why?"

"You'd have to ask him that."

"He's not here," Lincoln said. "I'm asking you."

"His story is not ours to tell," Hannah said, handing a plate to Lincoln. "Cake?"

He took the plate but did not eat the cake. Perhaps I could sneak it onto my plate and no one would notice.

Jack set down his plate, his slice of cake also going uneaten. What was wrong with these men? The cake was delicious. "Your letter mentioned that you think Alice might be a portal," he said to Lincoln. "How can that be? She's a person."

"A seer called her a door to other realms," Lincoln said.

I expected Seth to clarify that the seer had been Lincoln's own mother, but he did not. It was just as well. I doubted Lincoln wanted the Langleys to know he was also a seer, although a less powerful one than Leisl.

"Alice has dreams that sometimes become real," Lincoln went on.

"When I'm upset or frustrated, mostly," Alice added.

"Become real?" Jack hedged. "In what sense?"

"In the sense that the objects and beings from her dreams exist outside of her dreams," Lincoln said. "They have physical form. They can touch and be touched. They are, in every essence, present in our time and space."

"Remarkable," Hannah said on breath.

"We suspect the dreams are a conduit between this realm and another, and Alice is the portal."

"What form do the beings take?" Hannah asked. "What do they do and say? Do they remain here or return?"

"So many questions!" Alice attempted a smile but it

quickly faded. She set down her cake too and clasped her hands in her lap. The knuckles turned white. "To answer your first question, they take the form of humans, mostly, but I've also seen a talking rabbit."

"He wore a waistcoat," Gus added. "And trousers."

Seth glared at him and shook his head in discouragement. Gus stuffed the rest of his cake in his mouth and glared back.

"They speak English," Alice went on. She looked to me and I encouraged her with a nod. "They seem to want me to return with them to a place called Wonderland, to answer charges of treason. The Queen of Hearts rules there and sent her subjects to fetch me. They have not remained here, as yet. It used to be that when I awoke from my dream, all characters from it would disappear."

Gus clicked his fingers. "Just like that. Into thin air."

"But the last time the rabbit came, he did not disappear when I woke up. He remained until he spoke a spell. Before he disappeared, he seemed quite surprised and pleased that he was still in my bedroom after I awoke."

"As if he'd spoken a spell to remain but hadn't been sure it would work," Lincoln added.

Jack and Hannah exchanged a glance.

"You have something to say?" Lincoln asked.

"We're wondering if the spell is the same one that opens the portal at the abbey," Jack said.

"Show it to us and we'll compare."

"The answer is still no, Fitzroy."

"Did the rabbit change into a human?" Hannah asked.

Alice shook her head. "It remained a rabbit."

"But you've encountered some shape shifting demons, yes?"

"Too bloody many," Gus muttered. "I've got the scars to prove it."

"So I see." Hannah indicated the ragged scar that marred Gus's cheek and pulled at the corner of his eye.

"Ah, not that one. That's an old one. There's a good story behind it but it ain't for the ears of ladies."

"Now I am intrigued."

Seth rolled his eyes. "He got in a tavern brawl. There's nothing more to it than that."

"A brawl that *you* started," Gus shot back.

Seth cast a sideways glance at Alice and swallowed heavily. He didn't like Alice knowing much about his past. I thought it a shame that he felt he needed to hide it from her. His past was a part of him; it helped shape the man he'd become. If he wanted Alice to be permanently in his life, she should know all there was to know about him, even the horrid or shameful parts. I only hoped he told her before she found out through other means.

"We know some shape shifters who can shift between human and wolf-like creatures," I said. "Another could change to look like anyone or anything but he's dead now."

"Those are the rarest kind and pose the greatest threat," Jack said, nodding. "Have your shape shifters caused problems?"

"Some," Lincoln said but did not elaborate. "They're under control and being monitored."

"By you?"

"And others."

"You have spies?"

Lincoln didn't answer. From his small smile, I don't think Jack expected to get one.

"They're not all dangerous," I said. "One is even our friend, married to a committee member." Who was decidedly not our friend, but I didn't add that. "Those who have caused us problems in the past know they're being monitored and if they put a foot wrong, we'll see that justice is served."

The truce between Sir Ignatius Swinburn's pack and the ministry was uneasy at best but it had held so far. We promised to leave him and his pack alone to roam as long as they harmed no one. There'd been no more mauled bodies since poor Roderick Protheroe had been found dead in Hyde Park in the spring. Swinburn had also vowed not to pursue his ambitious plan to mix shifter blood with royal blood through marriage. Two months later, I felt somewhat optimistic that he'd given up on his scheming.

"What precisely *are* demons?" Seth asked. "Can they all change shape?"

"No." Jack clicked his fingers and fire danced on his palm. A swirl of his hand made the flames disappear.

Alice gasped. "Did it leave a mark?"

He showed us his hand. It wasn't even red. "It doesn't hurt."

"Jack is a demon, although I don't particularly like that word," Hannah said with a twist of her mouth. "He can't shift shape. The fire is his only supernatural trick."

"Only?" her husband teased. "How many more would you like?"

"One is quite enough, thank you."

"And your baby son?" Lincoln asked. "Can he make fire too?"

"Clearly you know nothing about babies," Jack said. "He has only just learned to crawl."

"Let me know if he develops the trait."

Jack bristled. "Why?"

"So I can add him to the ministry files."

"You will *not* put my son into your records."

"I will if he exhibits fire-making skill. You have your own file."

"It's all right, Jack," Hannah said. "We discussed this." To Lincoln, she added, "We agree, but you must promise to keep his file under lock and key. No one outside the ministry must be allowed to see it."

"That is already so with all the records," Lincoln said. "Not even the committee members see them."

We talked them into showing us the abbey ruins and headed down there after finishing our tea. Jack carried their baby, relieving the nanny of her duties for the rest of the afternoon. The sun hung lower in the sky but the warmth of the day lingered on, and I was hot by the time we reached the lake and ruins.

"It's so atmospheric," I said, taking in the view. Most of the stones lay scattered in the thick grass where they'd fallen centuries ago, but some remained in position and formed the floor and base of the abbey walls. Its layout was clearly defined; the doorways and window enclosures easy to spot. I could easily imagine monks bustling along its corridors or congregating for prayer.

A breeze brushed the blades of grass and brought the scent of summer flowers from across the lake. Alice drew a deep breath. "So peaceful."

"Its demise wasn't peaceful," Jack said. He leaned against the wall and made a face at the baby in his arms to win a smile. He was rewarded with a giggle.

I wandered around the ruins with Hannah, only half listening as she pointed out the function of each of the rooms we found ourselves in. The rest of my attention was focused on Lincoln. He'd wandered off on his own but kept coming back to a particular spot. Perhaps he'd sensed something about it with his seer's eye. Jack watched him too, a small frown connecting his brows.

"You're getting married soon," Hannah said, following my gaze to Lincoln.

"In eleven days." I twisted my engagement ring and smiled. Sometimes it was hard to believe how much my life had changed in twelve months. Not only did I have a home and security, something I feared I'd never have again, but I had friends who were like a family to me. And I was about to marry the man I loved, who loved me in return.

"You both look very happy," Hannah said.

"You think Lincoln looks happy? Usually only I can tell when he is."

She laughed. "To be honest, I'm guessing. He's rather hard to read." She took my arm in hers and gazed at her husband and baby. "I hope you will be as fortunate in your marriage as I am."

"Thank you. I hope so too."

"Jack's friend, Tommy, who married Jack's cousin, Sylvia, once said that the key to a happy marriage is never ending the day angry with one another."

"And what does she say?"

"That her husband is so amenable that she always gets her own way."

We both laughed.

"And what of Seth and Alice?" Hannah asked.

I followed her gaze to where Seth helped Alice down from a low wall, his hands on her waist. "They're a work in progress."

Alice caught us watching her and quickly pulled away from Seth. He trailed behind before seeming to think better of it and changing his direction to join Gus.

"It would seem he has quite some work to do," Hannah said.

* * *

WE WOKE EARLY the following morning to catch the train back to London. It had been a pleasant overnight stay, and we'd learned a lot from one another, but I sensed Lincoln was eager to leave after breakfast. I was too. While our brief country sojourn had been idyllic, it was too close to the wedding date to be away from home for long. Lady Vickers could have got up to all sorts of mischief in my absence. I half expected to find some of her friends added to the guest list or the flowers to be changed. At least I knew Cook wouldn't alter the menu without consulting me first.

While I liked to involve her, since I had no mother to share the experience with, she could be a little too determined to have her own way sometimes. Seth scolded her once, reminding her she was not the mother of the bride. Seeing her crestfallen face, I'd vowed not to do the same, but it wasn't always easy.

"It was good of Hannah to invite us back whenever we liked," Alice said, settling on the seat in a vacant first class compartment. "Perhaps we can return again after your honeymoon, Charlie."

I sat beside her and removed my gloves. It was too hot to wear them. Alice frowned at my impropriety but didn't scold. "So soon?" I asked.

"Of course. It's lovely in the country. And what a grand house! I adored it."

"You found it cold and uninviting at first."

"The people made it feel welcoming. Hannah and Jack were very kind. Even if you don't come back with me, I'll visit again for certain."

I wondered how much of her enthusiasm for Freak House had to do with the portal at the ruins and the possibility of learning more about herself from it and the Langleys. I felt a little sad that she never spoke so effusively about Lichfield Towers, but I shouldn't be surprised. She'd often told me it wasn't her home, merely a temporary roof over her head. She hated the idleness of her life there. I understood the need to feel useful, but I did wonder why Lichfield held no appeal for her while Seth resided there.

I said nothing, however, as I listened to the men approaching along the corridor.

"As the role of father-of-the-bride has fallen to me," Seth declared, "I must insist that we have a discussion before the wedding, Fitzroy."

Lincoln did not respond, perhaps because he knew they were nearing the door to our compartment. He could sense my presence when I was near.

"I'd shut up if I were you," Gus hissed.

"Charlie's like a little sister to me," Seth barreled on. "I'm warning you, Fitzroy. If you ever—" He stopped outside the door when he spotted us. "Ah. Charlie, Alice, I didn't know you were in here."

Gus shoved Seth inside and filled the doorway with his big, grinning face. "That'll teach you to flap your jaw."

"I doubt it," Lincoln said, coming in behind them. "He's a slow learner."

Seth hoisted his small bag onto the luggage rack above us. "If I weren't so affable, I'd take offence at that. Besides, I know you love me like a brother, Fitzroy."

"More like a cousin."

"A distant second cousin," Gus said, adding two more bags to Seth's. "On the side of the family no one mentions in polite conversation."

Alice giggled behind her hand.

Seth dug his elbow into Gus's ribs. "My apologies," he said through a strained smile. "It's crowded in here and you're the size of an elephant. Please sit down before you fall on the ladies and squash them."

Seth and Gus sat opposite us while Lincoln squeezed next to me. His thigh touched mine as the carriage jerked forward and remained there as he removed the newspaper tucked under his arm. He spent the next several minutes reading the front page while the rest of us conversed above the rhythmic *click-clack* of the train. The intimate connection between Lincoln and I was oddly distracting in a pleasant way, and I wanted to make eye contact to see if it affected him too. But he kept his gaze strictly averted from mine. He seemed quite disinterested, damn him.

Because we were touching, I was able to feel when he suddenly tensed after turning the page. "Lincoln? Is something the matter?"

He lowered the newspaper and pointed at an article near the top. MAN MAULED TO DEATH the headline screamed. A body had been found in the Old Nichol area of London with deep gashes to his throat and chest that resembled claw marks. The article suspected a wild dog attack, but made no connection to the death of Protheroe two months ago. There was nothing to suspect the mauling had been done by a shape shifting wolf.

Yet I knew it to my bones. I felt sick. "He broke the truce," I said heavily. "Swinburn and his pack are killing again."

CHAPTER 2

*L*incoln informed us that he would not remain long at Lichfield but leave to speak with Swinburn immediately after arriving home. He wanted Seth and Gus to accompany him.

They didn't need to go anywhere, however. Swinburn was waiting for us, along with Lady Harcourt. Lady Vickers looked relieved to relinquish the role of hostess to me when we entered the drawing room.

"Excuse me," she said, rising to her full, commanding height. "I must go. There's so much to do this close to the wedding."

Lady Harcourt picked at the copper colored thread embroidered into her skirt. "Speaking of the wedding, I assume I am not invited."

"You assume correctly," Lincoln said.

"I didn't think I would be, but I wanted to be certain. I may have plans for then." Lady Harcourt's tone was equal parts sweet and sour. "Now that I know I'll be free, I can go ahead with them." She wrapped her fingers around Swinburn's arm and bestowed him with a pretty smile.

He smiled back, his gaze dipping momentarily to her lush bosom before rising again to her face. She looked as beautiful as ever, but not as youthful. Small lines fanned from the corners of her eyes and the bones in her face were sharper. Worry and turmoil was wearing her down. Not that I felt sorry for her. She'd brought misery on her own head by alternately flirting with her stepson, Andrew Buchanan, and casting him aside. Their vindictive natures meant they could not leave one another in peace and so they both got hurt. She'd thrown him out of her house, even though he had a right to live there according to his late father's will. As far as I knew, he was living with his brother on the family's Oxfordshire estate. It may not be the best place for him, considering he and his brother did not get along, but it must be infinitely better than living with his stepmother. Their destructive relationship did neither of them any good.

I expected her to have shed the unhappiness Buchanan's presence inflicted on her, but looking at her now, it was clear she wasn't content. There was a certain air of victory in the way she held herself but there was no true contentment. I couldn't quite fathom it.

Lady Vickers exited the drawing room, taking Alice with her. Gus closed the door behind them and stood with his hands at his back. Lady Harcourt perched on the sofa's edge, Swinburn at her side. He was twenty years her senior with a stocky build. None would call him handsome, but that wouldn't matter to her. His wealth and connections were more important. She'd set her hooks into him two months ago, and it seemed she'd finally reeled him in after his initial resistance. I wondered what had changed his mind.

She clung to him in a way that Lady Vickers would describe as vulgar. It would seem Lady Harcourt had won her prize and planned on keeping him. *That* must be why she seemed victorious. He was wealthy and, although not titled, he was knighted. It was perhaps the best she could hope for, given that her background as a dancer had been made public. Her friends had dwindled in number and her prospects for another advantageous marriage dried up after the revelation. If she wanted to maintain the life she'd become accustomed to, she needed to marry a man like Swinburn. It would seem marriage might be on the cards if they were this close. Clearly it didn't concern her that he was a shape-shifting demon.

"You've been away." Swinburn eyed Lincoln with caution, as if he expected Lincoln to lash out at any moment.

"Where did you go?" Lady Harcourt asked.

"That's not your business," Lincoln said.

She stiffened. "It most certainly is! As a committee member—"

"It is not your business," he said again, punching out each word.

The muscles in her face worked as she battled not to bite back at him.

"You broke the truce," Lincoln said simply.

Swinburn held up his hands but it was Lady Harcourt who protested. "He did not! How dare you, Lincoln! How dare you suggest such a thing. Sir Ignatius has abided by the terms of the truce. That death last night had nothing to do with him or his pack."

"Swinburn?" Lincoln prompted.

"Julia is correct," Swinburn said. "That death wasn't caused by anyone from my pack. That's why I came here today—to reassure you before you jumped to the wrong conclusion. Indeed, Julia suggested I come."

"I know how you can be," she told Lincoln.

"Meaning?" Seth snapped.

She ignored him. She didn't even look his way. They'd

been lovers once, after she'd been Lincoln's lover, but Seth had grown to despise her after he learned her true nature.

"I know you well, Lincoln," she went on, "and I knew you'd assume Sir Ignatius broke the truce when you read about the mauling in the papers."

"We all came to the same conclusion when we read it," I said. "Not just Lincoln."

She ignored me too. At least I was in good company. "Lincoln, you do believe us, don't you?" Lady Harcourt clasped her hands together, an earnest frown crossing her brow. "The truce still stands. Look elsewhere for the killer."

"Gawler, perhaps," Swinburn said smoothly. Everything about him was smooth, unruffled, from his neatly trimmed moustache and slicked back hair to the curve of his lips. "The murder did occur in the East End. It seems more likely it was one of his pack than mine."

"Gawler wouldn't sanction it," Lincoln said. "He's no killer."

"We're *all* killers, Fitzroy. It's in our nature. Some of us suppress the instinct better than others—and for longer. Can he? Is he strong enough? Is he strong enough to control his pack?"

Gawler had lost the leadership of his pack to the shape-changer known as King, but he inherited it back again after King's death. Earning the leadership by default wasn't the same as winning it through strength, the defining trait of a pack leader. Gawler's East End pack was ripe for a stronger creature to oust him and take command. Such a person may not have the same ethics as Gawler when it came to murder. We knew it, and Swinburn knew we knew it. The curve of his lips didn't falter.

He stood and buttoned up his jacket. "If you don't mind, I'm a busy man. Julia?"

She took his offered hand and rose from the sofa. She

used her left hand, not her right, and wasn't wearing gloves, which was odd. Then I noticed the large diamond ring on her finger and understood why—she wanted us to see it.

"You're getting married?" Seth blurted out.

She bestowed a condescending smile on him. "Why, yes. I wasn't going to tell anyone until *The Times* ran the official announcement, but we might as well inform you all now. Sir Ignatius proposed and I accepted. We'll be married a few weeks after you, Lincoln."

"Huh," was all Seth said. It was difficult to gauge his feelings on the matter from that one word.

Lincoln offered stiff congratulations and I followed suit. Lady Harcourt thanked Lincoln but said nothing to me. At least I got an incline of the head from Swinburn. While his lips remained frozen into their curve, he did not look pleased to find himself shackled in matrimony to Lady Harcourt. I didn't think that was because he knew what she was really like, but more because he was an avowed bachelor.

So what could possibly have induced him to propose? According to gossip, he never settled with one woman, preferring the carefree life of a bachelor. He hadn't shown any particular interest in Lady Harcourt in the past, so why now? Perhaps she'd simply worn him down over the last two months.

"Good luck, Swinburn," Seth murmured as the couple passed him. "You're going to need it."

Lady Harcourt's eyes flashed.

"I'm sure we'll make the most of it," Swinburn said.

He sounded like he'd lost a fortune, not gained a wife.

"I know what you're going to say, Lincoln," Lady Harcourt said.

"I wasn't going to say anything," he said.

"You were going to remind me that ministry business cannot be shared with him, even when we are married. Don't

23

worry, Sir Ignatius understands my position. He won't ask me anything and I won't tell him anything. There. The key to a happy marriage is in those words. You should take heed of them, Lincoln, Charlotte. I have more experience than you both. I was happily married to Lord Harcourt and I shall be happily married to Sir Ignatius."

Seth snorted. I didn't bother to comment. Her definition of a happy marriage probably did not equate to mine. She was happy if her husband gave her gifts and status rather than his unconditional love. I was not.

Lincoln nodded at Gus to open the door for our guests.

Swinburn stopped and patted Lady Harcourt's hand. "I'll join you in a moment, Julia."

She blinked at him. "Ignatius?"

He smiled and shooed her on. Her nostrils flared but she complied and joined Whistler, the footman, near the staircase.

"One other thing," Swinburn said quietly to Lincoln. "I was speaking to your father—"

"My what?" Lincoln growled.

"Your father, the prince." Swinburn's lips curved up more. "Ah. You're surprised that I know. It seems you underestimated the friendship between His Highness and myself. He relies on me, you know. I give him advice on financial matters. Anyway, the point is, he informed me that Lord Ballantine's appointment as special envoy to India has been delayed."

Delayed! Where was the justice? Ballantine had tried to trick the Prince of Wales's son into marrying his daughter. It hadn't worked, but the royal family had been furious at the blatant manipulation. We suspected Swinburn, as leader of the pack Ballantine belonged to, was the one behind the scheme, but the Prince of Wales and his brother, the Duke of Edinburgh, refused to blame Swinburn. They'd organized it so that the Foreign Office would post Ballantine to India, essentially exiling him. It seemed Swinburn had successfully persuaded them to change their minds.

"Why?" Lincoln asked, not sounding at all surprised by the announcement.

"You would have to ask His Highness," Swinburn said. "Perhaps he just had a change of heart. He can be somewhat fickle like that, haven't you noticed? Or perhaps not. You don't know your father well, do you?"

"As well as I wish to know him."

Gus stepped aside and allowed Swinburn to walk ahead of him. He escorted them both down the stairs and Seth shut the drawing room door.

"What an arse," he declared.

"Which one?" I asked.

"Both. I can't believe they're getting married! Has he lost his mind? Has she? He's a bloody wolf, for Christ's sakes!"

Gus returned and threw himself into a chair. "I didn't think Swinburn and the prince were close enough to share that kind of secret. Seems he treats Swinburn like a brother. That's worrying."

"I'm not so sure." Lincoln leaned against the mantel and crossed his arms, as casual as can be. "Swinburn didn't actually say the prince told him he was my father."

"True," Seth said, nodding. "He led us to think that's who told him but never confirmed it."

"Nor do I believe the prince would have told anyone outside the family. It's highly sensitive information, and he's no fool."

"He did vehemently defend Swinburn when we accused him of Protheroe's murder," I pointed out. "As did his brother, the duke."

"Defending a man's reputation is one thing. Trusting him with this information is another entirely. Besides, the duke likes his brother. He wouldn't risk his reputation, no matter how much he respected Swinburn."

"That's not why I think the prince and duke are innocent, however. Swinburn sent Julia from the room for a reason."

"Blimey," I muttered as it dawned on me.

"Bloody hell." Seth flopped into a chair and his hair fell across his forehead. He swept it back and slumped. "You think *she* told him, but he didn't want her to know that he was telling us?"

"She probably asked him to keep the information to himself," Lincoln said.

"Bloody traitor!" Gus growled. "Are you sure, though? She's got too much history with the ministry. She knows it'll be a betrayal."

"It was her," Seth said heavily. "It's the only explanation that makes sense. She must have given him the information in exchange for marriage. I did wonder why he agreed to it. The man's a womanizer. He wouldn't settle down unless he got something out of it."

"The nerve of her!" I stormed to the door and wrenched it open.

"They're gone, Charlie," Gus said.

"She's a fool if she thought we wouldn't work it out," Seth said. "A bloody fool. And he's a fool for agreeing to the union. Give it a year and he'll decide the information wasn't worth it. What's he going to do with it, anyway? Go to the papers? It might cause a scandal, but only until the next scandal comes along. What will he gain?"

"Leverage for blackmailing me," Lincoln said simply.

I sighed. "So what do we do now?"

"She has to be ousted from the committee," Seth said.

"Aye," Gus agreed.

I looked to Lincoln and he nodded. "I'll do it tomorrow,"

he said. "A committee meeting will need to be held to inform the others."

The notion of cutting Lady Harcourt loose appealed to me. Without her on the committee, there'd be no more reason to associate with her. We'd be rid of her completely, since we rarely moved in the same social circles. "I'll come with you when you tell her," I said to Lincoln. I didn't want to miss this.

Seth stretched out his arms and cracked his knuckles. "She told me I was going to take her place on the committee if anything happened to her. Looks like I'm moving up in the world."

Gus rolled his eyes. "It don't give you any real power, you pompous prig. It don't pay, neither. Does it?" He looked to Lincoln.

Lincoln shook his head.

We sat in silence a few moments as we each contemplated Lady Harcourt's reaction to the news that she was off the committee. At least, I thought that's what we were all thinking.

"I wonder if Buchanan will be invited to their wedding," Gus said.

Seth crossed his legs at the ankles. "It could prove to be quite the spectacle if he is. Makes me wish I was getting an invite after all."

Gus snorted. "You're the last person she'd want there, along with Buchanan. Past lovers don't make good wedding guests."

"Then half of the nobility will be missing."

"You're both wrong," I said. "*I'm* the last person she'd want attending her wedding, just as she's the last person I'd want at mine. Anyway, I can't think of a single reason why she'd invite Andrew Buchanan."

"I can." Seth looked at me as if it were obvious. "When I

shrugged, he went on, "Her new husband won't allow her to have lovers. Swinburn's not the sort who likes to be cuck- olded. Buchanan has lost, and what better way to rub his nose in it than have him at the wedding so he can see what a big fish she caught. How she would love to twist that vindic- tive knife of hers further into his heart."

That I could believe. "You sound as if you feel sorry for him."

"Part of me does. He wasn't always such a turd." Seth huffed out a humorless laugh. "And there but for the grace of God go I."

"You were never like him," I said. "Perhaps your circum- stances were, but you, as a person, are not."

"Charlie's right," Lincoln said. "If you were like Buchanan, I wouldn't have employed you. You are his opposite in almost every way."

Seth straightened and his cheeks pinked a little. "*Almost* every way?"

"You're a peacock. You have that in common."

Seth's face fell. Gus roared with laughter.

I made my excuses. It had been a long journey from Hert- fordshire and I still wore my traveling outfit. I didn't get far up the staircase when a strong arm circled my waist. I hadn't heard Lincoln's footsteps.

"Can you spare me a moment?" His voice rumbled through his chest to my body, and his breath warmed my ear.

I turned and looped my arms around his neck. I teased the hair tied back with a black ribbon at the nape of his neck. "I can spare several for you." I kissed him lightly on the lips but found it wasn't enough and deepened the kiss.

His hands splayed across my back, holding me firmly in place, and he kissed me, thoroughly and completely. We were in danger of being seen, but I didn't care. Nothing mattered except Lincoln and his mouth, his body, and my visceral reaction to him. I ached for him, for more than mere kisses. Our wedding night couldn't come soon enough.

He pulled away and filled his lungs with a deep breath. He touched my cheek with the back of his hand. "I've missed you, Charlie."

"I was with you the entire time," I said, laughing.

"Not the entire time. I never did find a secret passage to your room."

"You wouldn't have entered even if you had. You're far too much of a gentleman, despite what you want people to think."

"Don't let Seth and Gus know." He took my hand and led me upstairs, out of view of the drawing room. "I'm enjoying their attempts to both lecture and threaten me. Gus said he'd castrate me if I ever upset you."

"That's positively medieval. Good for him. And good for you for taking it in your stride. Once upon a time you would have growled and snapped at them."

"And they would have feared me. Unfortunately, my reputation is ruined and I'm left with finding amusement instead."

"That's the spirit."

"Until they bore me. Then I'll send them on futile errands into dangerous slums."

We reached my bedroom and he kissed me again before disappearing along the corridor to his own rooms. It wasn't until I closed my door that I realized I hadn't asked him the plan of action. We needed to find out more about the victim, and the attack, and perhaps question Gawler. Lincoln found him easy to read, with his seer's senses, and would know if he was guilty or not. I'd speak with Lincoln after dinner.

I changed and went in search of Lady Vickers. I found her in the parlor, enjoying the last of the afternoon sunshine before dusk settled in. She opened her eyes and patted her hair. Finding several strands loose, she clicked her tongue.

"That Briggs," she muttered. "She's quite hopeless. I don't know what to do with her." Bella Briggs was Lady Vickers' maid, and a previous mistress of Seth's. I was surprised she was still in her employ, since Lady Vickers complained incessantly about her ineptitude. "You ought to get rid of her, Charlie."

"Me? But she's your maid."

"*You* are the mistress of the house."

"Seth employs and pays her. Ask him to dismiss her." We both knew he would not. He may no longer have dalliances with Bella, but he was much too good-hearted to dismiss someone he'd known intimately.

"It's not his place," Lady Vickers said. "You should speak to Mrs. Cotchin. While Bella isn't under her jurisdiction, it's acceptable for the housekeeper to dismiss the ladies' maid if the mistress permits it. Ask her to place an ad on your behalf for a new maid. It's time you got one. We'll keep her busy between us, and there's Alice too, for now."

It would seem she was economizing on her son's behalf. Although Lincoln had increased Seth's wages to cover the expense, I doubted he would decrease it accordingly after Bella Briggs left.

"So many rules!" I perched on the window embrasure and stared across the lawn. "Who can and cannot dismiss staff, who speaks to whom and when. What to eat and drink, and when. How will I remember them all?"

"You'll grow into your role, my dear. Until you do, I'll help you. Just think how lucky you are."

"I know I am, and I'm grateful to you."

"Many young brides have to put up with a mother-in-law who still rules the house. You have the best of both worlds. You get the benefit of my wisdom, yet *you* are the unchallenged mistress here."

I laughed. It wasn't quite why I thanked my good fortune.

"You're right, Lady V. Thank you for all your assistance with the wedding preparations."

She patted the sofa beside her. "Come sit by me. I've got an idea for your gown. Have you thought about a bow on each sleeve?"

"The gown is almost finished. I can't change anything now. The dressmaker would skin me alive."

"Tosh. Of course you can change anything, and right up to the day. It's your right as a bride to have exactly what you want."

"I do have what I want. I love my wedding gown."

"Wait until you see this." She plucked a periodical from the embroidery basket at her feet. "It arrived this morning from Paris." She flipped pages until she came to the one she wanted. "If you'd been away any longer I would have sent a request to the dressmaker on your behalf."

It was fortunate I'd come home when I did. The bows on each of the capped sleeves on the dress in the picture were excessive. "I think I prefer it as it is."

"No bows?"

"No bows."

She sighed. "Very well. Now, what about the guest list?"

"What about it?"

"Do you really need to have Lord Gillingham?"

"He's married to Harriet, whom I consider a friend."

She whipped out a copy of the seating arrangements from her basket. "Then he cannot sit next to me."

"But you're such a good conversationalist, Lady V. Your charm and wit are second to none, and you always know the right thing to say. You're comfortable talking to people from the upper classes. Imagine if I sat him next to Gus!"

"Flattery won't work this time, my dear. I can't sit next to him because he's much too small."

I spluttered a laugh. "What has that got to do with anything?"

"We'll look ridiculous seated beside one another. No man likes to feel small and weak, and no woman likes to feel like a giraffe. You'll have to put him next to his wife. She's the only one who'll put up with him. Besides, it's her fault he'll be at the wedding at all."

"So be it."

"With any luck, he'll come down with a sore throat and won't be able to come."

"Or perhaps he'll simply think of an excuse and let his wife come alone."

She scoffed. "I doubt he'll do that. Your wedding will be the event of the year, and he'll want to be included. Everyone is already talking about it."

"Who?"

She waved her hand. "All my friends. Several have requested an invitation, and of course I've had to tell them it's extremely exclusive. Or I will, at the last moment. Until then, I'll enjoy their luncheons and teas and other attempts to pander to me."

"Why is everyone so interested in us?"

"Mr. Fitzroy was highly sought after, at one time. His air of mystery, his good looks and wealth made him popular when I first arrived back in London. You were away at school then. Those girls who didn't need or care for a title threw themselves at him at every opportunity. When he went off the market, several wanted to claw your eyes out."

I stared at her.

"Seth is still popular, of course," she went on. "If only he would attend more parties, he'd have his pick of girls. Some of them are even heiresses. Of course, he'd have to secure them quickly, before their parents remembered why the Vickers name has mud attached to it." She sighed. "His father ruined everything for poor Seth. Do you think you could bring him back for me so I can kill him again?"

I threw my head back and laughed. She did not join in. "Oh. You're not joking. Lady V, you do know people only die once?"

"Can't you banish his spirit to hell?"

"No!"

"Somewhere similar, then. A place where there's fire and brimstone and horrid diseases. And ugly women. That would be his kind of hell." She patted my knee then used it to push herself to her feet. "There must be books in Mr. Fitzroy's library about banishing spirits to hellish places. Reading up on it will take your mind off the upcoming wedding."

"I don't need to take my mind off it. I'm looking forward to it."

She picked up her embroidery basket and rubbed her back as she straightened. "That reminds me, we need to have a talk before your wedding night. But not today."

Thank God for that. It wasn't a conversation I wanted to have with her, ever. Considering what I'd seen while living on the streets, I suspected I knew more than she did about the things a man and woman could get up to on their wedding night.

I went to the kitchen to speak to Cook but he was busy barking orders at his assistant while basting a leg of lamb and stirring the contents of a pot. "Find me later and we'll discuss wedding food," I said to him.

He stopped stirring and basting. "Something be wrong with the menu?"

"No." I winked and lowered my voice. "I haven't seen you for two days and wanted to catch up on news."

"Right you are. You there!" I thought he was shouting at me, but it was a maid who'd caught his attention. "What is it you want, Annie? Get it and go. It's too crowded in here for anyone who ain't kitchen staff."

"I'm looking for the cutlery," the girl said. I liked her pluck. She wasn't frightened of Cook in the least.

"The cutlery in here be for staff only. You be wanting the silver for the dining room. Ask Mrs. Cotchin."

Annie bobbed a curtsy and hurried off.

"She's new and still learning," Cook said to me with a shake of his head.

"Her hair was done nicely," I said.

He returned to his stirring and basting. "So?"

"I wonder if she did it herself. If so perhaps she'll make a good ladies' maid. Don't tell Bella yet."

"Lady V finally had enough, eh?" He chuckled. "I knew Seth's choice would come back to bite him on the—" He glanced at the girl stirring a mixture in a bowl at the table. "Speaking of Lady V, you can learn a lot from her, Charlie. She's got taste. I don't mean in clothes and the like, but this." He poked out his tongue. "She knows what sauce goes with what, and the like. Comes with being so well traveled."

"You ought to tell her that."

"She's too grand to speak to me, except when you be away and she gets hungry."

I patted his shoulder and assured him she wasn't like that. But, in truth, she was quite the snob. She rarely stepped foot in the service area, and it required a great inducement for her to put even a toe into the kitchen. Considering her second husband had been a footman in her household, it was strange that she kept her distance from the staff. Perhaps that was why—she didn't trust herself not to cross that line again.

I left Cook to his work and found Alice. We walked around the walled garden with its rambling vines and on through the apple orchard, my favorite part of the estate. Dusk hadn't yet rolled in and the day was still warm enough that we didn't need wraps. The air smelled clear and fresh here, compared to the cloying denseness of the city where I grew up, although not nearly as fresh as the air at Hertfordshire.

Alice and I spoke quietly, mostly about her dilemma but about the wedding too. After a time, I noticed she was distracted and followed her gaze. Ahead, the gardener studied one of the trees lining the drive.

"Is something the matter with our gardener?" I asked her.

"Not at all." She nudged me with her elbow. "He's quite handsome, isn't he?"

She was admiring a "quite handsome" gardener when she had a very handsome lord at her disposal? Was she blind, foolish or both?

"Not as handsome as Seth," I pointed out.

She sighed and tore away from me. "Don't spoil it, Charlie."

"Spoil what?"

"Our walk, our friendship…everything."

"I didn't think I was spoiling anything, merely pointing out that Seth is more handsome than the gardener."

She strode ahead. "Perhaps that's the problem."

I hurried to catch up. "Alice, what's the matter?"

She sighed again. "I don't really know. All I know is, I'm tired of everyone thinking Seth and I would make a handsome couple. Everyone except Lady V, that is. I just want to be his friend at the moment. Indeed, I can't even think about anything else, with any man, until I know how to fix my predicament." She stopped and waited for me to catch up. "Do you understand, Charlie?"

I took her arm in mine. "Completely. I won't mention Seth's good looks to you again."

The dinner gong rang out from the house. "Already?" Alice said. "But we haven't changed."

"I wasn't planning to change again. I already have once today."

"Lady Vickers won't like it. She says if a lady doesn't wear at least three different outfits a day she's being idle."

I laughed. "Come on. Let's shock her with our idleness."

* * *

LINCOLN DIDN'T CHANGE for dinner either as he arrived back at the house after the gong. He'd snuck out without telling me he was leaving.

"You've been to see Gawler, haven't you?" I asked as we sat at the table.

"Yes," he said. "And you can stop scowling at me like that. I didn't avoid you on purpose. You weren't around when I left."

My scowl deepened. He picked up his knife and fork and tossed me a smile, which only proved to me that he had purposely avoided me so that I wouldn't insist on going with him.

"What did Gawler say?" Seth asked.

"Do we have to discuss this at the dinner table?" Lady Vickers chided. "It's vulgar."

"It can wait," Lincoln said when Seth opened his mouth to disagree with his mother.

We congregated in the sitting room after dinner, joined by Cook. Lady Vickers pursed her lips when he entered and he turned to leave again, but I called him back. Honestly, she was such a stickler for rules despite knowing how things were at Lichfield. She'd long ago given in to having Gus associate with us; she could bend the rules for Cook too.

"Come sit by me," I said to Cook. "Gus, pour a brandy for him."

Cook had removed his apron but he brought the smells of roasted meat with him. He sat beside me and sighed like a man who'd been on his feet all day. Lady Vickers gave him a curt nod, her way of apologizing for her rudeness. He nodded back.

With that out of the way, I said, "Lincoln was just about to tell us what Gawler said when he questioned him about the murder. If Lady Vickers doesn't mind such a discussion, that is."

"I don't mind." She sipped her sherry slowly, peering over the glass in my direction. Or was it Cook's direction?

"Gawler denied any wrongdoing," Lincoln said. He sat in a chair near the window, looking relaxed yet alert. "He questioned his pack mates this morning, after he heard about the mauling, and they too denied any involvement. He believes them."

"Did you believe him?" I asked.

"I didn't detect a lie, but without questioning his pack, I can't vouch for their honesty."

"It might be worth speaking to Harriet. She ought to have some idea if any of them are murderously inclined."

Lady Vickers made a sound of disgust in the back of her throat but offered no comment.

"Gawler is worried about the blame being laid at his feet," Lincoln went on. "He knows how it looks. The murder happened one street from his own residence."

"I hate the Old Nichol," Gus grumbled. "It's packed with human scum. It don't surprise me that someone got murdered there."

"Murders happen there all the time," Seth agreed. At his mother's and Alice's raised brows, he added, "So I hear. Very gruesome murders. Mother, you'll probably want to leave before you hear any more."

"My constitution is quite strong, thank you," she said. "Do continue."

Seth muttered something under his breath but I couldn't

hear it. Why was he trying to get his mother to leave? I glanced at her, only to see her looking at me again. No, not me. At Cook. He, however, didn't notice. I smiled into my glass.

"If his pack didn't do it, who does Gawler think is responsible?" Alice asked.

"A random attacker?" Seth offered.

Lincoln shook his head. "He believes Swinburn did it and is trying to blame Gawler's pack, with the intention of forcing us to take action and disband it. Gawler thinks it's a power play by Swinburn."

"To become the top wolf pack in the city," I said, nodding. "It's a sound theory and fits with what we know of Swinburn."

"We need to talk with him again," Seth said.

Lincoln lifted a finger from his glass to halt the suggestion before it gained momentum. "I need to learn more details from the police first—the victim's name and place of residence, as well as the exact nature of the injuries. I want to know if they match those of Protheroe in the Hyde Park attack."

Lady Vickers set down her glass. "I think I'll leave you to it after all." She rose and all the men stood until she exited.

"I can raise the victim's spirit to find out more," I said as they sat again.

Lincoln gave a single nod and we set out our plans for the following day. A day that would begin with the most difficult task of all—confronting Lady Harcourt and advising her that she was off the committee.

CHAPTER 3

It was too early for making calls on members of polite society, but Lincoln didn't care for propriety, and our visit to Harcourt House in Mayfair wasn't a social call. We found ourselves having to wait in the drawing room, however, while Millard, the butler, fetched his mistress. It gave me time to admire her exquisite taste in furnishings, although it was spoiled by the memory of Marguerite Buchanan's brother shooting himself in this very room several months ago.

Lady Harcourt swanned in fifteen minutes later with her hair unbound. The glossy black locks fell to the middle of her back in waves that didn't bounce in the slightest as she glided across the floor. Her dancer's training served her well in her latest role as a noblewoman, although she would have given anything for it to have remained a secret.

"So early!" she declared, sinking onto a chair. "You will recall that I don't like to rise before nine, Lincoln, and take my breakfast in bed."

Despite steeling myself for this meeting, I was still shocked by her crassness. What sort of woman spoke to a gentleman like that in front of his fiancée? Not a kind one, that was certain. I hoped I managed to school my features and not show my feelings. I didn't want to give her the victory.

"This business couldn't wait," Lincoln said.

"Do sit down." When neither of us did, she added, "I know we haven't got along well of late, but I hope that will change now. We three are getting what we want after all. You two want each other, and I am marrying Sir Ignatius."

"And Swinburn," Lincoln said before I could. "He also got what he wanted."

She smiled. "Thank you, he did. I'm a fine choice for him, if I do say so myself."

I managed to turn my choke into a cough without making it too obvious.

Or so I thought. Lady Harcourt's gaze turned flinty. "Is there something you wish to say, Charlotte? Do you think me a poor choice of wife?"

"I think you and Swinburn deserve one another," I said.

"*Sir* Ignatius," she corrected me. "His origins are humble, but—"

"So are yours."

She sniffed. "What do you want, Lincoln?"

"To tell you that your membership of the committee has been revoked," he said.

She shot to her feet, all pretense of elegance gone. "You can't do that!"

"I've sent letters to Lords Marchbank and Gillingham requesting their presence at a meeting at Lichfield this afternoon. I'll inform them then. This is just a courtesy call to inform you. Considering your service to the committee in the past, I didn't think a letter appropriate."

She gasped as if she couldn't quite catch her breath, and pressed a hand to her stomach. "I told you yesterday that my relationship with Ignatius wouldn't affect my loyalty to the ministry."

"You told him who my father is."

A slight pause, then, "I did not."

"Don't lie to me. You know I can detect them."

She fell back a step, her chest heaving with her breaths. "I can't believe he told you," she whispered. "I can't believe he'd betray me like that."

It was confirmation from her own lips that the secret had come from her, not the prince or duke. Whether Lincoln could indeed detect her lie didn't matter. He'd forced a confession.

"You breached the trust bestowed on you, Julia," Lincoln said. "You gave me no choice but to remove you from the committee."

She spluttered a laugh but it quickly faded. "You can't."

"I can."

"No," she said, shaking her head. "No! Don't do this. Don't remove me from the committee. It won't happen again."

"You can no longer be trusted to keep ministry secrets."

"*No!*"

Lincoln said nothing.

"How dare you!" She flew at him and went to grasp his shoulders, or perhaps hit him, but he caught her wrists and held her at bay. She tried to pull free, her teeth gritted, her jaw hard. Her hair fell across her face, over her shoulders, the strands tangling in her struggle to free herself.

I'd seen her wild, mad side before, but I hadn't expected it today over this. I'd expected her to argue and fight with words, not fists. Had being on the committee meant so much to her?

"Calm yourself," Lincoln intoned.

"Why does everyone betray me?" she growled, her voice

low, masculine. "You, Andrew, Ignatius and now this! You *men*," she spat.

"Stop fighting me or I won't let you go."

She tried to kick him, but her skirts hindered her and Lincoln easily dodged it. She sobbed in frustration but seemed to lose much of her fight. "Don't do this, Lincoln!" she whined. "Don't cut me out of the ministry, out of your life."

His life? So that's what her tantrum was about? She was still clinging to the hope of being friends with Lincoln again? Or even his lover?

Lincoln blinked at her, the only sign that her words had surprised him too. "You thought I wouldn't find out that you'd told him?" he said quietly. "You know me better than that, Julia. I know everything about you. I know who you talk to, who you dine with, who you take to your bed. I know which are your favored servants, and how much money you spend, and the contents of your late husband's will. I know what your plans are before you plan them, and I know what you're thinking before you think it, because I know *you*."

She stared up at him, her eyes huge, deep pools. He let her go and she took two steps back, bringing her close to me.

"You thought you could betray me like this and not suffer the consequences?" Lincoln went on in that same quiet voice that held more power, more command, than a shout.

She straightened and thrust out her chin, every inch the noblewoman again. "I had to do it. He threatened me."

"No, he didn't. I'll say it again, don't lie to me."

She swallowed.

"You did it so he would marry you," I said. "He promised marriage in exchange for information about Lincoln. What else did you—?"

She swung around, her hand out to strike me across the face. It was so quick, yet I saw it coming from the moment her body began to twist. That small sign allowed me to block her blow with my right forearm and slap her face with my left hand.

She reeled back and would have fallen if Lincoln hadn't caught her. He righted her but didn't let go. She made odd gasping sounds that were almost sobs yet she shed no tears. A red mark marred one of her cheeks while the rest of her face was bloodless.

"Get out," she snarled. "Get out of my house."

Gladly. I went to leave but Lincoln remained. "You must send me a letter officially handing over your committee membership to your heir. If it hasn't been received by the end of the week, I'll just give the position to Seth anyway."

We exited the townhouse and Lincoln assisted me into our waiting coach. He directed the coachman to drive us to Lord Gillingham's house.

"How's your hand?" Lincoln asked as we settled in the cabin.

"Fine. It would have stung if I hadn't been wearing gloves." Now that it was over, I was glad I hadn't broken the skin on her cheek, although I suspected she may sport a bruise. "You didn't even move when she went to hit me. You're not as quick as you used to be," I teased.

"I knew you could stop her without my help."

"How could you know that?"

"Because I've seen the improvement in your training. Your reflexes are exceptional, and they were already very good. Next time, hit with a closed fist not an open hand. Although perhaps save that for a fight with a man."

"You think I can beat a man in a fight?"

"I didn't say that."

"But you would like to see me try against someone other than Seth or Gus?"

His brow crashed together. "No. I would not."

43

"Come now, Lincoln, admit it. You're curious. I've been training for a year now, and I've been involved in very little real fighting. You must be wondering if it has helped or if you're wasting your time."

"It hasn't been a waste of time. You have some skills that will help you if you're attacked. I don't regret that at all."

I switched seats to sit next to him. He narrowed his gaze as if he expected me to ravish him. "Don't worry," I said. "I only wish to hold your hand."

He took my hand in his own and brought it to his lips. He kissed my glove. "In all seriousness, Charlie, are you all right?"

"My nerves are settling." I indicated our linked hands and moved as close to him as I could get without sitting on his lap. "What do you think will happen now?"

"Usually a deceased committee member officially notifies us of his or her heir via their will, but since she's living, she needs to confirm Seth as her successor in writing."

"I meant with her and Swinburn."

He merely shrugged, but I suspected he had an answer.

"I think she'll confront him over his betrayal," I said. "They'll probably argue."

"She won't mention it." I knew he had an answer, it only required some encouragement to extract it from him. "Nor will she tell him she's off the committee until after the wedding, otherwise he'll break the engagement. She desperately wants to marry again to secure her future while she's still young, and Swinburn is the best man on offer right now. No other gentleman wants her as a wife. And he only wants her as long as she can pass on sensitive ministry information."

"I see," I said quietly. "You did say you know her so well that you know what she's thinking."

He frowned. "Does that bother you?"

"No. Yes. I don't know."

He touched my chin and gently forced me to look at him. His gaze searched mine. "I cannot change my past."

"I wouldn't want you to."

He didn't look as if he believed me.

"I don't," I said again. "What's done is done."

"Don't let her come between us, Charlie."

I kissed him lightly on the lips. "I won't. I know she's not a part of your life anymore."

"Not part of my life or my thoughts. And now we'll see even less of her."

I leaned my head against his shoulder, but not for long. Lord and Lady Gillingham lived only a few streets from Lady Harcourt and the coach already slowed.

Lord Gillingham was not at home, but Harriet was pleased to see us. As always, she welcomed us enthusiastically. How this vivacious young woman had ever come to like a toad such as Gillingham was beyond me. Their marriage had been arranged when she was just a girl. At twenty years her senior, and a nasty, self-important man at that, she had every reason to hate him. Yet she didn't. Instead, she enjoyed marriage now that she'd leveraged her shape changing abilities and shifted the balance of power in her favor. Now *she* appeared to rule *him*. It probably helped that she was carrying his child.

"We're sorry for calling at such an early hour," I said.

She waved a hand. "You just missed Gilly. He has gone to see a man about horses."

"It's not him we wish to see," Lincoln said. "Although if you could pass on a message, I would be grateful." He asked her to tell her husband to come to Lichfield for a committee meeting at three.

"Is something the matter?" she asked, directing us to sit on the sofa in the drawing room. "Why the urgency?"

"Yesterday's papers reported another mauling death."

"I don't read the newspapers." She pulled a face. "They're always filled with such ghastly things. Another mauling you say? By a werewolf?"

"I cannot say without seeing the victim's injuries."

"But it's likely," I told her. "How many wild dogs are there in London's East End?"

"You'd be surprised," Harriet said. "I've seen some poor starved animals attack out of sheer hunger."

"But why attack a man? Why not another dog or a rat, something easier to kill and eat?"

"I see your point." She pressed a hand to her stomach. It was not as flat as I expected. At three months along in her pregnancy, I thought she wouldn't be showing much yet, but clearly that wasn't the case. Perhaps she'd got her dates wrong.

"Do you still run with Gawler's pack considering...?" Lincoln indicated her swollen belly.

"Not run, no, but I do visit them. As much as I adore my Gilly, I do want to speak with people who understand me. They're my friends now. I'm looking forward to running with them again after the baby's born."

"You won't switch allegiance to Sir Ignatius Swinburn's pack?" I asked, genuinely curious. Harriet was a countess who'd led a very sheltered life. She seemed more suited to Swinburn's shifters than Gawler's, and yet she'd not shown signs of wanting to run with people more like herself.

"Of course not. One does not merely change one's allegiance as one would an outfit. I belong to Gawler's pack and that is that. I have no intention of following Sir Ignatius, particularly after he and his friends showed their true colors. I don't associate with murderers."

I wondered how much of her allegiance stemmed from her dislike of those with humble beginnings who'd risen high thanks to their money. She could be quite the snob when she wanted to be.

"Did you see anyone from your pack yesterday?" Lincoln asked.

She shook her head. "Surely you don't think one of them attacked the victim. Come now, Lincoln, you're not being fair. The last attack was orchestrated by Lord Ballantine, a member of Sir Ignatius's pack. You must look there for a murderer, not to Mr. Gawler. They have a history of doing that sort of thing; we do not."

"This attack occurred in the East End."

She bristled. "So?"

"So Gawler's pack runs in the East End, and Swinburn's pack contains itself to the West End. That's the agreement they came to themselves."

"That doesn't mean Sir Ignatius would keep his word and stay out of the East End. He's a slippery upstart. I don't trust him, and you shouldn't either."

"If you could find out what you can from your pack mates, I would appreciate it."

"I will, but I can already assure you they're innocent. Gawler isn't a killer, and his pack does as he asks."

"And yet he's weak," Lincoln pressed. "He inherited the pack because King died, not because he won the leadership. Doesn't that make you question his worth? Surely there is talk of overthrowing him."

"Certainly not. No one mentions such a thing. We are quite happy with his leadership, thank you, and kindly do not imply otherwise. We're loyal to Mr. Gawler."

"Even you?"

"Yes!"

"A countess loyal to an itinerant laborer?"

Why was he challenging her like this? She was our friend, for goodness' sakes. I tried glaring at him but he did not look my way. I doubted he would have stopped even if he had seen.

"Rank and fortune do not have a bearing on one's position within a pack," she said stiffly. "Only strength does."

"And yet Gawler is not strong. He lost the leadership to King. Perhaps he'll lose it again to another challenger."

"That's the point, Lincoln. There are no challengers. None of us are strong enough to defeat him."

"Swinburn is."

She blinked owlishly at him. Her lips parted to speak then she closed them again.

"And strength does not always imply physical capability," Lincoln went on. "There are other kinds of strength, such as courage, fortitude and an ability to understand and lead people."

"That's where Swinburn fails," Harriet said. "He does not understand *good* people, only wickedness. Take his affection for Julia. What a horrid pair! I suppose that makes them quite suited to one another. I do see your point, but I must reassure you that Mr. Gawler's pack won't make the same mistake they did with King. He risked their lives and the very existence of the pack itself. They won't let that happen again, particularly not with me there to remind them." She gave us both a smug look.

"You have influence with them?" I asked.

"I do now that I've settled in. At least, I like to think so."

She offered us tea but we refused and bid her good day. She walked us to the front door, her hand resting on her belly. I couldn't help saying something, and I only hoped she wouldn't take it the wrong way.

"When are you due?" I asked.

"December."

"Are you sure?" Lincoln asked, saving me from posing the question. "You look further along."

Her spine stiffened. "Quite sure. Gilly and I were not..." Her face reddened and she looked away. "We only became reacquainted with one another this spring."

"You mistake me," Lincoln said with an apologetic lift of his hand. "I believe you when you say you are only three months along. I'm questioning the fact that you are one third of the way through the pregnancy."

Harriet and I gave him blank looks. "You're not making sense," I told him.

"The gestation period for a wolf is less than three months."

Harriet glanced at the footman, standing by the front door. "But I am not a wolf," she whispered. "Not really."

"You are not human either but something else entirely. It stands to reason that your pregnancy will not follow the pattern of a human woman's."

"Oh. I must ask my pack mates. They'll know." She rubbed her belly and smiled. "I do hope it will come soon. I can't wait to tell Gilly the good news. He'll be quite shocked at first, but he'll grow used to the idea of a little wolf prowling around the house soon enough."

She had more faith in Lord Gillingham than I.

We left the Gillinghams' residence and traveled to New Scotland Yard to speak with Lincoln's police informant. The corrupt detective owed his job to Lincoln and proved to be a good source of information on occasion. It was easier going to him than attempting to sneak into the secure building. Lincoln ordered me to remain in the coach, however. I acquiesced on this occasion so that I could save my battles for more interesting and important occasions.

He returned fifteen minutes later and ordered our coachman to take us home.

"What did you learn?" I asked.

"The victim's name is Reginald Lander, a baker's apprentice who worked in Threadneedle Street," Lincoln said as the coach rolled forward. "He was killed on his way to work in the early hours. His body was found by two constables at four-thirty in the morning. There were no witnesses, although the police continue to question the local residents. Considering the extent of Lander's injuries, they speculate that someone must have heard him scream."

"No one heard the Ripper victims scream," I said darkly. "How extensive were his injuries? Did they match Protheroe's?"

"In every way, according to the report." He indicated where the wounds had been inflicted and described claw marks.

"That does sound like Protheroe's injuries." Once upon a time, such injuries would have sent a shiver through me, or made me nauseated, but I'd seen so much death in the last year, it no longer shocked or sickened me. "We need to find out if Reginald Lander was known to either Gawler's or Swinburn's packs."

"We can ask them now," he said.

"Or we could simply ask Lander's ghost."

"I had a feeling you might say that."

"And I can see you've already decided that I will question the ghost." At the arch of his brow, I added, "You told the driver to return home, not travel to Gawler's or Swinburn's house."

He huffed out a laugh. "Would you rather do it now or wait until we arrive at Lichfield?"

"Now will do. What's his middle name?"

"William."

"Reginald William Lander," I intoned. "I call on the spirit of Reginald William Lander. I need to speak with you about your death."

The ghost filled the cabin like a sketch come to life, and

settled on the seat beside me. The baker's apprentice had been huge, as big as Gus, with shoulders and arms that strained the seams of his clothes.

He looked around then addressed Lincoln, sitting opposite. "How'd I get here?"

"I summoned you," I said. "You're dead."

"Aye." Usually the newly deceased were a little confused, but Reginald Lander was quite composed. "But why summon me?"

"I called you here because I need to speak with you about your death. I'm sorry to rip you from your afterlife—"

"I weren't in my afterlife. I stayed near where I died."

"You remained to haunt?"

He passed a massive hand over his face, but it went right through, disturbing the outline of his bulging forehead. His face resettled in the same pattern of oversized nose, lips and brow. "Aye. I wanted to catch the dog what did this, but don't seem to be able to leave the street. I need to go further."

"You can't," I said. "That's a limitation of haunting—you must remain where you died."

"Then what's the bloody point?" The spirit dissolved into wisps that swept around the cabin twice before reforming again on the seat beside me. "Who're you and why'd you bring me here?"

My name is Charlie Holloway and this is Mr. Fitzroy, my fiancé. We're investigating your murder," I said. "We hope to bring your killer to justice."

"Murder? By a human?"

"We believe so. A human in wolf form, that is."

"A what?"

"You called your killer a dog just now, so I thought you knew, or had guessed, that a shape shifter murdered you."

He screwed up his face, drawing his heavy brow to plunge

51

over his eyes. "You ain't making sense, miss. What's a shape shifter?"

I quickly explained the situation. He didn't look like he believed me but he didn't outright dismiss me either. "Is there anything you can tell us about your killer?" I asked. "Anything we could use to identify him or her?"

"It were a big dog," he said with a shrug. "Could have been a wolf, I suppose, although I ain't never seen one before. It were all brown fur and big teeth. And claws." He looked down at the shredded clothing at his chest. "You saying that were a person in there?"

"Yes."

"Why did they kill me then?"

"Did you have enemies?" I asked.

"No." Another shrug of those big shoulders. "I worked hard, helped out my ma at home, got me a nice sweetheart, too."

I repeated his answer for Lincoln. "Were there any rivals for her hand?" he asked.

Lander shook his head. "None. She weren't the prettiest, but I ain't either." He laughed, revealing crooked teeth. "She's the daughter of my employer. Her parents were happy for me to court her. They said we made a good match, being alike in temper and all." He sighed. "I'm going to miss her."

"I'm sure she'll miss you too," I said. "Mr. Lander, does the name Gawler mean anything to you?"

He shook his head. "That your suspect?"

"Not at this point. What about a man named Swinburn?"

Another shake of his head. "You got clues? Witnesses?"

"No, nothing."

He grunted. "You're going to give up, aren't you? Another body turns up in the East End and you don't care. You pigs won't find my killer, just like you didn't find the Ripper. What's it matter if a whore gets murdered, or a dock worker, or a baker's apprentice? It's just another less mouth to feed, another voice what won't rise up."

"Mr. Lander, I don't appreciate your insinuation that we won't work hard to find your killer. Besides, Mr. Fitzroy and I do not work for the police. Our organization accounts for the supernaturals, and I can assure you, we have every intention of finding your killer before he strikes again. So, it's important to answer my questions fully."

"I have, miss. I don't know no Gawler or Swinburn, and I ain't got any enemies what would murder me. I didn't see no one attack me, just a big dog." He spread out his hands, palms up. "Any other questions you want to ask?"

"Lincoln?" I said. "Do you have any questions for Mr. Lander?"

Lincoln asked if he knew the Ballantines and the other members of Swinburn's pack. Reginald Lander didn't. Nor did he know Harriet or any members of Gawler's pack. He had never ventured past any of their places of residence either, including Gawler's in Myring Place.

"I don't usually go through the Old Nichol," Lander said. "It ain't a good area, miss. But it's the shortest way to work and I got lazy these last few days. But I ain't been to Myring Place."

Lincoln ran out of questions and I had no more. I sent Lander on his way and suggested he might as well cross over.

He looked as if he'd refuse but nodded instead. "There ain't no point staying if I can't leave the place where I died. You promise to catch my murderer?"

"We do." I watched him until he dissolved into a mist and finally into nothing at all. "He's gone," I announced. "He wasn't very helpful."

Lincoln studied the view out the window. When we finally arrived home, he took my hand and assisted me down the coach step to the gravel drive.

"Care to walk with me through the garden?" he asked.

I took his arm and kept pace with his slow, easy strides. We ambled across the lawn and passed by the orchard. It was a lovely day, but I didn't care about that, and I didn't think that was why Lincoln invited me to walk with him.

"You have a plan," I said.

"No. Do you?"

"No. Do you want to toss ideas around away from prying ears and eyes?"

"Why does it matter if Seth or Gus hear us?" he asked.

"Because you don't want it known that you have no ideas and are asking me for advice?" It sounded rather stupid even to me.

He chuckled. "My self-worth isn't *that* inflated. Don't," he added when I opened my mouth to speak. "No need to disagree with me."

"I wasn't going to! I was simply going to ask you why you suggested a walk in the garden."

"Because it's a beautiful day." He glanced back at the house then diverted our path toward the brick wall surrounding part of the garden. "And because I wanted to kiss you without anyone observing."

He hustled me through the doorway and gently pushed me back against the wall. I reached up and linked my fingers behind his head. He settled his hands at my waist and skimmed his lips over mine.

"You're wicked," I said on a breath.

"Very."

"Kiss me properly."

He smiled against my mouth. "If you insist."

* * *

DUE TO EVENTS over the previous months, the ministry's

committee consisted of Lords Marchbank and Gillingham, and Lincoln. Marchbank arrived first, and on time, but Lord Gillingham was half an hour late. I thought he wouldn't come at all but then his gleaming black coach arrived. The gold family crest painted on the side glinted in the afternoon sunshine so that the serpent wrapped around the sword looked as if it winked.

"You're late, Gilly," Lord Marchbank said as Lord Gillingham strolled into the library.

He undid his jacket buttons and sat in one of the deep leather armchairs. "I only just received Fitzroy's message from my wife. If she'd given it to me earlier, I would have gotten here earlier. You know how she is."

"And how is she?" I asked sweetly.

"Stupid."

Well, that wasn't very nice. At least he answered me, I suppose. Once upon a time, he would have ignored me completely unless it was to goad or hit me. "I disagree," I said. "I think Harriet is quite smart but has never had the benefit of a good education to capitalize on it. Granted, she is quite naive regarding some matters, but it's hardly her fault since she has been treated like a child for so long. I'm just glad she now lives her life as a shape-shifting countess ought to." I shot him a winning smile.

He sank into the armchair.

Seth handed him a glass of brandy. "You look like you need this."

"I still can't fathom it," Lord Marchbank said. "Harriet is such a gentle woman. To find out that she has the strength of several men, the speed and senses of a wolf...it continues to amaze me."

Gillingham downed the contents of his glass and held it out. "Another."

Seth pointed his chin at Gus. "You get it."

"Why?" Gus whined. "Because I'm the servant and you're the lord?"

"Because you're closer to the sideboard. But if you insist on being the servant, then by all means, act like one and get him another drink."

Gus crossed his arms over his chest. "Ring for a footman. Let the proper servants do it."

Gillingham leaned on the silver lion's head of his walking stick and pushed himself to his feet. "This is a bloody circus." He marched to the sideboard, the walking stick hardly hitting the floor, and removed the stopper from the decanter. "Lichfield Towers has gone to the dogs."

Gus and Seth exchanged smiles.

"Not quite," Lincoln said. "Although a dog or two running about would liven the place up."

"I've never had a pet," I said, warming to the idea.

"Where's Julia?" Gillingham snapped. "Let's get this over with. I have things to do."

"Like discuss the pending birth of your baby," Lincoln said.

Gillingham, his back to us, drank the contents of his glass and refilled it.

"The birth is months away," Marchbank said.

Lincoln shook his head and waited for Gillingham to say something. He did not. He merely pressed a hand to the sideboard and hung his head. I couldn't feel sorry for the weasel. He was revolting to his core.

"Harriet is wolf-like, in a way," Lincoln told Marchbank. "The gestation period for a wolf is much shorter than a human."

Marchbank absently stroked one of the scars marking his cheek. "Then how long has she got?"

"I cannot guess."

"Intriguing. Did you know about this beforehand, Fitzroy? Was this information in any of your books or files?"

"No."

"Then I hope you're studying her and taking notes. We can learn a lot from her pregnancy, eh, Gillingham. Harriet won't mind, will she?"

"I mind," Gillingham growled.

"But if your wife doesn't then you should not." Marchbank lifted his glass in salute. "Should you?"

Gillingham groaned and turned back to the sideboard and his glass. He downed his third brandy in one gulp. Seth got up and removed the glass from Gillingham's hand before he refilled it.

"We need you sober for this meeting," Seth said.

Gillingham shoved him off. Two blotchy red patches stained his cheeks and his mouth twisted. He'd never looked more ugly. "Where the hell is that whore?"

"Julia won't be coming," Seth said, sitting down again. "Not today or ever again. I'm the fourth committee member now. She named me as her heir for the position."

"Julia has been removed from the committee," Lincoln finished.

"What?" Gillingham exploded.

"Removed?" Marchbank echoed. "By whose authority?"

"Mine," Lincoln said.

"You can't do that!" Gillingham slammed his hand down on the sideboard, rattling the decanter stopper. "You have no authority to remove anyone, Fitzroy! Only we as a group can do that. God, man, has taking over General Eastbrooke's position gone to your head already? *You* are not superior to any of us. *You* are not in charge here."

"She left me no choice," Lincoln said icily. "Immediate action had to be taken and there was no time to consult you.

If you prefer a vote, then let's do so now, after you hear her crime."

Marchbank put up a finger to stop Gillingham's spluttering protest. Surprisingly, it worked and Gillingham quieted. "What did she do?" Marchbank asked.

"Gave our secrets to Swinburn in exchange for marriage."

Marchbank scrubbed a roughened hand over his face and swore. The elderly gentleman never swore. He must be deeply troubled by the news to do so now.

Gillingham stood very still, his mouth ajar. The two blotches on his cheeks had disappeared and he looked very pale. "The fool," he said. "The stupid fool. I cannot believe she'd do such a thing."

"Can't you?" Seth grunted. "I can. It's entirely in her nature to stomp over other people to get what she wants. Since you are not someone she has ever stomped on, I suppose I can forgive you for not believing us now."

Gillingham sat on the nearest chair and blinked stupidly at Seth.

"What secrets did she divulge?" Marchbank asked Lincoln. "Is there reason to worry?"

"I don't think so. She told him who my father is."

"Is that all?" Gillingham blurted out. "You removed her from the committee for that?"

"Where will it end?" Seth said. "What secret will be next?"

"Do be quiet, Vickers. Your opinion doesn't count since everyone knows you'd like to see her punished for her rejection of you."

Seth rose, but Gus's hand clamped around his arm. Seth looked as if he were considering shoving Gus off and attacking Gillingham when the door burst open.

Andrew Buchanan strolled in, his step cock-sure, his smile oily. "Good afternoon, my fellow members. I'm here.

The meeting can get underway now that *all* committee members are present."

Both Gus and Seth rose. "Get out, Buchanan," Seth said, approaching him.

"My first proposal is to stipulate that only committee members may be present in meetings. What say you, Gillingham?"

"It seems you've heard that Julia is no longer a member," Seth said. "But what you haven't heard is that you're not her heir. I am."

Buchanan plucked off his gloves and slapped them into Seth's chest. "Pour me a drink, Vickers, there's a good man. Make it a large one. I'm gasping, and it seems I have some catching up to do."

"Clearly you have quite a bit of catching up to do," I said. "Seth is right, and you are not Lady Harcourt's heir for the committee position. He is."

Lincoln finally rose and blocked Buchanan's path. He did not order Buchanan out, however. "You spoke to her today?" Lincoln asked.

Buchanan smiled. "I've just come from Harcourt House. She informed me of your decision and then told me I was her replacement." He stretched his arms out wide. "So here I am. Shall we begin?"

CHAPTER 4

"*Y*ou'd better explain yourself, Buchanan," Marchbank said. "Julia told us that Vickers is her heir."

"As Fitzroy seems to have guessed, there's been a change of plans," Andrew Buchanan said. "Julia never did get around to making Vickers her heir on the committee. Ask her, if you like. She'll even show you her last will and testament. Her *unchanged* will and testament." He threw himself into an armchair and snapped his fingers. "Make yourself useful, Vickers, and pour me a drink. It's all you seem to be good for, these days."

Gillingham snorted a laugh. Seth stepped up to Buchanan, but Lincoln caught his wrist. He shook his head in warning.

I poured a glass of brandy for Buchanan instead. Then I marched up to him and threw the contents in his face. "There's your drink."

Buchanan spluttered as brandy dripped off his chin and nose, soaking his clothes. His lips peeled back from his teeth in a grimace and he went to get up. Lincoln stepped in front of him and a glare was enough to force Buchanan to sit again.

He plucked at his damp clothes. "Waste of good stuff."

I took Seth's hand and hauled him out of the library. "There's no point listening to what he has to say," I said when we were out of earshot. "It won't be interesting." I shut the door and drew in a deep breath, gathering my wits.

Beside me, Seth shook with anger. Perhaps Lincoln should have let him strike Buchanan. It wasn't as if he didn't deserve it, and it would make Seth feel better.

"Miss Holloway," Doyle said, joining us. "I tried to stop Mr. Buchanan but he marched right past me."

"It's all right," I told the butler. "Come on, Seth. Let's find Alice."

I hoped being with Alice would calm his nerves a little, but it did not. For one thing, his mother was with her in the music room, and for another, he seemed to hardly notice Alice as she played the piano. His charm was nowhere in evidence as he brooded by the window.

A brooding Seth was not something I was used to, and I found I couldn't settle into the conversations that Lady Vickers and Alice attempted to draw me into.

"Charlie?" Alice prompted, her hands stilling on the keys. "Are you listening?"

"No. Sorry. I'm distracted." I regretted leaving the meeting now. I ought to be in there, contributing and supporting Lincoln. Not that he needed my support with the committee members, but surely it was the thought that counted.

"The mail is being delivered," Seth announced, pushing off from the window frame he'd been leaning against.

"Where are you going?" I asked.

"To see if there are any letters for me. A newspaper was on the hall stand too. I need something to distract me."

"Are we not distraction enough?" Alice asked, her fingers racing along the keys.

"Not at the moment." He stormed out, leaving a deafening silence in his wake.

"He didn't mean it quite the way it sounds," I assured Alice.

"I think he did," she said.

"My son is a man of action," Lady Vickers said. "He doesn't like being cooped up in music rooms and libraries for long."

Except when there are pretty women in those music rooms and libraries, I could have said. But I bit my tongue and followed Seth out. The hall stand was very close to the library, and I didn't want him to succumb to the temptation to rejoin the committee meeting.

His longs legs and purposeful stride meant I didn't catch up to him until the entrance hall. He flicked through the mail, tossing each letter back into the salver after a cursory glance.

"Are you even reading the names?" I asked.

With a sigh, he dropped the rest of the letters into the salver. "I'm going back in."

"Very well."

He narrowed his gaze. "You won't try to stop me?"

"No. I'm going to join you."

The corner of his mouth lifted and he held out his hand toward the library door. "After you."

"Miss Holloway! Lord Vickers!" Doyle rushed up to us, out of breath, and held out a newspaper. "This just arrived. I think you'll want to read it."

"Oh no," I murmured as I read the front page headline.

"'*Is the Ripper back?*'" Seth read.

"There's been another mauling death in the East End. We have to tell Lincoln."

Seth grabbed the newspaper as I went to move off. "Wait." He pointed to a spot near the end of the article. "That's an interesting development."

"'*Werewolf*,'" I read, my stomach sinking. "The reporter has made the connection."

Seth and I exchanged glances then we both headed to the library and pushed open the door together. All heads swiveled to face us.

"Do I need to remind you *again*," Buchanan said with a smirk. "You're not part of these meetings, Vickers, unless you're serving or taking notes."

"Shut your mouth, Buchanan, or I'll shut it for you," I said sweetly. I handed the newspaper to Lincoln. "It happened again."

He quickly read the article and passed it to Gus.

"What's happened?" Gillingham said. "What's in the papers?"

"Hand it to me." Buchanan clicked his fingers at Gus. "Come on, man, you're taking too long."

"Aye," Gus said, absently. "On account of my low education."

"And stupidity," Gillingham muttered. "Honestly, you shouldn't even be in here." He snatched the paper from Gus's hand. Buchanan and Marchbank joined him and read over his shoulder.

Gus looked at Lincoln. "Werewolf."

"The reporter's use of the word is interesting," Lincoln said.

"And concerning," Seth added. "To have come to that conclusion based on only two mauling deaths is a large leap. Do you think he has some sort of connection with the shape changing community?"

"Perhaps we need to speak with that reporter."

Gillingham slapped the paper with the back of his

gloved hand. "It's a poorly written piece. Clearly sensation-alist to sell more copies. The headline speaks to the Ripper crimes but the article itself concludes that a werewolf is responsible for this death and the last one. The reporter doesn't actually link these two latest deaths to the Whitechapel murders of two years ago. The headline is purely to catch the attention of passersby. Look at the size of it!"

"It's what newspapers do to sell more papers," Buchanan said. "Sensationalist news stories, scaremongering and gossip are their trade."

"You would know all about that," Gillingham muttered. "You're quite the expert on feeding gossip to journalists."

Buchanan swallowed and looked away. So he still felt guilty for informing the papers about Lady Harcourt's past as a dancer. It never ceased to amaze me to be reminded that he had a conscience.

"This meeting is adjourned," Lord Marchbank said with a nod for Lincoln. "Fitzroy has work to do."

Work that would begin with finding out why the reporter mentioned werewolves in his article.

* * *

A FRENZY of activity at the office of *The Star* in Stonecutter Street near Ludgate Circus was a testament to the daily's popularity. It was one of the few newspapers that circulated widely in the poorer parts of London. When I slept in derelict houses, there were always a few pages of *The Star* that could be found to stuff down the front of my shirt for warmth.

Lincoln and I met Mr. Salter in the front reception room. I guessed the tall slender man with the crooked teeth was a good ten years older than Lincoln, but it wasn't easy to tell.

He had a receding hairline but smooth skin and no gray in his beard.

"My name is Lincoln Fitzroy and this is—"

"Fitzroy!" Mr. Salter rubbed his hands together. "Well then, this must be Miss Holloway."

"You know of us?" I asked.

"I do."

"How?" Lincoln growled. He would not like it that this man knew about him when Lincoln knew nothing in return.

"I'll tell you that when you tell me why you're here." Mr. Salter sniffed the air, as if he could sense a good story. "We'll talk in private. Come this way." He led us down a corridor, past several rooms, some occupied, to a small office containing a desk and bookshelves. A mechanical typing machine took pride of place on the desk, an open notebook beside it. Mr. Salter closed the notebook and placed it in a drawer.

"How do you know us?" Lincoln asked again.

Mr. Salter wagged his finger. "Uh-uh. You agreed. You answer me first. Do you have information about the murders I reported on? Or something else entirely?" His accent was almost East End but not quite. In fact, it sounded like my own speech pattern in the years when I tried to blend in with the other urchins but hadn't quite shed my middle class roots. I suspected Mr. Salter had gone in the other direction to me—he'd been born an East Ender but earned a good education at some point.

"Your article mentioned a werewolf." It would seem Lincoln refused to agree to terms. "Why?"

Mr. Salter sighed. "I can see you have nothing for me, only questions. Pity."

"Answer my question."

"Please," I added.

Mr. Salter smiled knowingly, almost as if he expected

Lincoln to be abrupt and me to be conciliatory. Someone had told him all about us.

"I wondered if you would come here to speak with me," Mr. Salter went on. "I admit to using the word werewolf specifically to draw you out."

"How do you know about shape changers?" Lincoln asked.

"I heard rumors after that fellow was found in Hyde Park two months ago. When these latest murders happened, I couldn't help thinking of that one. So I entered into my own investigation. I came to the conclusion that the wild dog story put about by the police was just that—a story."

"And a werewolf attack seemed more plausible?" Lincoln asked.

Mr. Salter lifted one shoulder. "It does when you know they exist right under our noses."

"And what makes you think that?"

Mr. Salter sat forward and linked his hands on his desk. "Come now, Mr. Fitzroy. I am not a fool. I observe, listen and investigate, much as you do. The existence of the supernatural is nothing new to me. I belonged to an organization known as the Society for Supernatural Activity. It's disbanded now, but was quite prominent in the field of supernatural research."

"I've heard of them," Lincoln said.

"I haven't." I appealed to the journalist. "What did they do?"

"They investigated the supernatural," Mr. Salter went on. "Anything unexplained, they dug deeper to find answers. Their library containing supernatural texts was extensive, I believe. A private buyer bought the contents. Anyway, the society is no longer, yet I am still investigating rumors of the inexplicable whenever something inexplicable comes across my desk."

"And do many come across your desk?" I asked.

"Very few, I admit."

"So the term werewolf simply occurred to you in the case of this latest mauling?" Lincoln said.

"It did."

"Even though a more obvious answer is the wild dog theory?"

"I question whether a wild dog attacking people in an urban area is *more* obvious, Mr. Fitzroy."

"Something else led you to the werewolf conclusion. What is it?"

Mr. Salter smiled amiably. "I assure you, I am not privy to any other information. Scotland Yard have not been forthcoming, which implies they know very little. They've already admitted there were no witnesses to either murder. My conclusion of werewolf was simply a guess, based on my interest in the supernatural."

A good guess. *Too* good perhaps?

"You say you've heard about us," Lincoln went on. "What have you heard?"

"That you are the leader of an organization called the Ministry of Curiosities."

I sucked air between my teeth. I hadn't been expecting him to say that. Lincoln gave nothing away. If he was surprised by Mr. Salter's answer, he didn't show it.

"Go on," Lincoln said, as calmly as can be.

"There's little more to tell. I am aware that the ministry keeps records of supernatural families through the ages, and that you investigate paranormal phenomena from time to time. I am not aware of very many of the particulars, however, just generalizations."

"Is that why you haven't written an article mentioning the ministry?"

Mr. Salter merely smiled.

"Don't believe everything you hear, Mr. Salter."

"If you are trying to convince me that the ministry doesn't exist, you are wasting your breath. I trust my source."

"Who is your source?"

Mr. Salter chuckled as he leaned back in his chair. He seemed quite unconcerned. Clearly his source hadn't told him how dangerous Lincoln could be. "Come now, Mr. Fitzroy. You're smarter than that."

"It doesn't matter if you tell us or not," I said with more confidence than I felt. "We can discover who told you on our own." I stood and Lincoln followed suit.

"Be careful, Mr. Salter," he said. "Don't write anything too speculative in your newspaper or you might reveal too much. There are some people who wish to keep the supernatural a secret and they'll try to silence you."

Mr. Salter shot to his feet and squared his shoulders. "Is that an idle threat?"

"I don't make *idle* threats. Ask your source. They'll tell you."

"In that case, let me advise you to be careful too, Mr. Fitzroy. If these murders were in fact committed by a wolf-like shifter, and you are found to be harboring one, you might find your ministry coming under intense scrutiny."

Lincoln watched him from beneath hooded lids, that fierce gaze of his never wavering. Tension made his features hard, his body rigid. I hooked my arm through his and steered him toward the door before he created a scene.

We made our way out of *The Star's* office and climbed back into our waiting coach.

"The nerve of him!" I snapped as we drove off. "He doesn't care about the trouble he's stirring up at all. Imagine if people believe that article. They'll panic if they think there are werewolves roaming the city."

"They will if there's another murder," Lincoln said darkly. "It'll be like the Ripper murders all over again."

"Who do you think told Salter about the ministry? Swinburn? Ballantine?"

"It's possible, but if they also suggested the werewolf theory to Salter then they're putting themselves in danger of being exposed. I can't imagine Swinburn would jeopardize his pack by inviting scrutiny."

"I suppose," I muttered, not entirely convinced. Swinburn was so slippery that I suspected him of everything at the moment. "Lady Harcourt, in revenge?"

"We only removed her from the committee this morning. But if Salter had information about her past then it's possible she exchanged this information for his silence. It wouldn't surprise me. She doesn't want to lose Swinburn."

"It wouldn't surprise me either." I looked out of the window and watched the long shadows of the late afternoon slip past. "There's also Buchanan and any number of people we've met in the past—Lord Harcourt and his wife, Miss Redding from the theater... Sometimes it seems as if the entire world knows about the ministry."

"It hasn't been a priority to keep it a secret. Just your necromancy."

I turned to face him. "Do you think Mr. Salter knows about that?"

His brow creased in thought. "He didn't mention it."

"And he didn't give me odd looks, like most do when they learn what I am." I drew in a deep breath and let it out slowly. "I suspect he doesn't know." But how long before he found out?

He leaned forward and closed his hand over mine. "The question is, did his source leave that piece of information out deliberately, or did he or she not know?"

The answer to that would change the list of suspects.

"The Society for Supernatural Activity is an organization that had entanglements with the Langleys," he said.

"Are you implying the Langleys are Salter's source?" I shook my head. "Surely not. Jack Langley is a demon himself, and there is a portal on his property. He didn't like discussing the supernatural with us at first. Despite all that, I can't believe it of them anyway."

"Why not?"

"I liked them."

His features softened. "That isn't a good defense."

"And this is not a courtroom."

He stroked my wrist with his thumb. "There's another possibility. Someone I expect you to defend."

I snatched my hand back. "You are not going to accuse Alice or Lady Vickers! Who's next? Seth or Gus?"

He sat back and folded his arms. His eyes banked with a coldness I didn't like. "You think I'd do that?"

I bit my lip. "No. You're right. You wouldn't. I'm sorry, Lincoln. Who do you suspect?"

"The royal family."

I stared at him for so long my eyes watered. "You think your father is the source? I cannot believe it. He likes you, and his brother the duke likes him. They wouldn't talk about you to anyone. Besides, the royals are not the sort to trust newspapers. They dislike that sort of attention."

"Unless it helps them."

"How does telling a reporter from *The Star* about you and the ministry help them?"

"I don't know yet."

"It's a working men's daily anyway, and far too left wing for the royals. They'd probably go to the *The Standard*. No, I still think it's Swinburn."

"Then if Swinburn is confiding in newspapermen, we

have another problem." At my raised brow, he added, "He could tell Salter who my father is."

I considered that a moment then shook my head. "The risk is too great. He wouldn't want to offend the royal family, and he knows he'd be our number one suspect, since so few are privy to that piece of information."

"Whoever it is knows about Harriet being a shape changer. Salter mentioned the ministry harboring one. That can only mean her."

"Then we can rule out the royal family," I said.

"Unless Swinburn has informed the prince or duke."

"Could Mr. Salter be referring to Gawler and the fact you have not held him accountable for these murders?"

He nodded thoughtfully. "That is a very good point."

I sighed. We were not getting any closer to answers, only more questions. "So what do we do now?"

"I look through that notebook from Salter."

"Oh! Yes, the one he placed in his desk drawer. Why hide it from us if it's not important? It probably contains the name of his informant." I rubbed my hands together. "Shall we break into *The Star's* office tonight?"

"I will do the breaking in without you. That is not negotiable, Charlie, so don't attempt to change my mind."

"But—"

He lunged toward me, planted his hands on the seat either side of me, and pressed his mouth to mine before I could say anything more. The kiss sent a thrill through me, right to my toes. It was full of ferocious desire, of a need that came from deep within him. I could not push him away. Didn't want to. I clung to his shoulders and deepened the kiss.

He finally sat back opposite when the coach turned a sharp corner. I was gratified to see that his cheeks had colored. He looked as flustered as I felt.

"You are diabolical," I said.

He flashed me a wicked grin.

"But you can't silence me forever," I said.

"Seth and Gus will come with me. There's no need for you, too."

I didn't bother to contradict him. It would only end in an argument.

I SLEPT through the night and missed Lincoln's nocturnal excursion to *The Star's* office and his subsequent visit to Mr. Salter's lodgings. It was a pity, as I would have liked to scramble through windows like I used to. It turned out that he didn't take Gus or Seth either. I did not admonish him for it in front of them as we all sat in his study in the morning, but planned to do so later.

"Did you find the notebook?" Seth asked.

"No," Lincoln said. "It wasn't in his office, and I couldn't find it in his rooms. I didn't check his bedroom for risk of waking him."

"You never used to worry about that," Seth said with a laugh.

Lincoln glared at him and Seth gulped.

"Might be worth going back when he ain't there," Gus suggested.

"I disagree," I said. "I suspect he keeps the notebook close, perhaps even on his person."

"My money's still on Swinburn being Salter's source," Seth said. "Or Julia. Perhaps both together."

I no longer felt so sure. Lincoln was right; Swinburn wouldn't jeopardize his pack by drawing the ire of the public. Imagine if Salter's articles led to vigilantes roaming the streets at night or an extra police presence. At best, they would be seen during their runs, and at worst, they'd be shot at.

A knock sounded on the door and Lincoln asked the visitor to enter. It was Alice, biting her lip and looking drawn. She seemed out of sorts since returning from Freak House. She was often distracted by her own thoughts and frequently took out her frustration on the piano keys. When I asked her what the matter was, she simply shook her head and refused to answer.

"I'm sorry to interrupt, but we have visitors," she announced. "The Cornells wish to speak to you."

"Just Lincoln?" Seth asked.

"All of you. Leisl particularly asked for you, Seth."

He tugged on his cuffs. "She finds me charming."

Gus thumped his arm but had no cutting remark to offer. Perhaps because Seth was right and it was his presence that Leisl liked. Older women in particular found him charming.

I hung back with Alice, allowing the men to go on ahead. "Is everything all right?" I asked her.

"My nerves are frayed. The lack of progress regarding my situation is torture. I thought going to Frakingham would bring answers, and a plan to help me, but it hasn't. In fact, the investigation into my condition has stalled altogether."

"We're busy with solving the murders. That must take priority."

She sighed again. "I know. But that doesn't mean I can't feel irritable. You cannot understand how important this is to me. I must find a way to stop these dreams coming to life. I must find answers."

"What if the answer is that they cannot be stopped? What if this is how you'll be forever?" I felt awful for pointing it out but she ought to prepare herself for the worst. "Just as I have to live with the fact I'm a necromancer."

"At least you can control when you raise the dead. I can't control my affliction."

"Perhaps you'll learn to."

She threw her hands in the air. "When? I need to learn *now*, before something awful happens or that horrid little rodent returns."

"Rabbits aren't rodents." I didn't tell her that I found the creature rather adorable with his floppy ears and waistcoat. He'd not tried to harm anyone, he'd merely urged her to go with him. "You must relax, Alice. You know what happens when you're frustrated."

"I'll try."

"As soon as we discover who has killed those people, we'll investigate portals and realms. I promise."

She hugged my arm and we headed down the stairs, catching up to Seth who'd paused on the step. I followed his gaze to see his mother emerging from the hidden door that led to the service stairs. The stairs ran through the house between the walls with a door to each level for the servants to easily come and go. We used them, from time to time, if we didn't want to be seen by other members of the household, although those times were rare now Lichfield housed more staff. I'd never seen Lady Vickers venture through any of the doors before.

She headed in the other direction, not having seen us. Her light hum drifted along the corridor. It was a pretty, happy tune.

"Your mother seems content lately," I said to Seth.

He grunted. "That's what worries me."

I exchanged a glance with Alice. "Why?" I asked him.

"Because I've noticed her talking to Cook a lot."

I pressed my lips together to suppress my smile.

"You're worried they're developing a *tendre* for one another?" Alice asked.

"She has a history of it."

"And what is wrong with Cook courting her? He's a fine man."

Seth turned a sharp glare onto her. "You wouldn't understand."

"I understand that you don't like people from different stations courting each other."

"That's not why," Seth said and walked off.

"I think my charm is wearing off," Alice said, sounding pleased. "Thank goodness for that."

"Don't goad him," I said as we followed Seth at a distance. "He's sensitive about his mother's second marriage, and it seems she may be heading down the same path again. Her choices affect him."

"He's old enough not to let it matter. He should be pleased that she seems to have found happiness again."

It was impossible to argue with that.

All three members of the Cornell family waited for us in the drawing room. Lincoln greeted them stiffly while I gave them each a kiss on the cheek. We'd seen them twice in the last two months, including at a dinner held here. While it had been a pleasant evening, on the whole, David was still rather frosty toward Lincoln, his half-brother. Their mother had told me to give them time. I wondered how long it would take before he accepted Lincoln into his family.

I wondered how long it would take for Lincoln to want to be a part of it.

"What can we do for you?" Lincoln asked, getting straight to the point.

Out of the corner of my eye, I saw David's lips flatten in irritation at Lincoln's curtness. His sister, however, kept her face averted. Eva studied her lap, her hands clasped tightly. I got the distinct impression she was avoiding meeting anyone's gaze but couldn't fathom why. She'd been amiable and kind to us since discovering she had a half-brother, with a wicked sense of humor. I liked her.

"I had a vision about you, Lincoln," Leisl said. "I come to warn you."

Heavy dread settled in my heart. "Warn him?"

"I see you trapped in a small room."

"Where?" I asked.

"I do not know." Leisl wrung her hands together, her handsome brow deeply furrowed. "I am worried, Charlie."

Lincoln remained unmoved as he stood by the fireplace. He didn't ask his mother any more questions, so it would seem it was up to me.

"What did the room look like?"

"Dark, damp, bare. The walls are dirty. I do not see the door or windows, if there are any, but my seer's senses know he cannot get out."

"Any idea how he got in there?" Seth asked.

"It doesn't work that way," David snapped.

"Then how does it work?" Seth snapped right back.

"She sees or senses only a moment in time, not the before or after."

Eva cleared her throat. "The visions act as a warning of what is to come."

"So they only reveal the bad?" Gus said. "Never the good?"

"Good too," Leisl said with a glance at Eva. "But not this time. This is bad. You must be careful, Lincoln."

Lincoln inclined his head in a nod but didn't speak.

"He will be," I told her. "I'll make sure of it."

Leisl looked expectantly at Lincoln. He studied the hearth at his feet. I could hear my own breathing and the tick of the clock on the mantel in the hush. Why didn't he reassure her? She only needed to hear a word or two from him telling her he would be careful, even if he didn't mean it. I almost scolded him then and there, but it was David who finally broke the tension.

"Don't you care, Fitzroy?"

"David, don't," Eva said.

"We came all this way to warn you," David went on.

"*You* didn't have to come," Eva hissed.

"Thank you," Lincoln finally said to Leisl.

It wasn't nearly enough but I knew it was all Lincoln would offer, and I think Leisl understood that. She smiled tentatively.

"Let's go," David said, rising.

"Won't you stay for tea?" I asked as Mrs. Cotchin and Doyle entered carrying trays laden with tea things and cakes.

"We can't," Eva said, also rising.

"We can," Leisl said. Her children exchanged glances then sat again.

"Do you think this vision is connected to the one you had about the queen, Eva?" I asked as I poured the tea. "Where you think she will be a danger to us?"

Eva shook her head and accepted the teacup. "I don't know. Mama sensed no regal presence in her vision."

"Too many bloody warnings and not enough information," Gus muttered. "Pardon me, ma'am, miss, but what're we s'posed to do with 'em? How can we be careful if we don't know what to be careful of?"

It was a question without an answer. We left behind discussions of visions and dire predictions and moved instead to talk of the wedding. Lady Vickers joined us, her mood still buoyant. I tried to imagine her having a rendezvous with Cook on the service stairs but only ended up giggling into my teacup.

Seth shot me a glare. I suspected he knew precisely what I was thinking.

Our guests remained for another half an hour, during

which I could see the men growing increasingly eager to leave the drawing room. When Eva reminded her mother that she had a lecture to attend at London Hospital, Leisl finally agreed it was time to depart. David was the first to stand.

"Thank you for the tea," he said to me. "It was a pleasure to see you, as always, Charlie." He spoke just as nicely to the others, but was as brisk as ever with Lincoln.

Eva caught my elbow and held me back, allowing the others to go on ahead. "I'm sorry we all descended on you like this."

"Don't be silly," I said. "We're happy to see you."

"My mother insisted on coming and having me with her. David insisted on joining us."

"To see his brother again, perhaps?" I teased.

She grinned. "I do think he's thawing to the idea of having a brother."

"That was David *thawing?*"

"Oh yes. He didn't grumble once on the way here, whereas he used to. The real test will be what he says about Lincoln on the way home." She took my arm and squeezed it. "Don't worry. He'll thaw out altogether eventually."

"I'm not worried. He's exactly like Lincoln in that regard. They may not like one another by the wedding day, but I'm sure their greetings will move on from polite nods and graduate to grunts soon enough. Grunts are practically hugs in Lincoln's book."

She laughed and we strode toward the door arm in arm. Ahead, Seth placed a hand to Alice's lower back to steer her down the front steps.

"May I ask you a question about Seth and Alice?" Eva whispered, her head bent to mine.

"Of course."

"Is there an understanding between them?"

"He would like there to be, but she doesn't seem interested. I do think that will change when she gets to know him better and sees that there is substance behind his handsome face. Why do you ask?"

"No reason."

"Come now, Eva, you can share with me. Have you had a vision about them?"

She blushed and I knew I was right. "Not *them*," she said.

"Just Seth?"

She went to stride off but I clung to her and kept her at my side.

"Please, Eva, just tell me if it's something to be worried about."

She stared at Seth's back as he spoke to Alice. He flashed her a dazzling smile but Alice didn't respond. His smile faded quickly and he lowered his hand. Poor Seth. He needed to stop trying so hard. She would grow to like him in her own time, when he was acting more like himself.

"Yes," Eva said heavily. "Yes it is something to worry about, but I suspect I will be the only one who sees it that way."

No matter how much I pressed her, she would not tell me more. We rejoined the others at the door then walked with them down the front steps to their waiting hackney cab.

"Are your nursing studies going well, Eva?" Seth asked.

"Fine. Thank you."

"Excellent. What a grand profession you're entering into. The medical field is an exciting one these days. Lincoln has a subscription to a medical journal, and I flip through the pages from time to time. I'm amazed by all the developments. You must be clever to keep up with them all."

"You sound surprised that a woman can be clever."

"Do I?"

"Eva is studying to be a nurse, not a doctor," David said. "A noble profession, of course, and far more demanding in many ways. She's required to be nurturing as well as resilient and as proficient as any doctor."

"Not quite," Eva said tightly.

"When do your studies finish?" Lincoln asked. His question took me by surprise. He'd once said that Eva couldn't have been studying to become a nurse because nurses required no formal education before taking on a position within a hospital. I thought he might be wrong, but I wasn't sure. It did seem odd that Eva would keep the truth from us if she were actually studying to become a doctor. Why would she hide it? Anyway, her family also seemed to think she was going to be a nurse.

"Before the end of the year is out," Eva said.

"Or more," Leisl said. "If she marry. Her husband will not wish for her to work. He will want a wife at home, a proper lady."

"That's enough, Mama," Eva whispered.

David bundled both ladies into the coach and climbed in himself. It would appear he didn't want them to air their dirty laundry in front of us. Whether Eva was training to be a nurse or doctor, it was as if it didn't matter to her mother. She seemed to think Eva would marry and that would be an end to her career. Leisl could only know that if she'd had a vision about her daughter's future husband.

But why would Eva marry at all if it meant the end to her career before it even began? A career she seemed intent on having. Giving in to a man's demands on that score didn't seem like something she would do.

I watched the hackney until it left the grounds through the front gate. I was about to return inside with Alice, Seth and Gus, but Lincoln remained on the drive. He too had watched the coach until it was no longer in sight.

"What is it?" I asked, taking his arm.

"We have another visitor."

He'd hardly finished speaking before another coach raced down the drive toward us, dust billowing behind the hooves of two black horses. The coach gleamed in the sunshine, as did the gold embroidery on the coachman's crimson livery.

"What do the palace want now?" I muttered.

"I don't know, but it saves me from asking for an audience," Lincoln said.

I gasped. "You're not going to ask them if they are Salter's source, are you?"

"I am, among other things."

"You can't accuse the prince and duke of that!"

"Not accuse, merely ask."

I groaned. Sometimes Lincoln's interrogation technique didn't differentiate between accusing and asking. I wished I could drag him back inside and pretend we weren't home, but it was too late.

CHAPTER 5

The royal coach merely brought a note from the Prince of Wales requesting our presence at two PM at the palace. Lady Vickers insisted I change into my most fashionable outfit, an off-white day dress with two rows of black bows on the bodice that came together in a V at my waist.

"The queen may prefer dark clothes herself," Lady Vickers told me, "but she likes to see young people in lighter colors." She indicated I should twirl and I obliged. "Excellent. Now, pinch your cheeks." She pinched them for me. "Lift your chin." She lifted it for me. "And smile demurely."

I attempted a demure smile. She wrinkled her nose. "That will have to do. Remind me to have Seth teach you the art of smiling. He's quite good at it. It's why women adore him."

Perhaps too many women, but I didn't remind her of that.

"Are you an expert?" I asked her. "Does Cook like your demure smiles?"

She blushed fiercely and looked away. "We were going to have that talk about your wedding night."

"Not now." I picked up my skirts and hurried from the room. "We have to go."

* * *

THE PALACE FOOTMEN led us through grand and ornate rooms where the royals conducted formal business. We were met by the Prince of Wales in an office.

I curtseyed and Lincoln offered a shallow bow as his father welcomed us. The prince didn't take his gaze off Lincoln. He seemed fascinated by his illegitimate son. I wondered if, like me, he saw the similarity in their regal bearing and strong brow. They shared few other characteristics that I could see.

"I'll take you to Her Majesty directly," the prince said. "I simply wanted to take these few minutes to speak with you alone." He nodded at the footman who fell well behind as we walked.

"Is something the matter?" Lincoln asked, his hands at his back as we strolled through a room of intimate proportions compared to the state reception rooms.

"Not at all. Miss Holloway, I hope you're well."

"I am, thank you, sir. And you?"

"In excellent health." The prince placed his hands at his back the same as Lincoln. Lincoln immediately moved his hands to his sides. He caught me smirking at him and his eyes narrowed.

"And your moth— the queen?" I asked. "Is she well?"

"Well enough for her age. Her Majesty will be heading up to Balmoral soon for the rest of the summer. She prefers it there. The city gets far too stifling. My sister and her family will travel with her, of course, and I'll go up later in the summer."

"And His Royal Highness, the Duke of Edinburgh?" Lincoln asked.

"One never knows what my brother is doing from one week to the next." The Prince of Wales gave us a flat-lipped smile. "He's waiting with Her Majesty now. I must warn you, they both have a bee in their bonnet over some recent events that I'm sure I don't need to detail for you."

"Thank you for the warning," I said. "We're glad you called this meeting as we have some points of discussion to raise with you too."

"Oh?"

A stiff footman opened a door to the queen's private sitting room, cutting off our conversation. We'd been in this room before. I'd spoken to the spirit of the queen's late husband here. She'd been welcoming then, but she now looked unhappy to see us, her thick brow and pendulous jowls forming a severe frown. The Duke of Edinburgh greeted us with a flaring of his nostrils. We didn't even warrant a nod.

I curtseyed and Lincoln bowed. The queen indicated we should sit at the round table where both her sons now sat. She occupied the sofa, her black skirts spread around her like a storm cloud.

"You will have read the papers," Her Majesty began.

"Yes, ma'am," Lincoln said. "We've confronted the journalist who wrote the article for *The Star*."

"The one who mentioned werewolves? What an irresponsible thing to do! I hope you told him so."

"We certainly did," I said. "We asked him why he concluded that the attacks had been carried out by werewolves, but he wouldn't give a clear answer. He seemed to be guessing."

"An accurate guess?" the duke asked.

"In my opinion, yes," Lincoln said.

The prince sat back in the chair and rubbed his hand over his mouth and beard. "Good God," he muttered.

"And how will you stop them, Mr. Fitzroy?" the queen asked.

"When I find out who it is—"

"It's obvious," the duke said. "There's a pack of shape shifting wolves in the East End. Look there for your murderer, Fitzroy."

"How do you know about this pack?" the prince asked his brother.

"You know how."

And so did we—Swinburn or Ballantine had told him.

"I am not convinced it's them," Lincoln said. "We have—"

"Not convinced!" The duke scoffed. "It must be them. Slum dwellers are a lawless rabble, always making trouble, and the mauling deaths occurred in their very neighborhood. I knew you'd try to defend them, Fitzroy, but where's the evidence? Do you have any?"

"Only my instincts. The pack leader is not violent, and a member of their pack is known to us. We trust her."

"A friend, eh?" The duke snorted. "That explains it."

Lincoln stiffened. "We need more time to—"

"More time! And how many more murders will occur while you take time?"

The queen put up her hand, saving us from a prickly stand-off. "Enough, Affie. I'm sure Mr. Fitzroy and Miss Holloway are doing their best."

"I am not quite as convinced."

"Why?" Lincoln asked. Oh lord. This had the potential to deteriorate very quickly.

The duke blanched. "I beg your pardon?"

"Are you suggesting I am not impartial?"

"No one is suggesting that," the prince said with a sharp glare for his brother.

"I am merely playing devil's advocate," the duke said, sounding miffed. "There are some who would shut down the ministry."

"Who?" Lincoln said, his tone steely.

The duke straightened. "People."

"Affie," the prince warned.

"Would this be the same people who informed *The Star's* journalist about the ministry?" Lincoln pressed. "The same people who suggested to the reporter that a werewolf may be responsible for these recent deaths?"

"I wouldn't know about that." The duke stood and headed for the door.

"Affie," the queen bit off. "Sit down. We haven't finished."

The duke did as his mother bade. She was clearly still in command, despite her advanced years. Her sons dared not oppose her.

"The Ministry of Curiosities is a necessary organization," the prince said. "They will not be shut down."

"You would say that," the duke grumbled.

The prince gave his head a slight shake then his gaze flicked to the queen. So she still didn't know that he'd fathered Lincoln. If he hadn't informed her by now, he probably never would.

"If you attempt to abolish the ministry," Lincoln said, "then it will simply go underground. It has existed for centuries and will continue to exist, long after we're all gone."

"You think you're above authority?" the duke demanded. "Above the monarch, parliament, the will of the people? God, man, that is arrogant."

Lincoln didn't bother to answer him, which only made the duke's nostrils flare more. He looked as if he would storm off again and this time not heed his mother's summons to return.

"You mentioned that you were going to request an audience with us," the prince said quickly. "Why?"

"Have you spoken to my husband's spirit again, Miss Holloway?" The queen's voice sounded young, hopeful, and not at all like it belonged to the dour woman planted on the sofa.

"No, ma'am," I said.

"Oh." Her shoulders slumped and she fell into silence.

I appealed to Lincoln to get to the point before she requested I summon the prince consort's ghost now.

"Have you met with Sir Ignatius Swinburn since we foiled his plot to marry Lord Ballantine's daughter to His Royal Highness Prince Albert Victor?" Lincoln asked.

"That is none of your affair," the duke said.

"We have," the prince said, ignoring his brother's glare. "He is our friend and confidant. We trust him. He was not involved in *Ballantine's* plot."

"He was," Lincoln pressed.

"Look here," the duke said, sitting up straighter. "How dare you suggest our friends are conspiring against us!"

"He denied involvement," the queen said. "My sons chose to believe him and therefore so do I. They are very good judges of character."

"He's a shape shifting wolf."

"So you've already told us," the prince said. "That changes nothing. Even if he is, he's not involved in these latest deaths."

"He has far too much sense to wander into the Old Nichol, for goodness' sake," the duke scoffed.

I sighed and didn't bother to correct him. Neither did Lincoln. We had no evidence of Swinburn's wrongdoing, and until we did, there was no point accusing him in the presence of people who defended him. Swinburn was a trusted adviser to the royal family and until that trust was broken, they would choose his side.

The clock on the mantel chimed and the queen put out her hand. "Help me up, Affie."

The duke assisted his mother. Lincoln and I both rose and bowed as she exited the room. The duke followed her. I let out a breath once they'd gone, glad that the queen had not asked me to speak to her dead husband again.

"Forgive my brother," the prince said, walking with us out of the room. "He's a loyal friend to Sir Ignatius."

"Too loyal?" I suggested.

"Sir Ignatius isn't the sort of person you think he is. He may enjoy the odd party or two, but he's not a murderer, swindler or liar. He gives generously to a number of charities and is fiercely loyal. He has defended us in private and in public when others we called friends did not. He wouldn't harm a soul, nor condone anyone who does. I believe he has shed Ballantine as a friend and distances himself from the other members of his pack who were involved in the Hyde Park death."

"He may have distanced himself socially," I said, "but he still runs with them when in wolf form."

"How do you know? Has he told you that?"

I bit the inside of my lip. I didn't have an answer and I suspected any further attempt to tell him the truth about Swinburn would only raise his ire.

"We have a different experience of Swinburn," Lincoln said. At the prince's protest, Lincoln raised a hand for silence. To my utter shock, the prince closed his mouth. "But I see you'll need proof, sir. Hopefully I can give you that proof soon."

"Part of me hopes you do, if only so that I will have the pleasure of your company again. Yours too, Miss Holloway. Perhaps you'll be Mrs. Fitzroy the next time we meet." He smiled, and I forgave him his defense of Swinburn. There was no fault in being loyal to a friend, and it was only fair that he required proof before casting him out. I would agree to nothing less if I were in his position.

"His Royal Highness the duke seems intent on closing the ministry," Lincoln hedged.

The prince waved off the suggestion. "It was just a passing comment, said in the heat of the moment. My brother wouldn't do it."

"He can't anyway," I said. "He has no authority. Has he?"

"We may not sit in parliament, Miss Holloway, but we have influence with the nation's decision makers. If we wanted to shut down the ministry it would be within our power to do so."

I swallowed heavily and took Lincoln's offered arm. I suddenly needed something solid to hold on to.

* * *

"I expected better from two princes," Lincoln said as we drove home from the palace. I wouldn't quite say he seethed, but he certainly wasn't in a good mood. "I expected them to be more particular in their choice of friends. They ought to be, in their position."

"Politics and diplomacy are messy affairs," I said. "I suppose it's not easy to find true friends, so when one displays loyalty, they like to keep him close."

"They're naive."

"They merely want proof before they condemn a friend. What really concerns me is the duke's suggestion that the ministry could be shut down. If Swinburn is in his ear, he might just do it."

"Swinburn is definitely in his ear. Make no mistake about that."

I nibbled my lower lip and studied Lincoln's severe brow and the hard planes of his jaw.

"You're angry with the duke," I said.

He considered this a moment then shook his head. "Getting angry with an ill-informed fool is pointless. He'll change his tune when he learns the truth."

Perhaps I ought to take a leaf out of Lincoln's book. The duke made my blood boil. I couldn't wait to see him eat his words. "You said we'd go into hiding if anyone tried to shut down the ministry. Will I need to pass myself off as a boy again?"

"This isn't a joke, Charlie."

"I'm not joking. Not really. What does it mean to go underground? Will we lose Lichfield Towers?" A lump formed in my throat and tears burned my eyes. The old fear of losing my home, my friends, came unbidden and unexpectedly.

Lincoln leaned forward and rested his elbows on his knees. He took my hands in both of his and kissed my gloved fingers. "Lichfield belongs to me, not the ministry. If the authorities closed the ministry, we'll be forced to destroy our records and publicly state that we will no longer pursue paranormal matters. That's all. Nothing will happen to us or our home. This is the nineteenth century, not thirteenth."

I blinked back my tears and smiled to show him that I appreciated the reassurance. "But of course we won't actually destroy the files, will we?"

He merely smiled against my fingers.

* * *

LINCOLN SPENT the rest of the day and into the night talking to his contacts in the Old Nichol. He had a strong spy network consisting of people from various walks of life who gathered information for him. He paid them handsomely and got good results. This time, however, he insisted on staying in the East End himself to keep watch on Gawler's pack's movements. He returned before breakfast with Seth and Gus.

I'd woken at dawn and waited up for them. At the sound of footsteps outside my door, I threw a wrap around my shoulders and joined them in the corridor.

"Well?" I prompted. "How did it go?"

Seth dragged his hand through his hair. He looked ragged and disheveled, partly to blend in with the other East Enders, and partly because he'd spent all night outdoors. Of course he still looked handsome, perhaps even more so. I ought to wake Alice...

"I'm getting too old for this," he said. "Staying out all night is for young men."

"Lincoln looks fine," I teased.

"And I stink." Seth sniffed his armpit and pulled a face. "I don't know how you can stand it, Gus."

"I'm used to you," Gus said around a yawn. "I'm going to get an hour or two of sleep." He trudged up the corridor, Seth not far behind.

I appealed to Lincoln. "You didn't see any wolves, did you?"

He shook his head and his hair fell across his eyes making him look devilishly broody. "We did learn that Gawler's pack are doing some spying of their own. Gus followed one of the pack members to Swinburn's house. He did nothing, just watched for a few hours before being relieved by another."

"Why are they doing that?"

"Gawler is adamant that Swinburn is setting his pack up to take the blame for these murders."

"He may be right. Did Swinburn or his pack go for a run?"

Another shake of his head. "There were also extra constables on patrol and I saw some men with clubs roaming the streets."

"Vigilantes," I murmured. "So it has begun."

"It'll be hard for either pack to run now."

"Hard but not impossible."

He touched my chin and planted a light kiss on my lips. "Go back to bed, my love," he whispered.

I clasped my arms around his waist and held him to me. "Care to join me?"

"You are wicked. No wonder I adore you." He plucked my arms off and kissed my forehead. "Go back to bed *alone* and I'll see you for breakfast in two hours."

I pouted playfully. "You really are going to make me wait until our wedding night, aren't you?"

"I'm certainly going to try," he muttered as he walked off.

* * *

A MESSAGE CAME for Lincoln over breakfast that made him groan. Considering he rarely showed emotion, I knew it must be particularly awful. I asked to see it as I returned to my chair with a plate of bacon, toast and a boiled egg.

"It's from Andrew Buchanan," I told Alice and Lady Vickers, who'd joined us in the dining room. Seth and Gus still slept. I read further and groaned too. "He has called a committee meeting here in an hour."

"So soon after the last one?" Alice asked. "Why?"

"He doesn't say."

"It had better be for a good reason," Lincoln growled. "Or I'll make his life miserable."

"I think it already is. His lover is getting married, he has no home, no money and no prospects of earning any. Plus he's a turd."

Lady Vickers clicked her tongue. I thought she didn't

like my language, but it turned out to be because she didn't like Buchanan. "The man's a fool and a wastrel. He always was, and age hasn't improved him. He still acts like a petulant child. Look at the way he behaves over Julia! Quite pathetic."

"She does encourage it," I said. "Or she has in the past. That will probably stop, now that she's marrying." I pulled my toast apart but didn't eat. "Joining the committee might distract him, at least."

Alice lowered her fork to her plate. "Do you think it will give him some sorely needed purpose?"

"I do hope so," Lady Vickers said. "There's nothing more invigorating for the mind and spirit than a purpose. Don't you agree, Charlie?"

"I do," I said.

"My newfound purpose is to see that my son marries well and gets back on his feet."

I didn't think that a very sound purpose considering Seth already seemed to be well and truly on his feet. But I didn't say so.

"Good luck," Alice quipped as she got up to pour more tea into her cup.

Lady Vickers narrowed her gaze as if she were trying to work out if Alice meant something else by her comment. I detected nothing insincere, however.

The hour passed quickly and the three coaches arrived on time. Lords Marchbank and Gillingham drove up in their private coaches whereas Buchanan stepped out of a hansom that he then sent on its way.

"Good morning, everyone," he said as Doyle took his hat in the entrance hall. "Shall we adjourn to the library?"

"What's this about?" Gillingham asked before we'd all settled. Seth and Gus hadn't joined us since they were still asleep. Lincoln didn't look any worse for getting a mere two hours rest before breakfast. I'd once called him a machine—sometimes it didn't seem far from the truth.

Buchanan lifted a hand to ward off Gillingham's question, but it was me he addressed. "Charlotte, should you be here? You're not part of the committee—"

"She stays," Lincoln said.

"Get to the point, Buchanan," Gillingham snapped. "I've got things to do."

Buchanan snorted. "Like keep an eye on your wife?"

Gillingham had been about to take his seat, but he now rounded on Buchanan. "What are you implying?"

Buchanan hiked up his trouser legs and sat in an armchair. "Sit down, Gilly. You're not frightening anyone."

Gillingham's hand tightened around the head of his walking stick. "I should thrash you, you imbecile."

"Wait until *after* you hear what I have to say." Buchanan's laconic manner had *me* wanting to thrash him.

"What do you mean about keeping an eye on Harriet?" I asked, knowing I was playing into his hands.

Buchanan waved at the brandy on the sideboard. "Pour me a glass, Fitzroy."

"No," Lincoln said flatly.

"It's ten in the morning!" Marchbank said. "Get on with the meeting. Why did you call us here? What's happened?"

"Very well." Buchanan gave the brandy decanter a longing look then tore his gaze away. "I wanted to take Fitzroy to task. He hasn't reported in yet."

"There's nothing to report," I said.

Buchanan held up a finger. "The meeting with the journalist." He held up another finger. "The summons to the palace."

"The palace!" Gillingham spat. "Why haven't you mentioned it, Fitzroy? Buchanan's right, you need to report in on such important meetings immediately."

"No, I do not," Lincoln said. "There's nothing to report. I learned nothing at the palace. Her Majesty simply wanted to discuss the possibility that werewolves are roaming the city. She wanted reassurance that we will find them and stop them from killing again."

"And was she reassured?" Marchbank asked.

"I believe so."

"She was," I added. I waited to see if Lincoln would mention the discussion surrounding Swinburn and the duke's threat to close the ministry, but he didn't.

"You went too?" Buchanan said to me. "Was that necessary?"

Lincoln merely glared at him.

"You don't think I should have gone?" I asked sweetly. "Why not?"

"Because of what you are."

"You mean a necromancer? It's all right, Mr. Buchanan, you can say the word. I won't bring back your father and have him put you over his knee. Well, I may, if you really annoy me."

Buchanan's lips twitched and twisted with indignation. "You little—"

"*Don't.*" Lincoln's low growl sent a shiver down *my* spine.

Buchanan paled. "I'm merely pointing out that Her Majesty might not like having a necromancer in her midst."

"She knows," I lied. The queen did not know. She thought me a medium, a more acceptable supernatural than one who raised the dead.

"Very well then, but be sure to keep the committee informed of all your meetings, Fitzroy, not just the ones you choose to tell us about."

"I'll inform you when you need to know," Lincoln said. "Is that clear?"

"It's clear," Marchbank said before Buchanan tumbled into even bigger trouble. "Is that all, Buchanan?"

"No. There's another matter," Buchanan said, smugly.

Gillingham sighed. "This had better be worth my time."

"It's about you, as it happens. Or rather, your wife."

Gillingham stamped the end of his walking stick into the floor. "Harriet is not a *matter* that requires discussion. No one is interested in your gossip."

"She *is* a matter for discussion within the ministry. Just as Charlotte is. Anyone of an unnatural nature must be discussed, cataloged and monitored." Buchanan touched a finger to his lips then pointed at Gillingham. His theatricality made a mockery of Gillingham and his protest. "Indeed, didn't *you* say something similar once when it came to Charlotte's whereabouts?"

"How do you know about that?" Gillingham spluttered. "You weren't on the committee then."

"Julia," Lord Marchbank said with a shake of his head. "She told you everything that went on in our meetings, didn't she, Buchanan?"

Buchanan lifted one shoulder in elegant nonchalance.

"If you reciprocate and tell her what is said here, you will find yourself off the committee," Marchbank said.

"Or worse," Lincoln added.

"Right. Well." Buchanan cleared his throat. "Getting back to my point about the lovely Lady Gillingham. We all know what she is and the scum she associates with."

"She does *not* associate with scum." Gillingham's voice rose to a shout.

"She runs with Gawler's pack."

"That is different. Nobody knows about that but us, so it doesn't count."

Buchanan snorted. "Given that the attacks have occurred

in their jurisdiction, she is a suspect and must be treated as such."

Gillingham stamped his walking stick into the floor over and over. "Enough! Enough of this rubbish, Buchanan! My wife is above suspicion. She's a countess, for God's sake."

"She's a *werewolf*. She thinks and acts like a...an animal. They're wild creatures, Gilly, and cannot be controlled. Their superior strength, speed and senses make them even more difficult to manage. You know that." Buchanan bared his teeth in a twisted smile. "Indeed, I'd wager you know how strong your wife is better than anyone."

Gillingham shot to his feet, his face redder than his hair. "I won't listen to this."

"You need to listen to it," Buchanan shot back. "She's a suspect just as much as anyone in Gawler's pack is. You are the best person to follow and observe—"

"I will *not* spy on my wife!"

"Why not? If she is innocent, it's in your power to prove it."

Gillingham sat down again and shook his head.

"You're afraid, aren't you?" Buchanan goaded. "Afraid of what she'll do to you if she finds out."

"That's enough," Marchbank snapped. "Buchanan, be quiet. Harriet is not a suspect."

"I agree," I said. "A person's character is not suppressed when he or she shifts into their other form. Someone with murderous tendencies in human shape retains that in their wolf shape, and I can say with utmost confidence that Harriet is not a murderer. You know it, too, Andrew. You might be a turd but you're a good judge of character."

Buchanan made a miffed sound through his nose but, to my surprise, didn't challenge me. Perhaps because Lincoln stood close enough to throttle him.

"Charlie's right," Marchbank said. "Harriet is no murderess. That doesn't exonerate her pack, however."

We all agreed on that score, but Lincoln did say he believed Gawler himself was innocent.

"Even so," Marchbank said, "it might be wise for Harriet to stay away from them for now so she doesn't get caught up in this mess. That newspaper article has stirred up unrest."

Lincoln nodded. "There were vigilantes and extra constables in the East End overnight."

Gillingham groaned and rubbed his forehead.

"Harriet claimed she's not running with her pack until after the baby is born," I said. "She'll be safe."

"She still associates with them," Gillingham said heavily.

"Then forbid it," Buchanan said with a flourishing wave of his hand. "Oh, that's right, you can't tell her what to do anymore."

"This coming from a man who has had so much luck controlling *his* woman," Gillingham spat. "You couldn't forbid Julia to associate with other men while she was with you, and then you lost her altogether to another. Tell me, does she even let you in her bed anymore?"

Buchanan leapt from his chair and flew at Gillingham. Gillingham must have assumed Lincoln would stop him, so didn't try to defend himself. His misguided confidence meant that Buchanan smashed his fist into Gillingham's jaw, sending the earl's head slamming into the armchair's backrest. He cried out and put his hands up, his walking stick flailing aimlessly and in danger of hitting the books on the shelf behind him. Buchanan pulled his fist back and went to strike again, but Lincoln finally stepped in and caught his arm.

Buchanan stood down but glared daggers at Gillingham. Since Gillingham had closed his eyes, he didn't notice.

"This meeting is adjourned," Marchbank said, rising. "Buchanan, come with me. I'll take you home."

Buchanan tugged on his jacket cuffs and strode out of the library. He flung open the door and almost walked into Seth, who was about to enter. Seth took one look at Buchanan then Gillingham, rubbing his jaw, and grinned.

"I missed all the fun," he said.

Buchanan slipped past him, deliberately bumping his shoulder against Seth's and snatched his hat off Doyle.

Seth rolled his eyes. "Charlie? What happened?"

I led him to the parlor on the other side of the entrance hall and told him about the meeting. He chuckled through most of it.

* * *

LINCOLN, Seth and Gus went out for the rest of the day. Alice and I occupied ourselves in the attic, but I left her there when Whistler informed me Lincoln had returned and wished to see me. I looked forward to sneaking in some kisses in the privacy of his rooms, but he wasn't alone. Seth and Gus were with him in his office.

"Why are you pouting?" Gus asked me.

"No reason," I said on a sigh.

"Where's Alice?" Seth asked.

"In the attic."

"What's she doing in the attic?"

"Practicing her penmanship. How did you go this afternoon?"

"We spoke with all of the men and women in Gawler's pack," Lincoln said. "We asked them whether they were involved in the recent murders. They all denied it. Two definitely told the truth."

"And the others?"

"My seer's senses weren't strong enough to know for certain."

I perched on the edge of his desk. A pile of newspapers sat on the corner, all ironed by Doyle and ready for Lincoln's perusal. He liked to keep up with the news, but it was no more important than now. I picked up the pile and went through them. *The Star* was not among them. I glanced at the clock on the mantel. It was an evening paper so ought to arrive soon.

"I asked Doyle to bring me *The Star* as soon as it's delivered," Lincoln said, reading my thoughts. "No ironing necessary."

"He won't like that," Seth said. "He lives to iron newspapers."

The knock on the door couldn't have been more timely. Gus answered it and accepted the newspaper from Doyle. He closed the door again and handed the paper to Lincoln. It was *The Star's* latest edition.

Lincoln moved the inkstand, books and notebooks to the edges of his desk and spread out the newspaper. He tapped his finger on the main article on the front page.

"Damn," he muttered.

Seth, Gus and I crowded around his chair and read over his shoulder. *No. Oh no.* Once again, Mr. Salter's article mentioned werewolves being responsible for the attacks, but that wasn't the worst of it. He wrote about the Ministry of Curiosities and our role in controlling supernaturals. As if that revelation weren't enough, he then went on to claim we were an inept, corrupt, and biased organization.

"Fuck," Gus said. "This is bad. Really bad."

CHAPTER 6

There was nothing to be done about the article. It was already printed and a retraction would come too late. No sooner had the ministry been revealed to the public than our reputation had been ruined. A denial couldn't fix it. We'd begun our public life on the back foot. I thanked God Lincoln wasn't named in the article.

"I propose we kill the journalist," Seth said. At my glare he put up his hands in surrender. "A joke."

"I don't think Salter is entirely to blame for this." I leaned into Lincoln's back as he sat, and indicated the newspaper on the desk in front of him. "Someone is behind it. Someone has fed him the information about the ministry and is urging him to write this nonsense to destroy us. My money's on Swinburn."

"And mine's on the Duke of Edinburgh," Lincoln said.

"Since we're casting votes, I pick Julia," Seth added.

Gus shrugged. "Could be any of 'em. Or none."

"Thank you for your insight." Seth drummed his fingers on the desk. "We need to do something about this. Any ideas, Fitzroy?"

"We continue on as planned," Lincoln said. "Our priority is to protect the public and find the murderer."

"And what if the public don't want us to save them?"

"Aye," Gus chimed in. "Or what if we're shut down? We can't help no one if we shut up shop."

"No one will shut us down based on a newspaper article," Lincoln said.

I placed my hands on his shoulders and absently massaged. "We'll simply move our operations underground. Plans are already in motion."

Gus studied the floor beneath his feet. "Someone's digging tunnels under Lichfield while we were out?"

Seth thumped Gus's arm. "Idiot. She means *metaphorically* underground." He looked to me. "Don't you?"

I smiled. "I do. We're making a copy of the archive files. Now get to work. I suspect the only way to salvage our reputation and remain in operation is to find the killer and stop him or her."

"And find out who is leaking information to Salter," Lincoln added.

* * *

SETH WATCHED Swinburn overnight while Gus remained in the Old Nichol slum to spy on Gawler. Lincoln didn't specify where he would go, but I suspected he would travel between the two and speak with his own informants in an attempt to gather information.

It wasn't until he returned the following morning, and I questioned him, that he told me about breaking into Salter's lodgings again. This time he'd found the notebook—and brought it home with him.

"Let me know if you find anything in here," he said,

handing it to me. We stood in my bedroom, although he remained near the door. I'd got up to answer it upon his soft knock before dawn. I'd known it would be him so hadn't bothered with a wrap.

He studiously kept his gaze on my face.

"What are you going to do?" I asked.

"Sleep." He turned the chair at my dressing table around, put his booted feet on the trunk at the end of my bed, crossed his ankles and arms, and closed his eyes.

I kissed him lightly on the lips then returned to bed. He slept soundlessly for two hours while I scoured the pages of the notebook.

"Anything?" he asked, startling me.

I yawned and shook my head. "Nothing. No mention of Swinburn or any other names I recognize. He merely labels all of his informants as "Source" then assigns them a letter of the alphabet. Source K is ours."

He settled on the bed beside me but did not slip under the covers. I was acutely aware of his presence and the warmth his body exuded. I sidled closer, not that it was cold in the room but simply because I wanted to. To my surprise, he did not move away. In fact, he put his arm around me and nestled me into his side. This was my opportunity to take our relationship beyond kissing. Finally we were alone, in a bed, and it was early enough that only the servants were awake. Lincoln could sneak out afterward and not be seen. Perfect!

"Do you think the K refers to an initial?" he asked.

I blinked rather stupidly at him. "Huh?"

"The notebook." He took it off me and flipped through the pages. "Do you think Source K's name begins with a K?"

"Oh. Right. I was thinking of..." I bit the inside of my cheek and looked away.

"I know what you were thinking," he said with a smile in his voice.

"It's unfair that you can read my mind."

"Not always. But this time your thoughts are clearer than the words on these pages. So back to my question, do you think Source K's name begins with a K?"

"No. It's just the next letter of the alphabet. If you look through the book at the previous sources, they're lettered A to J." I slumped back into the pillows. "There is nothing of an identifying nature in there. Salter has been very careful."

He kissed my temple then scooted off the bed. "Try and get more sleep. I suspect it'll be a long day ahead."

"Why?"

" I hear other newspapers are picking up the story. That means more public interest in it, and more public interest means the authorities will need to act."

"Against us?"

"I don't yet know but I want to be prepared."

With that news ringing in my ears, sleep was impossible.

* * *

A LETTER from the Prince of Wales arrived over breakfast, warning Lincoln to be careful. He'd heard that certain members of parliament were looking into the reports of werewolves and the existence of the ministry. He suspected they'd demand to know more about it and we must be prepared to be questioned.

"And what is *he* going to do about it?" I said irritably.

"He says he'll use his influence to diffuse their interest." Lincoln passed the letter on to me then buttered his toast. "He can buy us time."

"To do what?" Lady Vickers asked.

"To get our stories straight," Seth told her. He and Gus

had only slept for a few hours, like Lincoln. They were too on edge to rest. "And to hide the evidence."

"What would you like us to say if we're questioned?" Alice asked, peering at Lincoln over her teacup.

"Don't deny our existence, but play down our influence and knowledge," he said. "Don't tell anyone about the records, don't mention our recent spying jaunts, or any of our previous investigations." He lowered his knife and fork and fixed a glare onto each of us in turn. "Do not mention Charlie's necromancy or I will—"

"Lincoln," I said sweetly, "pass the butter."

His lips flattened but he took my interruption well.

"And for God's sake, don't mention your dreams, Alice," I added. "If the authorities know an army came here through you, they'll lock you up."

"It wouldn't do any good," Gus said, knocking the top off his boiled egg. "They'd still come."

"Gus!" Seth scolded.

"Well they would."

"Who will question us anyway?" Lady Vickers asked Lincoln. "Who are these so-called authorities and what authority do they have over me?"

"The police will be sent," Lincoln said. "I suspect the members of parliament will request that Scotland Yard question us."

"I want nothing to do with the police," Lady Vickers snipped. "I'm not a common thief. I'll refuse to talk to them."

"Then you'll look guilty," Seth said. "It's better to just lie."

"I do not *just* lie, Seth. I'm a Christian woman. I tell the truth in all things."

"Is that so?" He set down his knife and fork then leaned forward. "Tell me, Mother, when did you last see Cook?"

She pushed her chair back and got to her feet. "I don't have to answer that."

Seth spread out his hands. "Then you're guilty."

"Of what?"

"Of...of... You know what!" He screwed up his napkin and tossed it on the table then stalked out of the dining room.

Lady Vickers sat again and lifted her teacup. "I need to find him a wife quickly. If only he wasn't so particular." She sipped calmly, putting on a good show of being unruffled. But I wasn't fooled.

I went in search of Seth after breakfast and found him in the attic. "You should apologize to your mother," I said. "You upset her."

"I know." He sat by the window, staring out at the overcast sky. Some of the ministry's records were spread on the desk near him but he wasn't making any attempts to copy them. "But she upset me too. She and Cook are..." He shook his head. "I can't believe it's happening again, right under my very nose *again*."

I clasped his shoulder. "Let it run its course. Their affections will wane soon enough. They're quite unsuited."

"That's what I thought about the footman, and look what happened—she ran off to America and married him."

He turned back to the window so didn't see my smile. I couldn't help it. The story was rather a romantic one.

"Besides," he added quietly, "Cook is my friend. I don't want her to ruin that friendship."

"It won't be ruined. Your friendship is strong." I took a seat at the desk and pulled a stack of ministry records toward me. "You know what will irk her?"

He eyed me sideways. "What?"

"You and Alice."

He sighed. "Charlie—"

"You've hardly paid Alice any attention of late. How do you expect to grow in her affections if you ignore her?"

"Paying her attention didn't advance my cause. Perhaps

absence will make the heart grow fonder." He joined me at the desk. "Or something."

Gus arrived but not to help copy the records. "Gillingham's here," he announced.

"What does he want now?" Seth muttered.

Gus's finger twirled small circles at his temple. "He's dolally. He's going on about the newspapers exposing him and his family, putting his wife and unborn child in danger."

"And Lincoln's just listening to him?" I asked.

"He ain't home. Gillingham's in Lady V's ear."

"I'd better rescue her," I said, rising. "Seth?"

He shook his head. "I'm staying here. I don't want anything to do with either at the moment."

I headed downstairs on my own and found Lord Gillingham pacing the parlor, his walking stick stabbing at the floor with each stride. Lady Vickers sat on a chair by the window but stood upon my entrance.

"I must leave you," she announced and swanned past me. I tried to appeal to her but she didn't meet my gaze.

I was alone with Gillingham, a position I'd not found myself in for some time. Lincoln saw to that. My history with the earl was turbulent, and even violent when I'd first come to Lichfield. A lot had changed since then. The balance of power had shifted and I even counted his wife among my friends. Despite all that, my nerves still jangled and my stomach tied itself in knots.

"Where's Fitzroy?" he demanded before I could speak.

"I don't know," I said. "Nor do I know when he'll return. Is something the matter?"

"Of course something's the matter!" he roared. "My wife's life and that of my unborn child have been put in danger!"

I drew in a deep breath and let it out slowly. "She has not been named in any articles."

"It's only a matter of time now that the ministry has been

exposed." He thrust his walking stick under his arm and stood stiffly by the mantel. "What if I am connected? Someone wants to harm my family. It's not on. Not on, I tell you."

"I don't think it's personal," I said. "If it is, then Lincoln is the target, not you."

"Does it matter who is the target? We'll all get injured in the crossfire. Can't you see that? No, of course you can't. You can't think beyond the scope of your own limited experience and education. If you were brought up properly, with a view to understanding how the world works, you'd be aware of the dangers." He sniffed. "Ignorance is bliss, as they say."

"Kindly refrain from insulting me in my home," I bit back.

"*Your* home. Ha! Just because you managed to twist Fitzroy around your little finger and trap him into marriage doesn't mean *you'll* ever own this place. It will always be his, never yours. He can throw you out like that." He clicked his fingers. "You won't keep his interest forever, Charlotte. Just wait until you've borne him a couple of brats, he'll grow tired and look elsewhere. And Julia will be waiting for him."

I stepped forward and slapped him across the cheek. "You never learn, do you?"

He rubbed his cheek and shot me a vicious glare. "You little whore."

I rolled my eyes and strode out of the parlor. "Whistler!" I called.

The footman emerged from the back of the entrance hall. "Yes, miss?"

"See that Lord Gillingham finds his way out immediately."

"I'm waiting for Fitzroy," Gillingham said.

"No, you are not," I said over my shoulder. "He's far too busy to bother with your hysteria."

"Hysteria? How dare you?"

I suppose it was rather awful of me to assign him an

affliction usually attributed to nervous women, but it felt quite satisfying listening to his protests as I walked up the staircase.

"I will not be so insulted!" he continued to declare behind me. "Get your hands off me!"

I looked down when I reached the landing, just in time to see Whistler close the front door on Gillingham. I smiled at him and the footman grinned back.

I informed Lincoln of Gillingham's visit when he returned, but didn't mention how I'd needed to slap him to stop his tirade. "He's anxious," I said. "He's worried about Harriet and the baby. It's good to see him being the dutiful loving husband, I suppose, but he's still obnoxious."

"He's more worried about his own reputation than his wife's safety," Seth said. We sat in Lincoln's study again after lunch, with the intention of going over the day's developments.

"I'm not so sure," I said from where I sat on the sofa in the area used as a sitting room. "But I could be wrong. Lincoln, where did you go today?"

"To speak to my contact at Scotland Yard," he said, leaning back in the chair at his desk. "He'll see what he can find out, but he doesn't have enough authority to be involved at a high level."

"Another letter arrived for you from the palace," I said. "Have you read it yet?"

He opened his top drawer and pulled out the thick paper with the broken seal. He handed it to Seth, sitting on the other side of the desk. "It's from the Prince of Wales. He says the queen and duke are campaigning against the ministry now. They're using their influence to drum up support to close us down."

"The queen too?" I whined. "But she's on our side! She likes me! I summoned her husband for her."

"She has the realm's interests at heart and if she believes we are harboring a murderer, she'll put her personal feelings aside."

"Then she ought to listen to her eldest son. The prince has the realm's interest at heart too."

Seth handed back the letter. "She's listening to the duke on this. God knows why."

"This is what Eva warned us about," Gus said. "The queen will cause us danger."

I rubbed my forehead, trying to wade through the fog in my brain. What began as an article to be scoffed at had developed into a dire problem. I only hoped common sense would prevail and the royal family would stop pushing for our abolition. For that to happen, they had to stop listening to Swinburn.

And therein lay our problem. He was too powerful. They would continue to listen to him if he continued to prove his worth and loyalty to them. It was a bloody mess.

"Leave us," Lincoln said to Gus and Seth.

They obliged and shut the door, leaving Lincoln and I alone.

He crouched before me and took my face in his hands. "It'll be all right, Charlie. Trust me."

"I do trust you," I said hollowly. "But some things are beyond even your control."

His thumbs stroked along my jaw. "This is our home and it can't be taken away from us. Our friends will always be our friends, and I will always be the one who loves you most." He kissed me with heart stopping gentleness and a longing that melted me. He broke the kiss all too soon and folded me into his arms. "Think about the wedding in five days' time, not this. I'll see that the persecution ends."

A knock interrupted us before I could ask him how.

"You're needed downstairs, Fitzroy," came Seth's voice through the door. "We have visitors."

"Not Gillingham again," I said on a groan as Lincoln opened the door.

"No," Seth said. "The police."

CHAPTER 7

*I*t was not just Detective Inspector Fullbright who demanded to speak to Lincoln. A member of parliament by the name of Yallop also stood in the drawing room. Behind the two men ranged four uniformed constables, all at attention with their hands by their sides, waiting for a command.

Mr. Yallop made the introductions, although he was not the older of the two. His position outranked the frothy whiskered Fullbright's, and the inspector seemed content enough for Yallop to do all the talking. Perhaps because he was too busy observing. His gaze took in his surroundings and each of us more than once. I felt like a freak in the circus, every inch of my person scanned and judged, his assessment to be imparted to others at a later point.

Mr. Yallop only had eyes for Lincoln. "I am the appointed head of the parliamentary Select Committee that was quickly formed in response to the articles in *The Star*," he said with a lift of his double chins. He was a much larger man than the inspector, with a girth that tested the seams of his waistcoat and jacket, and an unhealthy florid complexion.

"You're investigating the ministry," Lincoln said flatly.

"And, by extension, yourself. I am in charge of the investigation and Inspector Fullbright has been assigned to me. As one of the most experienced detectives at Scotland Yard, his insight will be invaluable."

"*The* most experienced," Fullbright said in a soft voice.

"Pardon?" Yallop looked as if he were annoyed at the interruption.

"I am *the* most experienced detective inspector at Scotland Yard. Sir."

"What's a select committee?" Gus asked.

"I'm glad you asked," Mr. Yallop said. "It is a group made up of MPs who investigate matters of national importance then report their findings and recommendations back to their respective department so that relevant policy can be formed. In our case, we are under the Home Office."

"So they're going to make a policy about us?" Gus looked to Lincoln. "Can they do that?"

"They can," Lincoln said.

"Let's not get ahead of ourselves," Seth said. "My name is Lord Vickers," he said to Mr. Yallop. "You have my word as a gentleman that the claims made by Mr. Salter are false. The ministry is not corrupt or biased. We exist to protect the public from—"

"Forgive me, sir, but your word means nothing to me as I do not know you," Mr. Yallop said. "I've never heard of Lord Vickers. Are you a sitting member in the House of Lords? Not all of them are familiar to me."

"I am not."

"Are *you* in fact the leader of this so-called Ministry of Curiosities? Is my source mistaken?"

"They are not." Seth didn't seem at all perturbed to be put in his place. "That honor belongs to Mr. Fitzroy, a more amiable gentleman you will never meet. I'm sure he'll be most obliging and answer your questions in full."

Lincoln gave Seth a sideways glance. "Who is your source?" Lincoln asked the politician.

"I cannot say," Yallop said.

"Then can you say why parliament responds to sensationalist reporting now?"

"We cannot afford another Ripper situation. News of these latest murders and *The Star*'s accusations has spread very quickly. The city is still on edge and fears have resurfaced. The Ripper crimes were not so long ago. Something must be done, and done quickly, to prevent another murder."

"Agreed. We are on the same side, Mr. Yallop."

"That remains to be seen."

"You have my attention," Lincoln said. "I'll answer whatever questions you have. There's no need for such a heavy police presence in my home. You're frightening my fiancée."

As much as I wanted to deny it, he was correct. I was anxious. There were too many constables for a mere interrogation.

"The constables are needed," Mr. Yallop went on. "The police failed to apprehend the Ripper monster and are eager to make amends for that disappointing outcome. Isn't that right, Inspector?"

Detective Inspector Fullbright's whiskers shook. "There are some who would agree with you."

"The ministry is not the vehicle for a political statement," Lincoln said. "Or for the police force to 'make amends.' It transcends politics and exists solely to maintain control over the supernatural, as it has done for centuries. Salter's claims of corruption are false, made simply to sell more papers. Kindly get on with your questions as I have an investigation to undertake."

I placed my hand on Lincoln's arm. It would do no good

for him to get angry now. He needed to be at his most diplomatic, if there were such a thing.

"Then let's begin." Fullbright turned to his constables, but Yallop interrupted him.

"Even if Salter's claims come to nothing, I should warn you that things will change." Mr. Yallop jutted out his jaw, making his chins wobble again. "Your group is far too secretive. It needs to be more open, more accountable, or it's ripe for corruption."

"Not while I am its leader," Lincoln said.

"And how long with that be? Hmmm? No, Mr. Fitzroy. You have had it your own way for too long. Such an organization cannot be allowed to possess as much power as your anonymity gives you."

"You're proposing that we answer to parliament?" Seth scoffed. "And be weighed down by factional politics? It will tie our hands. It's an absurd idea."

"I am yet to give my recommendations on how to run the organization," Mr. Yallop said stiffly. "Or whether it should exist at all. Perhaps abolition is a better alternative. We have a police force, after all."

Lincoln's arm tensed beneath my hand. I squeezed it hard, partly to hold him in check and partly because I needed to cling to him. I felt all at sea suddenly, as if my boat had been cast adrift with me in it.

"Get on with it, Fullbright," Mr. Yallop said. "I haven't got all day."

"Search the house," Inspector Fullbright said to his constables.

"Search the house!" I cried. Seth and Gus echoed my surprise.

"There's no need for a search," Lincoln said, sounding far calmer than I expected. His rigidity told another story, however. "I will answer your questions and cooperate fully."

"As I would hope," Mr. Yallop said with a sniff. "But Inspector Fullbright has a job to do." He nodded at the detective who in turn nodded at his men. They filed out of the drawing room.

The records! We hadn't completely finished making a copy of them all. Letters V to Z were still sitting on the desk for anyone to see. Once the constables found those, they would realize what we were doing and demand to see the other files.

I swallowed heavily and gripped Lincoln's arm harder. "Charlie?" he said. "Are you unwell?"

"It's a little hot in here," I said, flapping my hand in front of my face. "I think I'll retire to my room to lie down."

"No," both Fullbright and Yallop said.

"You will remain here while Fullbright's constables perform their search." Mr. Yallop's lips pinched into what I suspected was an attempt at a placating smile. "Can't have you hiding the files, can we?"

"Files?" Lincoln asked.

Mr. Yallop's smile widened. "So we've been told."

"You're mistaken. There are no files pertaining to the ministry. I keep none."

"We shall see. There are another two constables checking the outbuildings as we speak. We'll leave no stone unturned."

They didn't need to turn any stones, simply open the attic door.

"Are we all prisoners in here?" Seth demanded.

"In a sense," Inspector Fullbright said. "Sit, Miss Holloway. This could take some time."

Lincoln directed me to a seat and I gladly took it. If none of us could leave, how were we to hide the files? We couldn't even pass on a message to Cook, Alice and Lady Vickers. There was still Doyle...

"May I order tea?" I asked with a nod at the bell pull.

"I'll find your butler and ask him to bring refreshments," Mr. Yallop said. "Can't have you communicating with him now, can we?" That pinched smile again. He *knew* what I planned to do.

My stomach plunged. I wanted to scream in frustration but managed to act the demure hostess instead. "Please do not upset the servants. It's so difficult to find good ones nowadays." Lady Vickers would be proud of me.

Mr. Yallop left and some of my anxiety left with him. Inspector Fullbright didn't seem quite so unreasonable, merely a man doing his duty. He pulled a notebook and pencil out of his jacket pocket and settled on the sofa.

"What does the ministry do, precisely?" he asked.

There followed a series of questions that Lincoln answered honestly. Perhaps too honestly. He told the inspector about the types of supernatural abilities that existed, although he didn't mention necromancy, other realms, or portals. It was just as well. Fullbright seemed somewhat overwhelmed by the prospect of mediums, shape changers, seers and fire starters existing alongside ordinary folk. However, he didn't once scoff and tell us we were mad for believing in fairytales. He simply noted everything in his little book and asked another question.

Mr. Yallop returned carrying a tray with teapot and cups. He closed the door with his foot and set it down on the table near me. I poured and handed out the cups, eyeing the bell pull with longing.

Inspector Fullbright sipped his tea, dampening his lengthy mustache. He licked it only to take another sip and do the same again. "Who in the city has supernatural powers?" he asked. "I want names and abilities."

Gus scoffed. "We ain't telling you that."

Fullbright sat with his pencil poised over the notebook and arched his brow at Lincoln.

"As Gus told you, I can't divulge that information," Lincoln said. "Many wish to remain anonymous and I have promised to abide by their wishes."

"Dangers are afoot, Mr. Fitzroy. You cannot protect those who wish us harm or you'll be arrested for hindering a murder investigation."

"Arrested!" I cried. "You cannot arrest him! He's done nothing."

"He is colluding with these supernaturals," Mr. Yallop said. "And at least one of them is a murderer."

"There is no them and us in this equation," Lincoln said. "We all live in this city together. We will find the murderer without your interference."

"Being supernatural doesn't mean they're evil," Seth added. "We've met many who are as normal as we are."

"Yet one has committed an evil act," Mr. Yallop said. "Perhaps more. I suspect you are not telling us about those because you wish to protect them from our justice system. Why? Why are you protecting them?"

Seth took a long sip of his tea so Mr. Yallop focused his attention on Lincoln again.

"Some have committed crimes," Lincoln admitted. " I have meted out justice as I saw fit and will do so again when I catch the one responsible for the recent mauling deaths."

"So you're a vigilante too?" Yallop declared. "Or does your justice allow them to get off lightly?"

"No."

Inspector Fullbright cleared his throat. "The police need to know who to suspect when an atrocity of this nature occurs. It's always easier when we have a list of suspects to question at the start of an investigation."

"I am not here to make your work *easier*," Lincoln said. "I will not be giving you any names. They are *not* suspects any more than you are."

Mr. Yallop set down his teacup with a loud clank. "Of course they're suspects, man! One of them killed those poor devils in the Old Nichol! Who is it? Well? Who is one of those shape-changers you spoke of? Stop this pissing contest and just tell us!"

"No."

"Why are you are protecting them?" Mr. Yallop's gaze shifted to me. Did he suspect?

Or did he already know?

My blood ran cold. My throat dried. Too many times I'd been wanted for my necromancy. I'd been a magnet for madmen intent on raising an army of dead, and I'd been kept prisoner to keep me safe from them. Their deaths had bought my freedom.

And now that freedom might vanish again.

I looked to Lincoln, but he did not look at me. His gaze bored into the politician's. "I am protecting someone," he said. "Myself. I'm a seer." He spread out his hands. "I cannot predict the future, but I can sense lies on some people, and the presence of others."

I drew in a deep breath and let it out slowly.

Mr. Yallop and the inspector both stared at Lincoln. Finally, Inspector Fullbright spoke. "Why attempt to keep that a secret from us?"

"Because I suspect Mr. Yallop doesn't believe that I can't predict the future since that is, after all, the public's perception of a seer. He'll want me to work for him in some capacity, perhaps to predict elections or the way people will vote. I hoped to spare myself his attention. I have no political leanings and no intention of assisting him, even if I could."

His temper was fraying again, his tone growing more and more abrupt. He needed to maintain calmness or risk angering Mr. Yallop and Inspector Fullbright.

The detective flipped his notebook closed. "Tell me or not. It doesn't matter. My men will find your files."

Indeed they would, and the copies we were in the process of making. At least we still had Lincoln's formidable memory to reproduce them. He could probably recall most supernaturals listed in our records, but not all. But the police would still be in possession of the information, and use that to persecute some good people. I heard footsteps overhead, going through the bedrooms, and a woman's voice, but not her words.

Thank goodness I wore the amber orb necklace at all times. Not that the police would know a creature lived inside, but I felt better having it on me where they wouldn't search. I resisted the urge to touch it now and feel its reassuring shape.

Inspector Fullbright continued with more questions, asking about particular traits each type of supernatural showed. He also asked about crimes committed by or against supernaturals where Lincoln had solved them, and Lincoln gave what information he could without giving away the particulars. The detective seemed impressed with his honesty. I hoped it was enough.

From Mr. Yallop's scowl, I suspected not.

Finally the constables returned. They carried no filing cabinet drawers or pieces of paper. "We found nothing, sir," said one. "We checked top to bottom."

I didn't move. Didn't dare, lest I give something away. How could they have found nothing? Did they miss the attic altogether?

"As I already told you, there are no records," Lincoln said. "Now, my friends and staff have been inconvenienced enough. Kindly leave."

Inspector Fullbright stood, but Mr. Yallop huffed out a breath and shook his head. "Inept," the politician muttered.

"My men are thorough," Inspector Fullbright told him. "If they found no files then there are no files."

"There must be! My informant tells me that meticulous records are kept. Damn it, man, send them around again. We *must* find them or we have nothing to show for our efforts."

"Not today," the inspector said, striding to the door. "I have other lines of inquiry to follow anyway." He held Lincoln's gaze. "This investigation is not over. I intend to find out who committed those murders."

"As do I," Lincoln said. "We can work together, Inspector."

The detective merely grunted and left, his men trailing behind him.

Mr. Yallop came up to Lincoln and stood toe to toe with him. He was shorter but wider, his flushed face a red beacon. "I don't trust you, Fitzroy. You're hiding those files, I know it."

"Perhaps your source knows where they are," Lincoln said.

Mr. Yallop's jaw worked then he stormed off. "I *will* find evidence that you've been keeping information from us and when I do, you'll be arrested for conspiracy to murder."

"Murder!" I blurted out.

Mr. Yallop did not stop and Lincoln held me back from chasing after him.

I searched Lincoln's face. "Could he really do that?"

"Unlikely."

Unlikely still contained the word likely in it.

"What an arse," Gus said. "I hope his coach overturns and squashes him."

"Yallop's an eel," Seth said. "But he's dangerous. Select committees have a lot of power. If he recommends we be shut down then we'll be shut down."

"We'll go underground if that happens," I said.

"If he wants to arrest someone, then he'll be arrested," Seth added with a speaking glance at Lincoln.

"This is absurd." I threw my hands in the air. "We are on their side. We want to find the killer too."

"Someone wants the ministry abolished," Lincoln said, heading for the door. "And they are using the most powerful means at their disposal to do it."

"Their influence," I said heavily. "He must have a lot of it to have a select committee formed so quickly. I don't think the public's fear is the entire reason."

"Swinburn," Gus and Seth said together.

I nodded. It had to be. Lincoln stopped in the doorway then stood aside for Lady Vickers and Alice to hurry in. They both sported grins.

"They're gone," Alice announced, shutting the door.

"We did it!" Lady Vickers grasped Alice's hands in her own and shook them. "Well done, Alice, you brave thing. Well done."

"You were brave too. Seth, your mother was a marvel. She acted her role brilliantly, and with no rehearsal or prompting required."

Seth stared at them both, his mouth ajar. "You removed the files, didn't you?"

They both nodded.

"All of them?" I asked.

"Give us some credit, Charlie," Lady Vickers said. "We may not be able to raise the dead, see into the future, or strike a blow with fists, but we are not entirely useless."

"Then do tell how you managed it."

"I suspected what the police wanted," Alice said, taking a seat on the sofa. Lady Vickers sat next to her, quite close. They both still sported smiles. "As soon as I realized you were all in here being interrogated, I went up to the attic to hide the records. I removed the filing cabinet drawers and carried them out of the attic to my bedchamber. I even remembered the ones on the desk. It took three trips but I retrieved all of the records before the constables searched the attic."

"They searched the attic before the bedchambers," Lady Vickers said. "Indeed, they left those to last, and the attic second last."

"It gave me plenty of time," Alice went on, "and I was able to use the service stairs to quickly navigate between floors. By that time, Lady V was delaying them."

"I also knew what they were doing, but not Alice's activities. I thought only to slow their progress to give you time to convince them to leave, Lincoln. I carried on and on about violations of privacy and the like, and I even pretended to faint at one point."

"Faint!" Seth snorted. "Poor man who had to catch you."

"Indeed," his mother said with a laugh. Seth chuckled too.

"But they did search your room, Alice," I said. "So where did you hide the files?"

"I stripped the sheets from my bed and tipped the contents of the drawers into them. I then pricked my thumb with a needle from my sewing basket and gathered up the linen with the files inside the bundle. Of course some of the blood from my thumb got on the sheets. I stacked the drawers inside the cupboard where they did not seem out of place and waited until I could hear sounds of activity in the corridor. I opened the door and pretended to have just woken from a sleep and needed to urgently take the soiled linen to the housekeeper."

"And they just let you pass?" Gus asked.

"I pleaded the women's curse," she said, avoiding his gaze. "The young constable turned as red as a radish."

Gus suddenly didn't know where to look. "I don't blame him."

"He did," Lady Vickers said. "I'd followed them upstairs and performed quite the hysterical show, begging them not to violate us poor women. I saw Alice and realized what she was doing and went along with her story. I convinced them that her courses are a source of difficulty for her and they ought not embarrass her over it. She blushed on cue and hurried past them, her head bowed. It was quite the performance."

"As was yours, madam."

Lady Vickers touched Alice's hand. "We made a good team."

"What did you do with the files?" Lincoln asked.

"They're in the basement," Alice said. "Still wrapped up in my linen."

Lincoln strode off, but paused at the door. "Thank you, ladies. Your quick thinking and bravery saved us. Those records go back a very long way. The information they contain is invaluable to the ministry, both now and in the future."

"Invaluable and dangerous if the wrong hands get a hold of them," Alice said darkly.

I leaned down and hugged her. Like me, she had a lot to worry about if the government learned what we were. Our every move would be tracked to the end of our days, at the very least.

I suppressed my shiver and kissed her and Lady Vickers on their cheeks before picking up my skirts and racing after Lincoln. I thought he would go to the basement, but he went to his rooms. He slid the painting that hung on his wall aside and checked the safe behind it.

"Has it been opened?" I asked.

He shook his head but turned the dial several times and opened it anyway. He swiftly checked the contents then closed the safe door and spun the dial. "They didn't find it," he said, straightening the picture.

"That's a relief."

The safe contained several documents, the most important of which were details of a secret deposit box at the bank. As well as the ministry's financial documents, the deposit box contained a codebook that mapped all the codes Lincoln used when noting information about supernaturals. Since his memory was formidable, his notes were generally meant for the rest of us in the ministry. I was the only other person who knew the wall safe's code so if anything happened to him, I could access it. If the police had found the safe and the deposit box details, the ministry's secrets would be exposed.

"Shall we move the files from the basement?" I asked.

"Not yet. We'll do it under cover of darkness tonight. Wear something you don't mind getting dirty."

We left his rooms and met with Seth and Gus on the staircase on their way up. "Seth, find out everything you can on Yallop. I want to know why he wants to close down the ministry."

"You think he has a personal agenda?" Seth asked.

"I'm not sure."

"He did seem vehement in his enthusiasm," I said.

"Like it were more than his job," Gus agreed.

Gus, Seth, Lincoln, Cook and I buried the files in the walled garden at midnight while most of the household slept. We did not use lamps but moonlight to guide our path, and we didn't speak until we entered the secluded area and only then in whispers. Not only did we bury the files, we also buried the copy we'd made, but in a different location. After spreading manure over the entire area to obscure the freshly turned earth, we returned silently to the house and went our separate ways.

I got no further than my bedroom door. A male voice came from Alice's room. A voice I recognized.

Lincoln heard it too and pushed me behind him. He barged inside before I could stop him.

Alice sat up in bed, awake. The white rabbit from Wonderland stood near the window, his nose twitching violently.

CHAPTER 8

The rabbit's paw tightened around something in his hand. I couldn't see it, but I suspected it was the pocket watch he used to help him travel between realms.

"Wait!" Lincoln said, hands up in surrender. "Don't leave yet. We just want to talk."

The rabbit glanced between Lincoln and me, then back to Alice. He held out his hand to her. "You didn't give me your answer, Miss Alice."

"Answer to what?" Lincoln asked.

"Alice, are you all right?" I said, sidling closer to the bed. "Has he harmed you?"

"Of course I haven't." The rabbit looked horrified. It was not an expression I'd ever seen on an animal before. "What kind of brute do you take me for?"

"The large talking rabbit kind," I told him. "Forgive us, but we're not used to…this."

"I know. Your creatures run around naked. It's obscene. They should be ashamed of themselves."

The conversation had just taken a turn to the absurd. "Alice?" I prompted.

"I'm all right," she said. "We were just talking."

"About?" Lincoln asked.

The rabbit twitched his nose in Lincoln's direction. "Don't tell him, miss. It's between us. No one else need—"

"I beg to differ. Alice lives in my house and I am responsible for her wellbeing. What were you talking about?"

"He told me this is my last chance," Alice said.

"Miss!" The rabbit shook his head in warning.

I sat on the bed alongside Alice. "Last chance for what?"

"To go with him to Wonderland," she said.

"She's not going anywhere," I told the rabbit. "Not to another realm and not with you."

"And if you don't?" Lincoln asked. He had not looked at her but kept his gaze on the rabbit. The rabbit seemed unnerved by the attention, his nose in a constant twitch.

"The queen's army will come for me and take me by force." She clutched my hand in both of hers. Her brow creased into a deep frown. "The last time they came for me they almost destroyed the school."

They'd only stopped because they vanished from this realm when Alice awoke. Since then, the rabbit had learned to remain here after she woke up using a spell. If the army used the same spell…it didn't bear thinking about.

"The queen is desperate," the rabbit told Alice. "Every day you remain here, you anger her more. You *must* return and answer the charges laid against you."

"She's not going anywhere," Lincoln growled.

The rabbit jumped and swallowed heavily. "Please, Miss Alice. For the sake of your friends here, come with me."

"Perhaps I ought to go," Alice said in a small voice.

I clutched her shoulders and locked my gaze with hers. "No! You can't go to another realm, for God's sake! I won't let you."

"I said, she's not going anywhere." Lincoln's dark snarl

had the rabbit backing up against the wall.

He clutched the watch to his chest. "Please, Miss Alice. If you don't come with me, I, as the queen's emissary, will be blamed and punished."

"That's not Alice's problem," I said.

The rabbit ignored me. "Take my hand and we'll return together. If you don't, your aunt will be furious and when she's mad, she—"

"My aunt?" Alice echoed.

The rabbit's nose stopped twitching. "Ah..."

"Is the queen my aunt?"

"Alice has no relatives in your realm," I said.

"Does she?" Lincoln demanded, taking a step toward the bed.

"Stay back!" the rabbit snapped. "Miss Alice, you have to come with me *now!*" He reached toward her, his hind feet planted on the floor as far away from Lincoln as possible.

My fingers tightened on Alice's shoulders. "You cannot seriously be considering going with him."

She bit her lip and blinked watery eyes at me. "But the army..."

"We'll find a way to defeat them. At least we know what we're up against. If you go with him to another realm, you'll be alone in a strange land, facing charges of treason laid against you by a mad queen."

It was rather telling that the rabbit did not refute any of my claims. So the queen really was mad, and the charges were real. But the news that she was Alice's aunt... That had to be false.

Alice gave a small nod then addressed the rabbit. "I can't go. Tell the queen I'm sorry."

"Sorry!" the rabbit spat. "You think that will suffice? You think she'll care for your apology? She'll make me pay for my failure."

"And I'll boil you and serve you to my dinner guests if you try to take her," Lincoln said.

The rabbit gulped.

"Go away and don't come back. Tell your queen that if she sends an army, this realm will retaliate and send one to Wonderland."

"You would start a war between realms?"

Lincoln lunged across the bed. The rabbit squealed, clicked the watch's button, and quickly spoke some foreign sounding words. He disappeared before Lincoln could reach him. Although I suspected Lincoln delayed on purpose to give him time to speak the spell.

Alice drew her knees up and hugged them.

"Thank God he's gone," I said, scooting closer to sit alongside her.

"But when will the army arrive?" Alice wailed. "Tonight? Tomorrow night? Oh, Charlie, I think sending him away may have been the wrong thing to do. I should have gone—"

"No," Lincoln said. "You're not going to another realm on your own. You're my responsibility, and I won't allow you to put yourself in danger."

She nodded but didn't look convinced.

I hugged her and rested my chin on her shoulder. "Were you asleep when he arrived?"

"Yes. I don't want to go back to sleep now. What if he returns, or the army comes? I don't think it matters anymore if I am awake, but I still don't want to risk it."

"How about I sleep in here with you tonight?" I said.

"That'll help my nerves settle. Thank you, Charlie." She hugged me.

Lincoln left us and I headed to my room to change into my nightdress. I returned to Alice's room and slipped into bed alongside her. I yawned but predicted I would not get much sleep.

"Charlie," she whispered.

"Hmmm?"

"Do you think Lincoln would really have boiled the rabbit and served him for dinner?"

I laughed softly. "No, but don't tell the rabbit that if he returns. A little fear will keep him from attacking us."

"I don't think he's the attacking sort. He could have done so many times by now. In fact, I quite like him. He's very polite and even a little charming, in his own way."

I yawned again and pondered the absurdity of Alice finding a rabbit charming yet Seth false. And then I pondered how Alice could possibly be the niece of a queen from another realm when she'd been born and raised in England.

* * *

LINCOLN ASKED me to join him in his study after breakfast. Since he asked no one else, I thought perhaps a liaison of a personal nature was on the cards, but he did not so much as offer me a kiss. Indeed, I'd say kisses were not on his mind at all. He looked worried.

"Did you get any sleep?" he asked as he sat at his desk.

"A little," I said, taking the seat opposite. "But I doubt Alice did. I don't think she'll sleep tonight either. Poor thing. She's anxious. She feels responsible for bringing danger here."

"We'll worry about it when the army arrives," he said.

"But we must prepare for its arrival."

"I'll dismiss the servants today and ask Lady Vickers to find other accommodation. Then we'll reinforce doors and windows on the ground and first floors, and make sure we have a lot of ammunition. Gus and Seth will take turns watching for the army and must alert the household as soon as they appear. I'll also send word to Lord Marchbank of what may eventuate and try to get word to him if the army arrives. He'll notify the authorities and send reinforcements when the time comes."

I rubbed my forehead. At least he'd made plans, but with the murder investigation still underway, we were severely understaffed. It might be necessary to send Lords Marchbank and Gillingham to question our suspects while we prepared for the army's arrival. Even Andrew Buchanan could be put to use if we were desperate. Very desperate.

Lincoln picked up a notepad and studied what he'd written. Then he spoke some foreign words—the same words the rabbit had spoken to disappear.

"You memorized the spell?" I asked.

"I wrote it down immediately when I returned here." He handed it to me. "It's phonetic since the actual words are unknown to me. Unfortunately it's useless to us without the rabbit's watch. It seems to act as his portal."

"Do you think these are the same words that open the portal at Frakingham?"

"I don't know, but that portal exists only at the abbey so perhaps the spell that opens and closes it is also unique. It's not portable as with the rabbit's watch or a person, like Alice."

I handed back the notebook and he tore off the page. He moved the painting aside and opened the wall safe then placed the paper in it.

"What do we do?" I asked as he returned to the desk.

"You speak to the servants and Lady Vickers. Tell them they must leave but only temporarily. Give them funds for accommodation. Seth and Gus are already seeing to our defenses. I have to go out. I'll probably be gone all day." He cupped my cheek. "Don't worry, Charlie."

"I'm not," I said.

I suspected he saw right through my lie because his lips flattened into a grim line. Then he strode out of his office.

* * *

I EXPECTED Cook to refuse to leave but I was not expecting Lady Vickers to put up a fight.

"You're dismissing the servants *now*?" She threw her hands in the air then let them fall on her skirts. "The wedding is in four days!"

"Forget the wedding." I picked up my skirts and headed for the kitchen where I doubted she would follow.

I was wrong. She marched into the kitchen right behind me. Cook looked up from the array of vegetables laid out on the table.

"Cook, talk some sense into Charlie," Lady Vickers snipped off. "She's refusing to be reasonable."

"I am being reasonable," I shot back. "I don't want to postpone the wedding, but it's looking like it will be necessary. Cook cannot possibly work in here alone and the servants cannot possibly stay. It's far too dangerous."

"Don't be worrying about the wedding feast," he said. "Gus and Seth will help me. We'll get it done. We ain't postponing the wedding."

"No, we are not," Lady Vickers agreed. "It's too late to change the date now."

"It's far too much work," I protested.

"There ain't many guests," Cook said. He picked up a large knife and began chopping a parsnip.

"But the queen's army—"

"As long as they don't arrive on the day, you will be wed, Charlie." Lady Vickers had a way of making it sound as if she had the final word on matters, and this was no exception. "Nor am I leaving with the servants. If Seth stays, so do I."

Cook studied me then set down the knife. He took my hands in his and leveled his gaze with mine. "You'll be wed on Saturday if I have to chop off every soldier's head myself. Now, go get some rest. You be tired."

I was tired but I wouldn't sleep. There was far too much to do. Gus and Seth needed help with the barricades, Alice needed reassuring before she wore out the piano, and then there was the housework that would not get done now without servants. Yet I could not settle. My mind would not stop whirling. I flitted from one room to the next, checking windows and doors, helping Seth for five minutes then moving on to Gus before seeking out Alice.

Thankfully Lincoln returned after a few hours' absence with news that he imparted to us over luncheon at the kitchen table. Since the servants had all left, we decided not to use the dining room. Even Lady Vickers joined us, much to Seth's surprise and consternation. The more amenable she was to sitting in the kitchen, the more likely she was to be forming a relationship with Cook. It would be easier for them to have a liaison now with the rest of the servants gone. If I weren't so tense, I'd be amused.

"Yallop is an acquaintance of Swinburn's," Lincoln told us.

"I knew it!" Gus declared. "Swinburn's using all the friends he's got in high places. Scum. Begging my pardon, Lady V."

She merely narrowed her eyes at him.

"They are not friends," Lincoln said. "Yallop owes Swinburn money. A lot of money, according to Marchbank's friends."

Seth stabbed his slice of beef and studied it with a scowl. "So Swinburn will absolve the debt if Yallop succeeds in shutting us down."

"Scum," Gus said again before shoving half a boiled potato into his mouth.

"That explains why he wants to close the ministry," Lady Vickers said, "but does not explain how he knows about the records *et cetera*."

"Swinburn must have told him," I said. "And Lady Harcourt told Swinburn."

"There ain't no reason for her not to, now that she no longer be on the committee," Cook said.

"She told Swinburn our secrets *before* we ousted her," Seth said with a shake of his head. "She'll do anything if it'll save her own skin."

"Quite," his mother bit off.

We formed some more plans for the afternoon, and even Lady Vickers joined in. She volunteered to help Cook in the kitchen and see if any housework needed to be done. Alice remained quiet the entire time. I tried to catch her attention but she simply toyed with her food before giving up without eating anything.

She retreated to the piano room and played very loudly.

We finished our meal and Lady Vickers collected the plates. I patted her arm in thanks as she passed me then hurried after Lincoln. "Everyone has something to do this afternoon," I said. "Except me."

"You can stay here and speak with Alice."

"I've tried that. She hardly even hears me. She's lost in her own thoughts. I think I'll come with you to visit Gawler." He picked up speed so I lifted my skirts and raced after him. "Don't protest, Lincoln. I'm coming with you and that's final."

"I didn't say anything," he said.

"No, but you would have if I didn't get in first."

He smirked. "You think you know me so well."

"Do you deny it?"

"Yes." He stopped suddenly at the base of the staircase and rounded on me. "I leave in fifteen minutes. If you're not here, I'll go without you."

"I'll get my shawl."

* * *

THE PLAN WAS to convince Gawler to have a frank discussion with Swinburn about risking the lives of members of both packs, something that might happen if the ministry was forced underground. It wasn't a great plan, but we could see no other way. Swinburn wouldn't let us get close enough to spy on him. Sooner or later, he would catch us. His sense of smell was just too strong.

We didn't have to leave Lichfield, however, as Gawler came to us just as we headed across the courtyard to the coach house. Gus called out to us from the back door and we returned. We met Gawler in the drawing room, but he was not alone.

Lord and Lady Gillingham sat with him. Or, rather, Gawler and Harriet sat. Lord Gillingham paced the floor. His walking stick was nowhere to be seen. The last time I'd seen him, I'd slapped him and thrown him out. I doubted he would make trouble today with Lincoln present.

"Where's Doyle?" Harriet asked.

"The servants are having some time off," Lincoln said.

She gasped. "So close to the wedding?"

"That's why they needed time off," I told her. "They were overworked. Don't worry, everything is in hand for Saturday."

"I am pleased to hear it, but you are generous employers indeed to give your household the day off at such a busy time." She sat awkwardly on the sofa and rubbed her protruding belly. If I wasn't mistaken, she'd grown even more since I last saw her.

"Do you think your time is close?" I asked.

She nodded and smiled wistfully. "Mr. Gawler thinks so, don't you?"

"Aye, ma'am." The big, bushy-haired man clutched his scruffy hat in his hand and perched on the edge of the chair, as if he worried his clothing would soil the upholstery. If

Lady Vickers saw him, she'd make him stand and order him to leave his boots at the front door.

"Other shape-shifting women have had short pregnancies, as Lincoln guessed," Harriet went on. "I am glad I found out or I wouldn't have had the nursery prepared. We wallpapered it in a soothing yellow with white rabbits bounding across the border."

White rabbits. *Ugh*.

"Stop it," Lord Gillingham snapped, striding back to us. "Stop discussing this topic. We haven't come to talk about babies."

"Do hush, Gilly," his wife chided. "Stop pacing and sit down. You're making my head spin. It's not good for the baby."

He sat and picked up the small slender vase holding a single pink rose. He merely clutched it for a few moments then put it down again and closed his fist on his knee. It would seem he missed his walking stick.

Gawler also fidgeted where he sat. He peered out from under the mop of greasy black hair, his gaze flicking between the Gillinghams and Lincoln. He seemed to be waiting for an opportunity to speak, but even during a pause in the conversation, he didn't seize it. He simply waited.

"You must be wondering why we're here," Harriet finally said. "It's the police, you see."

"You've heard we had a visit from them," I said. "Don't worry, we told them nothing about you or your pack. They didn't take our records and any details we did pass on were limited. We gave them no names."

"Good. I am relieved." She smiled prettily. "See, Gilly?"

Gillingham grunted and didn't meet anyone's gaze. His fist rubbed his thigh slowly, up and down, up and down.

"My husband was worried," Harriet told us. "Of course, I

knew you wouldn't tell them anything, but he wanted to come here and find out for himself."

"They questioned me, too," Gawler said.

"A politician named Yallop and a detective called Full-bright interrogated poor Mr. Gawler," Harriet said. "They accused him of those murders. It was awful, wasn't it?"

He nodded. "They said I was a dog, that I should swing for what I done. I told 'em I done nothing and that I don't know nothing about changing into a wolf."

"A necessary lie in this instance," Harriet said with a nod.

"What I want to know is, how'd they know to speak to me if you didn't tell them no names, Mr. Fitzroy?"

"Swinburn," Lincoln said. "I suspect he told them."

"God damn it." Gillingham thumped his fist onto his knee. "Do you think he gave them Harriet's name?"

"No, since the police haven't called on her."

Harriet shook her head. "They have not. But poor Mr. Gawler. What an ordeal!"

"Forget him!" Gillingham shouted. "It's you I'm worried about, not your so-called friends."

"Gilly! That's enough. We've been through this. What affects my pack also affects me." She rubbed her belly again. "They're like my family."

Gillingham dragged his hand through his hair and sat back, deflated.

"You really do think Swinburn is to blame for setting Yallop onto us?" Harriet asked Lincoln.

Lincoln told her what he'd learned about Yallop's debt to Swinburn, and their association.

She was nodding by the time he finished. "It must be Swinburn," she agreed. "First he commits the murders near Mr. Gawler's place to make it look as if he did them, then he colludes with that blasted Yallop fellow. What say you, Mr. Gawler?"

"I say he's a low down mangy cur, ma'am. Pardon my language, but I don't know no better words to describe him."

"That's quite all right. I agree. He's a cur. So the question is, what do we do now?"

"Kill him," Gillingham said, winding up again. "Fitzroy, get onto it. Harriet, come. It's time to go." He went to stand, but Harriet put her arm across his chest, barring him from moving. The muscles in his face twitched but he settled back meekly enough. Harriet's mouth softened with her smile.

"We can't just kill him," I said. "It would look too suspicious."

"Why not simply tell Fullbright all about Swinburn?" Harriet said. "Put suspicion onto *him* by telling Fullbright he's a shape changer and a horrid person."

"If you have any thoughts on how to do that, I am all ears," Lincoln said drily. "Swinburn is too well connected for unfounded accusations to be taken seriously. Particularly accusations voiced by me, since I am already under suspicion thanks to *The Star's* reports."

"That bloody rag," Gillingham spat. "That journalist should be shot. His editor, too. They stirred up this trouble."

"Isn't there someone *you* can speak to?" I asked him. "Don't you have influence with other members of parliament?"

He looked away, chin lifted high, and didn't deign to answer.

"You got influence, ma'am," Gawler said to Harriet.

"Not really," she said with a sigh. "With the wives of MPs, perhaps, but that's all."

"What about with Swinburn's pack? Most of 'em like you, on account of you being a kind soul." Did I detect a blush above his whiskers?

"They're not MPs or related to MPs. None have any real

power except Swinburn himself. Even Lord Ballantine is only a minor baron."

"I meant to ask them to spy on Swinburn for you."

"You overstate my influence, you dear man. They wouldn't spy on him for me, or for anyone. They're much too loyal."

Lincoln rubbed his jaw in thought. "You could still speak to the members of his pack and—"

"No!" Gillingham shouted. "My wife will *not* speak to anyone associated with that reprobate."

Harriet jerked around to face her husband. "But Gilly—"

"No! Out of the question. It's far too dangerous."

"Nonsense. I'm quite capable of doing my bit and I intend to do it." She lifted a hand to silence Gillingham's protests.

He huffed twice, stood, and stalked to the window. He stared up at the sky.

"I have a better idea." Harriet's eyes brightened, and she clapped her hands lightly. "Instead of trying to influence them, and hoping they can influence Swinburn, I shall pretend to befriend him. I'll tell him I've had enough of the East End and its slum dwellers, and that I want to run with a more prestigious pack after the baby is born. He has been trying to get me to join them ever since he found out about me. He thinks I belong there, you see, and not with Gawler."

Gillingham groaned. "Do I have any say in this?"

"It's the best way, Gilly. You know that."

"But it's dangerous."

"It's good of you to worry about us." She patted her belly. "But I won't be swayed. I will call on him tonight and then I'll proceed to spy on him when he brings me into the fold. Isn't that a clever plan, Charlie?"

I glanced at Lincoln, but he did not give his thoughts away. He was staring at Harriet. "I...I don't know," I said. "Your husband's right, and it could be dangerous. If Swinburn finds out that you're spying, he'll…do something awful to you."

"Tosh." She waved her hand. "He won't find out. I'm very good at pretending. Aren't I, Gilly? Very good indeed. I'll see him tonight and report back when I have some information. Come Gilly, Mr. Gawler, we've taken up enough of Charlie and Lincoln's time. They seem quite busy." She held out her hand and Gawler took it, rather than her husband. He assisted her to stand then only dropped her hand when Gillingham glared at him.

"You know who I blame for all this?" Gillingham said to no one in particular.

"Swinburn?" I said.

"*The Star*?" his wife offered.

"Julia and Buchanan," he said.

Harriet shook her head. "I'm not sure Andrew is at fault."

"He is. He can't control Julia. Never could. If he'd been able to keep her, she wouldn't have run off to Swinburn and told him the ministry's secrets."

Harriet giggled then looped her arm through his. "You do say the oddest things, Gilly. Andrew never had a hope of controlling a spirited thing like Julia. He's no match for her. He knows it too."

Gillingham's nostrils flared and he walked with her to the door. Harriet let him go when they reached it, and told her husband to go ahead. "I want to speak to Charlie alone." She took my hand and placed it on her arm.

"Is everything all right?" I asked after the men were out of earshot.

She smiled sweetly. "Everything is perfect. I wanted to ask *you* how you are, with the wedding so close. Are you sure all is in hand? Lincoln hasn't scared off the servants, has he?"

I laughed. "No. They like him."

She screwed up her nose. "Really?"

"Yes! Thank you for your concern, but it's fine. Lady V has been helping me prepare everything. She's very organized and knows precisely what is required."

"It comes with having done it twice, I suppose. Speaking of the old dear, I must say that her association with you hasn't harmed your reputation a bit."

"I wasn't aware I had a reputation," I said as we descended the stairs.

"Oh yes. You're quite the topic of discussion at all the garden parties this summer. You secured Lincoln, you see, and *he* created a sensation when he was on the market. All the women were aflutter over him."

"So I heard."

"It seems Lady Vickers's reputation has risen too. She's almost an accepted member of society again. If she plays her cards right she ought to secure a good match for Seth."

"I'm not sure Seth agrees with his mother's idea of a good match."

"He ought to listen to her. Dalliances are all well and good, but there comes a time when a gentleman must marry and marry well. A solid marriage is not all about love, you know. Just because *you* are fortunate in that regard, doesn't mean everyone is."

I watched her husband walking ahead with Lincoln. Side by side, the physical difference between them was never more pronounced. "No, I suppose not."

She followed my gaze. "Oh, we're happy enough *now*, but it has taken time and some very big changes. Despite some resistance at first, he's quite content for me to have my way now."

"And you like getting your own way more?"

She winked. "I certainly do."

* * *

LINCOLN WENT OUT in the afternoon but wouldn't tell me why. He simply gave vague responses to my questions, but since he promised not to confront Swinburn or any of his pack, I didn't worry too much.

I assisted Gus and Seth a little as they checked the guns in the weapon room, then went in search of Lady Vickers and Alice. I found them both in Lady Vickers' bedroom, changing the linen. The room smelled like wood polish.

"Let me help you," I said, taking a corner of the sheet and tucking it under the mattress.

"There's no need," Alice said. "We have it in hand. We make quite the team."

"We do," Lady Vickers said. "Although I am glad this is the last room."

"We ought to dust the drawing room and library at the very least, in case there are more visitors. And I noticed scuff marks on the entrance tiles. The porch is a little dusty too."

Lady Vickers plopped down on the bed with a groan. Her hair had come loose from its arrangement and strands fell across her shiny face. She swept them aside with the back of her hand. "Housework is for youngsters."

"Mrs. Cotchin isn't young," I said.

"She doesn't *do* any housework, she merely orders the girls to do it." She rubbed her shoulder and tilted her head to the side, stretching her neck.

"You've done a lot today," Alice said. "Why not lie down for a while."

"And you? You haven't stopped."

Alice massaged Lady Vickers's shoulder and the older woman groaned in relief. "I need to keep busy or I'll go mad," Alice said.

"I thought you'd be assisting Cook, Lady V," I said with a wicked smile.

She didn't notice it, however. "He seems to have everything under control, and kitchen work is even more exhausting than housework. It's so hot in there! I don't know how he does it every day."

"The warmth is inviting in the winter." I'd spent many a morning or evening in the kitchen, warming icy hands by the stove. After living in a derelict tenement or on the streets for several years, coming home to a warm kitchen was like stepping into heaven.

"That feels nice, Alice." Lady Vickers closed her eyes and yawned.

"Why not lie down for a little while," Alice said. "Charlie and I can cope on our own."

"Perhaps I will. Just for ten minutes."

Alice and I left her and headed downstairs to the kitchen to make tea. The crunch of wheels on the gravel diverted us when we reached the base of the staircase, however. It couldn't be Lincoln. He would have driven around to the coach house out the back. This conveyance stopped.

I opened the door just as a middle-aged man alighted from the hackney. He was short with dark hair and a set of bushy eyebrows that almost connected in the middle as he gave me a stern appraisal. Since he was studying me so closely, he did not notice the other passenger emerge and so did not offer assistance. She was even shorter than he, reaching only his shoulder, and quite broad in hip and bosom. A wide brown hat perched on her head, matching the plain gown she wore. Neither hat nor gown sported so much as an inch of lace, embroidery or other embellishment.

"Charlie? Who is it?" Alice asked from behind me. She peered over my shoulder and gasped. "Oh no."

"You know them?" I whispered.

"Yes."

"Who are they?"

"My parents."

CHAPTER 9

*A*lice had once told me she looked nothing like her parents, and now that they drew closer, I could see why she thought she might not be their daughter. Alice had a natural grace and elegance that came with her tall, willowy figure. Her parents were both short and their gait as they stomped up the front steps was anything but graceful. Where Alice had fair hair, her father's was dark and her mother's red. Their features were unalike too, and although her mother had blue eyes, they were steely, whereas Alice's were the color of a summer sky. Not even Mrs. Everheart's anger could alter their shade *that* much. And she was very angry.

"Pack your things, Alice," Mrs. Everheart said as her sharp gaze darted around the entrance hall and up the staircase. "You are coming home with us. You cannot stay in this vile pit any longer. The good lord knows what debauchery you've been exposed to already."

Alice protested, but my voice rose above hers. "I beg your pardon! This is a respectable household and I would thank you not to suggest otherwise." I sucked in a breath to steady my nerves. "My name is Charlie Holloway and I am Alice's

145

friend and mistress of Lichfield Towers. If you'd like to have a calm, rational conversation with Alice then please come with me to the drawing room and we'll have tea."

"We are not staying for tea," Mrs. Everheart bit off. "We are collecting Alice and leaving. Things have gone on too long already."

"Things?" I echoed. "What things?"

Mrs. Everheart looked around the entrance hall again, as if she couldn't bear to look at either Alice or me. "You know what sort of things. Unmarried men and women living together...it's not right in the eyes of God."

Alice bristled. "Mama! That is not fair. And I am *not* leaving."

"Don't argue, Child—"

"I am not a child! If I'm old enough to marry then I'm old enough to make my own decisions."

Mrs. Everheart's gaze finally locked onto Alice. "You are *not* old enough to marry without our consent."

"That is not the point, Mama! I don't want to get married yet, and certainly not to Mr. Crossley. He's far too old, for one thing, and as dull as a puddle."

"He is our very good friend!" Mr. Everheart spluttered. "He is sensible, responsible and godly. He's everything one could hope for in a husband."

"Then *you* marry him," Alice snapped.

"How dare you!"

"Living here has infected your mind." Her mother wrinkled her nose, as if she could smell the so-called debauchery. "The morals we instilled in you are corroding from idleness and lack of purpose. Do you even attend church?"

Alice huffed. "I give up. You won't listen to me, and never have. I'm tired of being treated as if I carry some sort of disease that must be cured. I am your daughter, your only child now, not someone you need to wash your hands of."

Her father thrust out his chin and gave a triumphant smile. "If we were trying to get rid of you, why are we here collecting you?"

"Because you promised Mr. Crossley I would marry him and you were prepared to wait for me to come around to the idea, but grew impatient."

Mr. Everheart's smile slipped but he kept his chin out.

"You're worried that my reputation will be tainted beyond repair because I live with a gypsy, a pugilist and a thug as your last letter pointed out. You want me to be as pure as fresh snow for my marriage. Or, rather, that's what Mr. Crossley wants and *he* is becoming impatient. Well? Is that how it is?"

"Lower your voice," her mother hissed. "The servants will hear you."

"There are no servants at the moment." As soon as it was out of my mouth, I regretted it. I'd just given them the ammunition they needed.

Mr. and Mrs. Everheart exchanged glances. "Do you mean to say you are unsupervised?" Mrs. Everheart asked.

"Of course not," I said. "Lady Vickers is in residence. She's an upstanding pillar of society."

Mrs. Everheart snorted. "Our inquiry agent says she ran off with her footman."

"They married."

"After living in sin for several months."

"That is neither here nor there," Alice said.

"What my wife is trying to say," Mr. Everheart said, voice tight, "is that without a housekeeper, governess or other respectable woman living here, we must assume the worst."

Alice did not respond. I wondered if, like me, her father's use of "my wife" and not "your mother" had thrown her off balance. It may mean nothing, but considering Alice's doubts surrounding her parentage, the words dropped like stones at our feet. And there was the rabbit's statement about Alice's aunt, the queen, still ringing in my ears.

"The servants are usually here but have been given time off," I said to break the silence.

"Why?" Mr. Everheart asked.

"Er... Well..."

"What Charlie is too polite to tell you," Alice said, her eyes flashing, "is that the servants have been sent away for their own safety. My dreams have become more frequent and took a dangerous turn. You recall my dreams, don't you? The ones that come to life? The reason you sent me to that dreadful school?"

Neither parent met her gaze.

"The fewer people near me at the moment, the better. So you see, if I leave here with you, it's likely you'll wake up to soldiers on your doorstep tonight. Is that what you want? Are you able to defend yourselves against Wonderland's army?"

Mr. Everheart paled. "Army?" he whispered.

Mrs. Everheart clutched the collar at her throat. She stared off into space. "We should never have taken you in," she murmured. "We thought we were doing our Christian duty, but...what if it was the devil that led you to us?"

Alice gasped and staggered back. I took her hand in mine and steadied her. "I am..." She gulped and began again. "I am not your child, am I?"

"Why did we do it, Mr. Everheart?" Mrs. Everheart asked her husband. "Why did we take them in?"

"My brother and I..." Alice said again, her voice firmer. "We were adopted, weren't we?" Alice had told me about her little brother and how he'd died young. She'd adored him and his death had affected her deeply.

Mrs. Everheart reached a hand toward her husband. He caught it and patted it vigorously. "I feel faint," she muttered.

"The parlor," I said quickly, leading the way to the closest adjoining room. I directed Mr. and Mrs. Everheart to sit together on the sofa then drew close to Alice. "Are you all right?"

She nodded. "I feel as though I might finally get some answers." She sat on an armchair and addressed the couple sitting opposite. "Who are my real parents?"

Mr. Everheart looked to his wife and said something I couldn't hear.

"Pardon?" Alice pressed.

"We don't know," he said, louder. "You were found sitting on a pew at our church one morning. You were about three years old but could tell us nothing about yourself except that your name was Alice and that you were told you could not go home. We took you in while the authorities tried to locate your parents, but..." He shrugged. "No one came forward and there were no reports of missing children matching your description. The odd thing is, no one saw you arrive in the village. So we simply kept you."

"And did not think to tell me the truth?"

"It was better if you thought we were your real parents."

"Better for whom? Not for me, I assure you." Alice got to her feet and paced the room. "I have long suspected you were not my parents." She stopped abruptly. "What about Myron? Did you adopt him too?"

Mrs. Everheart dabbed the corner of her eye with her handkerchief. "My poor boy."

Mr. Everheart nodded. "He was found in the same way, in the church, but as a baby. He couldn't have been more than a few weeks old."

Alice suddenly plopped back down onto the chair. "Perhaps that was why he was never very strong...he was taken from his mother so young."

"*We* didn't take him." Mrs. Everheart's voice cracked and she dabbed her other eye.

"Alice didn't suggest we did." Her husband patted her hand again, but it was ineffectual in offering comfort. Mrs. Everheart's eyes continued to water.

"Have you received any communication about Alice or her brother?" I asked. "Either recently or in the past? Anything at all?"

Mr. Everheart shook his head then lowered it and slumped back in the sofa. He looked like a beaten man, as if he'd spent his entire life running only to stumble at the end of the race. He blinked dry eyes at Alice. "We'll never see you again, will we?"

"No," she said without hesitation.

Mrs. Everheart sniffed. Her husband passed her his handkerchief and she continued to dab the corner of her eyes.

"That has nothing to do you not being my true parents," Alice said, "and everything to do with how you have treated me since my dreams became real."

"You can hardly blame us for that," Mrs. Everheart said.

Alice rolled her eyes.

"Perhaps it's just as well that we part ways now considering..." Mrs. Everheart waved her hand to encompass the room, the house, and probably me.

Alice stood again and peered down her nose at the people she'd once called Mother and Father. "I think it's time you left."

Mr. Everheart assisted his wife to stand and placed her hand in the crook of his arm. After a hesitation, he gave Alice a nod. "Goodbye," he said simply.

Mrs. Everheart did not offer any parting words, but she did allow a tear to slip down her cheek as she walked out with her husband. I thought the tears meant she was sad to part with her adopted daughter, but her next words banished that notion.

"What will we tell Mr. Crossley?" she said to Mr. Everheart. "Will he insist on compensation?"

I walked them to the front door then rejoined Alice in the parlor. She stood by the fireplace, her arms wrapped around her body. She stared unblinking into the empty grate.

I touched her shoulder. "Are you all right?"

Her chin quivered but she nodded. "I think so. I'm not too shocked, since I have long suspected, but to hear it from their own mouths...it's still unsettling."

"And for them to leave on such poor terms too." I glanced toward the door. "I'm sure they love you but are just frightened of you and your dreams."

She shook her head and returned to staring into the grate. "You're kind to say that, Charlie, but I don't think you're correct. They never quite accepted me as their own."

I hugged her. "I was adopted too, remember. I know my adopted mother loved me. My father, too, before he learned I was a necromancer."

"If he loved you, he would have overlooked that. He would have continued to love you anyway. I'm sorry if that hurts you, Charlie, but that's how I feel about my parents. If they truly loved me, they would help me, not abandon me."

Perhaps she was right. Perhaps Anselm Holloway never did truly love me, but I was quite sure my adopted mother would never have treated me as cruelly as he did. I was blessed in her love. Perhaps it was time to visit her grave again and pay my respects.

"We're your family now, Alice. You'll always have a home here, and people who care about you."

She hugged me back. "Thank you, Charlie. Now, the question is, who are my real parents? And where am I from?"

"According to the rabbit, you're niece to the Queen of

Hearts from Wonderland." I drew away and gave her my sternest glare. "And no, you are *not* going there to learn more about yourself, so put that thought from your mind."

"I already have. I'll stay here."

The unspoken "for now" hung between us like a guillotine blade.

* * *

LINCOLN RETURNED in time for dinner so we were able to inform everyone together of the visit from Mr. and Mrs. Everheart. A profound silence followed Alice's pronouncement that she was adopted. No one even chewed.

"Someone say something," Alice said, nervously.

"So the rabbit most likely spoke the truth," Lincoln said. "You were once in Wonderland and the queen is your aunt."

Alice nodded at her plate. "It seems that way."

"Bloody hell," Gus muttered.

"You not be from this world?" Cook asked.

"It seems I am from that other realm," Alice said.

Gus studied her anew then waggled his knife. "If I cut you, will your blood be red?"

"Yes!"

Seth thumped his arm. "Idiot."

Gus blushed and apologized.

To my surprise, Alice laughed. "It's absurd, isn't it? Don't worry, Gus, the same questions that are going through your head have already gone through mine. As far as I am aware, I am physically like all of you. I don't shift shape as Harriet does, and I can't set things on fire like Mr. Langley. I am quite normal."

"Perhaps Wonderland is just like here," Seth said.

"Except for talking rabbits," Gus said pointedly.

"You must want to go with the rabbit now," Lincoln said,

focusing on his dinner again. "But I urge you to reconsider. We know nothing about Wonderland, and it seems as though you would be immediately placed on trial if you went. We don't know if their justice system is a fair one or not. I insist you stay here."

"We've already discussed it," I told him. "Alice agrees."

"I'm not leaving," she assured him.

"Good," Seth said. "Because I would have to insist on coming with you and I don't want to miss the wedding."

"Seth!" Lady Vickers cried. "You are not traveling to strange places, so put that from your mind immediately."

He picked up his glass and saluted her. "You traveled to a strange place."

"There are no talking rabbits in America."

We discussed the fortification plans as well as what Lincoln had learned from his informants. Unfortunately, it amounted to very little. Lady Harcourt had visited Swinburn in the evening and stayed the night. This morning, he'd gone to his club. The duke was already inside, as was the MP, Mr. Yallop. They'd emerged separately an hour later. Harriet visited Swinburn in the afternoon and left a short time later. As to the rest of Swinburn's pack, they'd gone to their various places of employment as they usually did, although the Ballantines remained indoors. They rarely left their residence nowadays, preferring to keep a low profile after angering the royal family.

"And Gawler's pack?" I asked. "What are their movements?"

"Nothing out of the ordinary," he said. "They're also spying on Swinburn, but they don't have the numbers to watch the entire pack. They all have jobs to go to. If they don't work, they don't eat."

Lincoln and I volunteered to wash the dishes after dinner. Seth and Lady Vickers assisted us to carry the plates and glasses into the scullery. As we left the others behind, she said to Seth, "She is certainly not a candidate for marriage now. She's not even human."

"Mother," he said on a sigh. "She *is* human. She's just not from this realm. Anyway, I don't care. If anything, it has only made her more intriguing. She is, after all, related to royalty. Don't you want me to marry a princess?"

His mother stopped in her tracks to gawp at him. We left her behind.

* * *

"I LIKE DOING the dishes with you," I told Lincoln when we found ourselves alone in the scullery.

"Why? Because I do this?" He flicked water at me.

"Very mature."

He grinned so I dipped my hand in the water as I leaned in to kiss him. Then I slid my wet hand down his cheek. I pulled away and smiled. "Now we're even."

He looked at the pail of water sitting by the door.

"Don't you dare!" I cried, passing him a stack of dirty dishes to keep his hands occupied.

"So why do you like doing the dishes with me?" he asked.

"We don't get time to talk in private much lately. This forces us to take the time."

"You want to talk to me? About anything in particular?"

"Yes, as it happens."

"Alice?"

"No."

He stopped washing the plate and looked at me. "Is this to do with Lady Vickers telling you what to expect on our wedding night?"

"No! It's about what you were doing today. Did you only speak to your informants?"

He resumed washing. "Why do you ask?"

"Because you were gone a long time and you smell nice."

"I don't usually smell nice?"

"Not after returning from the slums then settling the horse in the stables."

"I washed my hands in the stables before coming inside."

Keeping a cake of lavender soap in the stables did not seem like something Lincoln would do and I was about to question him further when Gus entered the scullery brandishing a newspaper. Seth followed close behind.

"This evening's edition of *The Star* just arrived," Seth said.

"Gawler is named as a suspect in the attacks," Gus added.

I groaned as I read it. "What an irresponsible thing to do! Do you think Yallop and Fullbright will arrest him now?"

Seth shook his head. "They don't have any evidence."

"Spoken like a toff," Gus said. "The police don't care about evidence. If they want to arrest a cove, they'll arrest him."

"And miraculously find the evidence later," I added. Like Gus, I had little faith in our constabulary. I'd seen too many innocent people in the slums get arrested for crimes they hadn't committed because the police couldn't be bothered to investigate properly.

Seth took the newspaper from Gus and slapped the article. "Swinburn's got a nerve feeding Salter this information. He's putting one of his own kind at risk. It's madness."

"That's Swinburn to a T," I said. "Mad. What will you do now, Lincoln?"

"Check on Gawler," Lincoln said.

"To make sure he hasn't been arrested?"

"To make sure he hasn't gone after Swinburn in retaliation."

* * *

THE FOUR OF us paid Gawler a visit the following morning but he wasn't at his home in Myring Place. His neighbor told us that he'd angrily stormed off after "a toff lady" visited. Further questioning proved Harriet was the visitor. She'd carried a newspaper under her arm and sported a grim expression, and she had departed separately to Gawler.

We traveled on to Swinburn's townhouse in Queen's Gate, Kensington, where he lived next to Lord and Lady Ballantine. They and the rest of the pack had moved to London from Bristol when Swinburn decided to move his shipping company's operations to the nation's capital. He was the first of his line to win leadership of the pack after Ballantine's ancestors had held it for generations. Seeing their townhouses side-by-side, identical down to their black doors and brass knockers, I wondered how Lord Ballantine felt about losing pack leadership to the grandson of a sailor.

"Gawler's here," Lincoln said as we stood together on the pavement. "I can sense his presence. But not inside."

"He's most likely watching from that alley over there," Seth said with a nod at the gap slicing through the row of grand townhouses. "He'd be a fool to go inside anyway. No wild creature would enter a closed enemy space for fear of being trapped."

"And Swinburn?" Gus asked from the driver's perch of our conveyance. "Can you sense him too, Fitzroy?"

Lincoln shook his head. "I've never been able to sense him. Some I can, some I can't."

"Then lets urge Gawler to go home before he does anything rash," I said, setting off toward the alley.

"He'll simply return tonight," Seth said, falling into step with me. "Perhaps that's a good idea. Let them fight and get it over with."

Tonight would be better than now. There were too many people about. A maid pushed a perambulator and two gentlemen hurried on their way, intent on reaching their destinations quickly. Coaches passed by and a footman stood on a stoop only a few houses down from Swinburn's. Gawler couldn't do anything today except watch. It was far too busy.

Lincoln caught my elbow and jerked me to a stop. "Wait."

Seth stopped too. "What is it?"

Lincoln's head cocked a little to the side and his gaze focused on the entrance to the alley. "Growling."

I listened but heard nothing.

Seth shook his head. "They won't confront each other in their wolf form now. They'd be seen."

The two gentlemen, walking in opposite directions to one another, drew closer to the alley entrance. They would not only see an attack, they would hear it too, and perhaps be in danger themselves.

"Charlie, stay here." Lincoln strode off toward the alley. Seth followed and I followed him.

Then I heard it too. Growling, low and deep. Deeper than a dog's growl. The sound vibrated through me. There was only one growl, not two.

Both gentlemen stopped and turned toward the sound.

Lincoln broke into a run.

"Get away!" Seth shouted at the gentlemen.

Either they didn't hear him or they chose to ignore him. One stepped into the alley while the other squinted into the shadows.

A shot rang out, its echo ricocheting off the walls.

CHAPTER 10

J pushed past the gentlemen and careened into Seth's arms.

"It's not a pleasant sight," he said in my ear.

I clutched him as my eyes adjusted to the dimness. The first shape I made out was Lincoln's familiar one, standing a few feet ahead. "Why?" he snapped at the figure obscured from my view.

No answer. I let Seth go and joined Lincoln. Behind me, the gentlemen spoke in shocked whispers to one another.

"You saw that," came Swinburn's voice, spoken loudly to carry back to them. He stood just beyond Lincoln, a gun in his hand. It pointed aimlessly at the ground. The furred body of a large wolf-like creature lay at his feet.

"Gawler?" I whispered.

"Is it him?" Seth demanded of Swinburn.

Swinburn looked to Lincoln then to the gentlemen, now approaching cautiously along the alley toward us. "You saw that, sir? And you too?" he asked the men. "You saw that beast attack me?"

"Y-yes," one said, voice shaking. "What *is* it?"

"A dog," Lincoln said.

"Bloody big dog," said one of the gentlemen. "Pardon my language, miss."

"Swinburn?" Seth said again. "Who is it?"

Swinburn turned back to the body on the ground. He nudged it with his toe then let out a long breath. "I couldn't begin to guess what it is," he said with an emphasis on "what." "I'll leave identification to the experts. All I can say is, thank God I was armed. Thank God I came across it before it attacked someone else."

"A woman and a baby walked past," said one of the gentlemen, glancing over his shoulder. "If it had got to them first…"

Swinburn went to move off but Lincoln grasped his shoulder. "I'm going to send for the police," Swinburn told him. "Everyone must remain here to give witness accounts, of course. Did you see anything Fitzroy?"

Lincoln merely glared at him.

Swinburn shook Lincoln off and strode out of the alley.

Movement in the shadows caught my eye. Something smoky floated in the breeze. But there was no breeze in the narrow alley. The wispy tendrils coalesced into a human shape, that of a naked man. Gawler. My heart sank. He ignored me and followed Swinburn, but only as far as the alley entrance.

"Gawler," I whispered to Lincoln and nodded in the spirit's direction.

The two gentlemen circled the dead animal, inspecting it from all angles. One crouched near its hind legs, but neither went too close to the head.

"Did it attack first?" Lincoln asked them.

One gentleman shrugged. "Sir Ignatius wouldn't have shot it if it hadn't," the other said.

"You know him?" Seth asked.

"We're his neighbors."

"What do you think of him?"

"A fine fellow, keeps to himself."

"He's always friendly," the other man said. "Lucky he was armed."

"Yes," Seth said drily. "How fortunate."

"Not for..." I swallowed down the name. "Not for that dog."

"Ugly beast," one of the gentlemen said. "Look at the size of its paws. That's no ordinary dog, miss."

"Do you think that's what killed those people in the slum?" the other man asked.

"Must be. Unlikely there are two of these things walking around the city. Someone would have noticed." He poked it in the back with his walking stick. "To think it could have killed someone here, in Kensington."

"If not for Sir Ignatius."

I walked out of the alley, unable to listen to any more, and stood near the hovering spirit of Gawler. I dared not speak to him, lest the witnesses overhear. Gawler took no notice of me. He simply drifted silently back and forth across the alley entrance, his gaze on Swinburn's house.

I wanted to ask him if he'd attacked first, if he'd been intent on killing Swinburn in retaliation for speaking to Salter and the police. But a more burning question bothered me. Had Swinburn lain in wait? If so, who'd warned him that Gawler was on his way?

Harriet?

I felt sick. I leaned a hand against the cool stone of the wall near the alley entrance and concentrated on my breathing.

"Are you all right, Charlie?" Seth asked.

I nodded. "A little shocked."

Voices and movement came from Swinburn's house. A footmen hurried down the street while another knocked on

Lord Ballantine's door. Soon, Swinburn returned, bringing Ballantine with him. Ballantine's nostrils flared upon seeing me, but he otherwise ignored me and strode into the alley.

"If you could wait on the street," Lincoln said to the gentlemen. Seth ushered the witnesses out of earshot and Lincoln faced Swinburn. "Who was it?" he asked, even though he already knew.

"Gawler," Swinburn said. "He'd accused me of being a traitor to our kind then he attacked me."

"How did you know he would be here?"

"Sir Ignatius doesn't have to answer your impertinent questions," Ballantine bit off.

Swinburn looked down at Gawler's werewolf body, while Gawler's spirit looked down on him. It shimmered. "You think I planned this?" Swinburn said quietly. "You think me that callous? He came to my house and challenged me. We entered this alley to talk without being disturbed but he didn't talk. He changed shape. I did not. I'd brought a weapon and when he attacked, I used it to defend myself."

"Liar!" The spirit swooped around Swinburn, circling so fast his head almost caught up to his feet. "What innocent man carries a gun with him around his house?" He did not refute the claim that he attacked first.

"He was unarmed," I said in Gawler's defense.

"Not in wolf form." Ballantine kicked the animal's paws. The claws had retracted in death, but the paws themselves were larger than a man's hand. I'd seen the deep wounds werewolf claws inflicted—as deep as a dagger.

"Will you tell the police who it is?" Lincoln asked.

"Of course," Swinburn said. "They already suspected him, thanks to the article in *The Star*."

"Which you orchestrated," Seth said.

Gawler's spirit swirled violently around Swinburn then whooshed upward before plunging again. A ghostly finger pointed at Swinburn's face. "You bloody done it! You bloody told 'em I killed those men when it was *you*!"

"Not me," Swinburn answered Seth. "I haven't spoken to any reporters."

"Ballantine then," Seth said. "Or someone else from your pack, either acting alone or under instruction."

"How dare you!" Ballantine pulled himself up to his full height. He was a large man with grizzly whiskers but for some reason, I didn't feel intimidated. He was all bluster and pomp with no substance. It was no wonder he'd lost the pack leadership.

Swinburn, however, was a different matter. There was a coldness to him, a calculated cunning that made him unpredictable. He played games with people's lives and reputations and gave his opponents no choice but to play along with him.

"I cannot control what others do," Swinburn said. "But I can assure you that I did not authorize anyone to speak to reporters from *The Star* or any other newspaper. That is not my way. But what's done is done. The secret of our kind is out and we must navigate these new, public, waters as best we can." He looked down at Gawler's body and shook his head. "Fool. It shouldn't have come to this. He shouldn't have attacked me."

Gawler's spirit screamed. He whirled around the alley, dashing from one end to the other, up to the roofline and down again, swooping on Swinburn and Ballantine. They didn't notice and Gawler's frustration mounted. I wanted to urge him to calm down, but I didn't want Swinburn to know he was here. The otherworldly screaming filled my head and hurt my ears. It felt as if the ghost himself were inside my brain.

Lincoln must have sensed my discomfort, even though I felt sure I didn't display any signs. He touched my chin and studied my face, a question in his eyes.

"She looks pale," Seth said. "Charlie? Do you need to sit down?"

Ballantine snorted. "She should be used to death."

The screaming suddenly stopped, leaving a profound silence. I glanced around but could no longer see Gawler's spirit. Perhaps he'd gone, too frustrated to listen to Swinburn any longer. I hoped his afterlife proved to be a better existence for him than this life.

I met Lincoln's gaze and offered a small smile. "I'm all right," I said.

He turned back to Swinburn. "You defeated Gawler. His pack will be yours now."

Therein lay the real reason for the murder. I had no doubts.

"No," Swinburn said. "To take over a pack that I don't belong to, I must defeat the leader when we are both in our other forms. I didn't change. In this situation the pack will elect a new leader in whatever way they see fit. I suspect it will be handed to Lady Gillingham."

"Harriet?" I blurted out. "Why? She's not as strong as others in her pack, surely."

"Particularly in her delicate state," Seth added. "She can't run with them at the moment, let alone fight."

"She is the only natural leader within that pack," Swinburn said.

"The rest are a bloody useless lot," Ballantine added. "Sir Ignatius is right. She'll get the leadership by default. No others will want it, and being a countess makes her the perfect choice."

Swinburn narrowed his gaze ever so slightly at his friend. Ballantine swallowed and looked away. It would seem no matter how far Swinburn rose, or how strong a leader he made, Ballantine would always consider him his inferior.

The arrival of Detective Inspector Fullbright with his

constables saw us all ousted from the scene. We gathered on the street where another constable questioned the two gentlemen witnesses. The sun rose high in the sky overhead, brightening the row of white houses so that I had to squint until my eyes adjusted. It promised to be a hot, sticky day in the city.

Several minutes later, constables carried the body on a stretcher and slid it into a waiting cart. It drove away and Fullbright joined us. He spoke with the gentlemen then dismissed them.

A two-wheeled hansom sped up the street and stopped alongside Gus and our carriage, blocking the road. Mr. Yallop, the MP, alighted and strode toward us, patting a handkerchief across his shiny forehead.

"We had a meeting," Mr. Yallop snapped at Detective Inspector Fullbright.

"I was called here unexpectedly," Inspector Fullbright said without glancing up from the constable's notebook he now held in his hand.

"Why wasn't I told about...this?" Mr. Yallop signaled toward the alley. "Your superior informed me when I went looking for you."

"There wasn't time."

"I want a full report."

"And you'll get one."

Mr. Yallop's jaw hardened.

"It was self-defense," Lord Ballantine said. "Sir Ignatius was attacked."

"Sir Ignatius?" Mr. Yallop looked at Swinburn for the first time. He nodded once and gave him a cool smile. "I didn't see you there, sir."

"What are *you* doing here?" Swinburn asked.

Mr. Yallop puffed out his chest. "I'm the appointed chair for the Home Office's select committee investigation into the

Ministry of Curiosities." Was the explanation just for show, or did Swinburn not help Yallop get the position after all? At least they didn't try to hide their acquaintance.

Ballantine smirked at Lincoln. "Is that so? Well, well."

"And you are?" Mr. Yallop asked.

"Lord Ballantine. Sir Ignatius and I are friends."

"Tell me what happened here," Yallop demanded. "I was told the creature was shot and killed."

Inspector Fullbright gave a brisk account of the events as he knew them. No one added to it, and no one stated or implied that Ballantine and Swinburn were also werewolves.

"Good." Mr. Yallop cupped his hands behind his back. "It seems we're now rid of the blasted werewolf creature. An excellent result. Thank you, Sir Ignatius. You'll be a hero when the newspapers get wind of this."

"No names, please," Swinburn said. "I'd like to remain anonymous. My friends don't like it when one of our circle garners publicity, even good publicity."

Mr. Yallop's thick brows wriggled up his forehead. "Your friends, eh? No, I'm sure they don't." Did he already know that Swinburn associated with royalty? Or merely guessed?

"I'd like to hear your version of events, sir," Inspector Fullbright said to Swinburn. "Yours too, Mr. Fitzroy."

"He didn't witness anything," Ballantine growled. "He was too far away."

"And you were in your house," Seth shot back. "So you have nothing of worth to say."

Ballantine opened his mouth, but Inspector Fullbright spoke first. "Thank you, my lordship," he said to Ballantine. "But you won't be needed."

"It's *your* lordship or my *lord*." Ballantine gave him a tight smile then strode off in the direction of his house.

"Would you like to step over here and tell us what happened, Sir Ignatius?" Inspector Fullbright said.

"There's no need for privacy," Swinburn said. "I'll tell you what I told Mr. Fitzroy."

He proceeded to tell the detective inspector a number of lies. For one, he made no mention of being a shape-shifter. I didn't expect him to, and we would not divulge his secret, something that he must have guessed. For another, he didn't admit to knowing the victim.

"A man came to my front door and asked for me," Swinburn said. "He introduced himself as Gawler—"

"Gawler!" Mr. Yallop nodded vigorously. "We knew it was him, didn't we, Fullbright?"

"What did Mr. Gawler want with you?" Inspector Fullbright asked.

"He spouted all sorts of nonsense, claiming I'm destroying his home," Sir Ignatius said. "I'm involved in the slum clearances in an advisory capacity, you see. The Old Nichol is on the list of areas to be cleaned up. Some residents don't want to go. It seems he decided to take his complaints to me personally."

"Fools," Mr. Yallop spat. "Why do they want to remain in those pig sties? Most of the buildings are only held together by the dirt."

"Because it's their home," I said. "If you clean up the slums, where will they live? They won't be able to afford to rent the new houses."

"They can move further out of the city," Mr. Yallop said. "They ought to be dispersed anyway. Keeping them all together like that only leads to an infestation of crime. Eh, Fullbright? Places like the Old Nichol keep your lot busy."

I closed my hands into fists at my sides. This was not an argument I could win.

"To the matter at hand," Fullbright said to Swinburn. "You say Mr. Gawler came to your home and confronted you."

"Over my involvement in the slum clearances, yes."

"And how did you end up in this alley?"

"I told him to calm down as he was getting agitated," Swinburn said. "He suggested we move into the alley where no one would hear us. I agreed."

Seth grunted. "Because it's wise to go into dark alleys with angry strangers."

"I had my gun on me," Swinburn told him coolly. "I hadn't yet removed my jacket as I'd just walked in the door myself. He must have been waiting for me to return home."

"So you went with him into the alley," Fullbright prompted. "And then?"

"And then..." Swinburn shook his head and shrugged. "He did the oddest thing. He undressed and then he...changed into that creature your men carried off. It was remarkable. A truly amazing transformation. I still cannot believe it."

It was a good performance, and it certainly fooled Mr. Yallop. He hung on Swinburn's every word, his face distorting as he imagined the gruesome sight. Inspector Fullbright offered no such opinion, either in the tone of his voice or his facial expressions. He simply made notes in his book.

"Then he ran at me," Swinburn went on. "It—he—bared his teeth. They were as long and sharp as knives. And the creature was enormous, as you saw. He would have gored me without hesitation if I hadn't shot him."

"Good lord," Mr. Yallop said on a breath. "Your bravery and presence of mind are to be commended."

Swinburn smiled. "Those two gentlemen saw everything," he said. "Mr. Fitzroy and his companions did not, but no doubt they heard the gunshot."

"Do you have anything to add, sir?" Inspector Fullbright asked Lincoln.

"No," Lincoln said.

Fullbright looked to Seth then me. We both shook our

heads. To Swinburn, he said, "Do you always carry a loaded gun when you go about your daily affairs?"

"These are dangerous times," Swinburn said. "I've carried a gun ever since the Ripper murders."

"It seems a little extreme."

"I'm not the sort who does things by halves."

"Quite right." Mr. Yallop nodded with enthusiasm and studied Swinburn anew. "No one becomes advisor to the royal family by treading lightly." So he was aware of Swinburn's importance to the palace.

Inspector Fullbright closed his notebook. "Thank you, sir. I'll be in touch if I have more questions."

"We will indeed," Mr. Yallop said. "Although I'm sure there'll be no need to trouble you again. You've told us everything you could. May I applaud you once again, sir. Your actions have saved this city from further chaos and fear. The public can breathe easier now that the murderous creature is dead."

I almost walked off in disgust. I was only glad the spirit of Gawler was no longer around to hear so many lies spewing from Swinburn's mouth. My ears couldn't cope with more screeching.

The detective inspector signaled to his remaining constables that it was time to leave.

"What will happen to Gawler's body?" Lincoln asked him.

"Why?" Mr. Yallop sneered. "Does the ministry want it? I can assure you, you won't be allowed anywhere near it. You are still under investigation—"

"An investigation that may prove the ministry is necessary," Seth cut in.

Mr. Yallop huffed out a humorless laugh.

"Scientists and doctors will want to study it," Inspector Fullbright told Lincoln. "They'll seek to understand these creatures in the hope that will help them develop a way to stop them in the future."

"Quite right," Swinburn said. "It's the only way." He didn't sound worried at all. Why wasn't he concerned about what they may discover about the body? Perhaps he knew they'd discover nothing of importance.

"I'm not convinced Gawler committed the Old Nichol murders," Lincoln said.

Fullbright studied him, his face blank.

"Don't be absurd," Mr. Yallop scoffed. "Of course he did it. You saw that beast!"

"There are others?" Inspector Fullbright asked Lincoln.

Lincoln's gaze locked with the detective's while Swinburn went very still. I didn't dare move, didn't dare glance at him, or anyone. I couldn't decide on the best course of action—let Fullbright know that Swinburn was a shape-changer, or keep his secret?

Somewhere in the distance a dog barked and Mr. Yallop jumped. He tried to hide his nervousness with a cough and stroking his waistcoat at his chest. "If there are, we'll catch them. Now that we know Gawler was one, we'll find the rest. All we need to do is find his associates."

We must warn Harriet. And yet it may have been her that set these events in motion, either accidentally or on purpose.

Inspector Fullbright walked off to his waiting coach. Mr. Yallop watched him leave out of the corner of his eye then stepped close to Lincoln.

"You've got a nerve suggesting it wasn't Gawler," Mr. Yallop hissed. "You ought to be locked up for defending him."

"We look at the evidence," Seth said when Lincoln offered no explanation. "And the evidence doesn't point to Gawler."

Mr. Yallop wrinkled his nose at Seth as if he smelled something foul. "Stop your bleating, Vickers. I asked my colleagues in the House of Lords about you. Laughter followed every mention of your name. If half the stories are true, I wouldn't show my face around London if I were you."

"Luckily I don't have your face. As to your colleagues in the House of Lords, I suspect some of their laughter was nervous. I know as many secrets about them as they do about me. But I'm not a tattler, Mr. Yallop, so don't bother asking me for information."

Mr. Yallop blinked owlishly, clearly unsure of what to make of Seth and his retort. He returned his attention to Lincoln. "I'm warning you, Fitzroy. If you don't hand over the ministry files, you *will* be arrested for hindering our investigation."

"I already told you, there is nothing to hand over," Lincoln said.

Beside him, Swinburn shifted his weight, catching Mr. Yallop's attention. "I do apologize, Sir Ignatius," Mr. Yallop said. "This discussion is irrelevant to you. Thank you for your time." He turned and strode off to his own conveyance.

"Nicely done, Fitzroy," Swinburn said as he watched Mr. Yallop drive off. "You're willing to risk arrest rather than betray those recorded in your files."

"No thanks to you," I said. "You told your cronies about us and that led to Yallop's committee being formed. You've put many lives in danger, Sir Ignatius. I hope that gives you what you want."

"Why would I do that? My name is in your files, as are those of my friends.'"

That was a good point. And yet I felt sure Swinburn was to blame for bringing the ministry to light, not only as Mr. Salter's source but also as Mr. Yallop's. I didn't believe him to be innocent.

"Your actions mean Gawler's body will be dissected," Seth said. "One of your own. Doesn't that concern you?"

"No," Swinburn said. "They'll discover nothing to help them eliminate us, if that's what you're thinking."

Lincoln held out his hand to me and I took it. He tucked it into the crook of his arm. "If you are responsible for the Old Nichol murders, Swinburn, I will turn your files over to Fullbright and Yallop. Is that understood?"

"And then what?" Swinburn asked. "He'll arrest me? Hardly."

"I agree. He won't arrest you." Lincoln smiled. "Because I will have already meted out the ministry's justice."

* * *

SETH SAT with Gus on the driver's seat as we drove to Mayfair. Considering his foul mood, it was the best place for him. Hopefully the fresh air would blow away his temper. Lincoln spoke little and gave nothing away. As usual, he kept his thoughts to himself unless I prompted him to share.

We both agreed that Swinburn could have provided information to Salter and Yallop anonymously, yet neither of us could think why he'd jeopardize himself and his pack. If Lincoln handed over the archives, his name would be there for all to see.

"Unless he trusts me not to hand them over," Lincoln said.

"That's a lot of faith he's putting in your ability to keep them hidden."

One corner of his mouth flicked up. "You doubt me?"

"Never."

It was midday when we arrived at the Gillinghams' house. Lord Gillingham was out and Harriet invited us into her private sitting room, where she sat with a plate of boiled eggs on her lap. Dressed in a lavender and pink dressing gown with her fair hair cascading down her back, she looked young and fresh, a picture of health.

"Charlie, fetch me that cushion, please," she said. "My back aches." She sucked in a sharp breath as she leaned forward, allowing me to slot the cushion behind her.

"Are you all right?" I asked.

"The baby kicks constantly. He's so vigorous." She smiled and rubbed her belly. "I don't think I have long to go."

We'd decided that I would give her the news, but now that the time had come, I wasn't sure how to deliver it. I glanced at Lincoln and Seth, standing by the door, both of them still looking frustrated over our encounters with Swinburn and Mr. Yallop. Perhaps I was the best choice for delivering news today.

I pulled a chair closer and took her hand. "Harriet, I bring sad tidings. Mr. Gawler is dead."

She dropped the egg she'd been nibbling. It missed the plate and fell to the floor. "Oh," she said heavily. "How did it happen?"

"Swinburn shot him."

She gasped. "He *shot* him?"

"After you met with Gawler today, he went to confront Swinburn. According to Swinburn, they went to an alley where Gawler changed into his wolf form. He attacked Swinburn who then shot him."

"Did you see it?"

"No. We heard the gunshot but were too late."

"Have you spoken to Gawler's spirit?"

I shook my head. "There is no need at the moment. We have no reason to doubt Swinburn. He admits to shooting Gawler and it's easy to believe that Gawler was angry enough to attack. According to his neighbors, he was seething when he left his home."

She nodded slowly. "I showed him the newspaper article that mentioned him by name. He became angry."

I glanced at Lincoln. He urged me with a nod. But I

couldn't bring myself to accuse her of encouraging Gawler. "Swinburn thinks you will now be pack leader because they respect you," I said instead. "He told us that since he didn't kill Gawler in a fair fight, he won't be accepted as their leader."

She nodded, not at all surprised by the news. "I am the logical choice, even though I haven't been with them long. None of them want the leadership, you see. They're all rather plodding in nature."

I blew out a breath and sucked in some courage. "Harriet, I must ask this of you. Did you stoke Gawler's anger?"

She picked up another egg. "He needed no stoking."

"Did you encourage him to confront Swinburn?"

She nibbled the egg.

"Harriet?"

"I planted the seed in his head, yes."

"And then went to Swinburn's house to warn him."

She glanced at Lincoln then nodded.

I sat back. "Why? How could you betray your own leader like that?"

"I didn't know Sir Ignatius would kill him!" She dropped the egg and rubbed her forehead. "I only warned him in an attempt to ingratiate myself into his good graces. I thought if I could show some loyalty to him and not Gawler, he'd believe me when I asked to join his pack. I did it for you, Charlie, and for the ministry. I need to become Swinburn's confidant to spy on him properly. He needs to trust me." She clutched my hands and her eyes filled with tears. "You must believe me, Charlie. I would never have encouraged Gawler to go if I thought it would be his final act." She drew in a shuddery breath. "Poor man. To think—Swinburn *shot* him. Why not simply fight him honorably? They could injure one another yet not have the fight end in death. We do it all the time to settle disputes. Why shoot to kill?"

"To blame him for the Old Nichol deaths," Lincoln said. "The police believe they have their murderer now. They won't look elsewhere."

"And Swinburn becomes the city's hero," Seth added with a twist of his lips. "All because he *happened* to have a gun on him."

Harriet grasped her throat above her lace collar. "What will they do with Gawler? Are they going to cut him open and fiddle around inside his body?"

"Yes," Seth said.

She covered her mouth. I tried to comfort her, but it felt awkward, stilted. I couldn't decide whether she was acting or if I believed her to be as innocent as she claimed. I decided not to tell her the other reason we thought Swinburn killed Gawler—to eliminate a rival pack's leader. Since she would now be leader, it would be an outright accusation directed at her. I couldn't do it without more evidence.

I hoped I would never find that evidence. I didn't want Harriet to be guilty of something so cruel.

"The police will investigate Gawler's associates," Lincoln said. "Expect a visit from a Detective Inspector Fullbright."

She whimpered. "Investigate me?"

Seth crouched before her and took her hands from me. He waited until she met his earnest gaze. "You're the wife of a peer and heavily pregnant. They won't accuse you of anything. But the rest of the pack may come under suspicion of being werewolves. If you're able to contact them, warn them to avoid going for a run until this blows over."

She nodded. "I will. Thank you, Seth. You're a dear man."

He was certainly better at comforting than me.

I asked Lincoln on the way home what he thought of Harriet's reaction to our questions. "Could you tell if she was lying when she said she didn't suspect Swinburn would kill Gawler?"

He shook his head. "My seer's instincts failed me. I had to use regular human intuition."

"Oh dear."

He laughed softly. "She did not seem too surprised or upset over Gawler's death, only that it was a shooting."

I slumped forward only to straighten again when my corset dug into uncomfortable places. I'd only just taken to wearing them on a regular basis because I grew tired of Lady Vickers *tsk tsking* every time I saw her of a morning. I was still getting used to the restriction of movement. "That was my thought too," I said. "Lincoln, I think she may have double-crossed us, and is not spying on Swinburn after all but has befriended him."

"Then we can no longer trust her."

CHAPTER 11

e got through the night without a visit from rabbits, armies or the authorities. Alice looked exhausted the following morning as she, Lady Vickers and I drove to the dressmaker's shop in Dover Street. I suspected her lack of sleep explained why we'd not had a visit from otherworldly beings.

Lady Vickers wrapped Alice's knee with her closed fan. "Alice! Wake up!"

Alice blinked furiously and straightened her spine. "I wasn't asleep. The motion of the carriage is making me drowsy, that's all. I'll be fine once we start shopping."

"Did you sleep at all last night?" I asked her.

"A little."

"You're worried the army will use your dreams as their portal to come here, aren't you?"

She nodded.

"You mustn't fret," Lady Vickers said, spreading out her fan. "Lack of sleep will dull your wits, and you will need them all if we are to face an army."

"She's right," I said."

"Of course I am."

"I'll nap this afternoon while the rest of the household is awake," Alice assured us. "Speaking of which, where did Lincoln go last night?"

"Nowhere," I said as the carriage slowed.

"I saw him crossing the lawn toward the house at about three."

He hadn't mentioned going out when I saw him at breakfast. Usually he summarized his nocturnal activities for all of us, but this morning he'd said nothing.

And two days ago he'd come home smelling of lavender.

"He was probably conducting some sort of investigation," Lady Vickers said, watching me closely.

"That must be it," Alice chimed in.

I forced a smile for their sakes but I didn't like it when Lincoln kept secrets from me. It usually meant he was doing something dangerous.

I put Lincoln from my mind as I submitted to the dressmaker's ministrations that began with the tightening of my corset laces. Apparently my waist wasn't tiny enough, although I thought her somewhat rude for suggesting it, as well as wrong. While the comforts of Lichfield and Cook's cooking had seen me put on weight in the last year, I was still on the thin side. My breasts were a particular disappointment, although the detailed beading on the bodice provided a distraction for the eye.

"There," the dressmaker said, stepping back to admire it on me. "It suits you very well."

"Oh, Charlie," Alice said on a breath. "You look lovely."

Lady Vickers flapped her fan rapidly but it did not hide the tears shining in her eyes. She simply nodded in agreement.

"Do not cry, Lady V," I said, smiling. "This is a happy occasion."

She nodded again and dabbed the corner of her eye with her little finger. "That fitted shape shows off your narrow waist, and the simplicity of the skirt is as elegant as you said it would be. It falls beautifully to the floor."

"It's a thoroughly modern style that suits you superbly," the dressmaker said. "You have an excellent eye for fashion, Miss Holloway."

"Miss Everheart has an excellent eye," I said. "I simply agreed with her ideas."

Alice smiled and blushed.

"I'll be sure to provide a detailed description to the newspapers," Lady Vickers said.

I twirled to get the full effect in the mirror. "The newspapers won't be interested in me."

"Nonsense! I've already scripted a headline for them— homeless waif marries one of London's richest men and second most eligible bachelor."

Alice laughed. "It's a little long."

"There's no point in such a beautiful gown if no one gets to see it or read about it."

"My close friends and Lincoln's family will see it," I told her as I did another twirl. I liked the way the white silk flared at the hem. "Admit it, Lady V, you just want to make your enemies jealous."

Her eyes shone, but not with tears anymore. "I have put it about that you are like a daughter to me for that very reason. Now it's time to show you off."

"I'm not sure I want to be shown off."

"Indulge me, Charlie. Seth is not likely to be wed soon if he maintains his stubborn attitude. You are my only hope to rub my good fortune in my enemies' faces."

The dressmaker and her assistant helped me out of the gown then buttoned me into my day clothes again. We finalized a delivery time and stepped out of the shop into an oppressive summer's day.

The syrupy air clung to my skin and weighed me down. We waded through it to our carriage, parked several feet away. Gus lounged on the driver's seat, flapping his hat near his face, his eyes half closed.

"This heat!" Lady Vickers wailed. "I can't stand it."

"There's an ice man over there," Alice said, pointing toward a cart on the opposite side of the street. "Shall we get one?"

"Good idea," Gus called down. "I'll have lemon."

We left Lady Vickers behind and darted through the traffic to the cart. We paid for four lemon ices in penny licks and were about to head back when I looked up, straight into the wintry gaze of Lady Harcourt.

"Working hard on the ministry's behalf, I see," she said in a tone as chilly as the ices I held in each hand.

"A bride is allowed time off for a wedding gown fitting," Alice said, matching the tone.

Lady Harcourt angled her face to peer up at Alice. "Did I address you? No, I did not. Why would I? You're nothing to me. As are you, Charlotte. Nothing."

I huffed out a laugh. The hint of madness in her response was hardly surprising, and I no longer felt the sting of her barbed words. Whether I was indeed nothing to her didn't matter—*she* was of no consequence to *me* anymore.

"It's far too hot to stand here talking to you. My ices are melting. Good day, Julia," I said, not using her title.

Her spine stiffened at the slight. "You little sewer rat," she hissed. "You always hated me, even when I tried to help you."

Now *that* I could not let pass. "Help me? You tricked me, betrayed me, belittled me, and more besides. But it seems that is not enough for you. You've betrayed us all by giving away ministry secrets to a man who would see us destroyed."

"Ignatius?" She scoffed. "Don't be ridiculous."

I stepped up to her so that we were mere inches apart. I could smell her perfume, as cloying as the heat swamping me. "Make no mistake, Swinburn wants the ministry closed. He's using you to find out everything he can to cause us problems with the authorities."

She stretched out her lovely, slender neck. She resembled an elegant swan…and then she spoiled the effect by opening her mouth. "You have no proof. Ignatius is merely protecting himself and his pack."

"If you believe that, you're more of a fool than I thought. He's using you, Julia. He's using you and will discard you the moment he succeeds in getting what he wants."

"And what does he want, Charlotte? Your head on a spike?"

"Not mine. Lincoln's."

The color leached from her face but she remained as stiff as a statue. "You do have a flair for the dramatic. Ignatius and Lincoln are not friends, but Ignatius wishes no harm to befall him. I wouldn't have helped him if he did. He simply likes to know things, but he rarely acts on that knowledge."

"Ask him how the authorities and *The Star* came to know about the ministry. Ask him how they know about our archives. Ask him why an MP by the name of Yallop wants Lincoln arrested for conspiracy to murder simply because he is protecting the names in those files. Then take a long look in the mirror and ask yourself if you're happy to have played a role in Swinburn's war against Lincoln and the ministry."

She drew in short, sharp breaths, as if she couldn't fill her lungs. Then her features sharpened and her eyes narrowed to slits. "How dare you accuse me? Me! I *love* Lincoln! I would never—"

"My ices are melting." I strode off, my blood at boiling point, my face hot. "Is she really so stupid?" I asked Alice as

we strode back to the carriage. "Does she truly believe Swinburn wishes us no ill will? That he simply wanted to acquire
knowledge but not use it?"

"It's hard to imagine she could be that naive, but she did
look shocked. Perhaps she simply thought Swinburn would
use the information she gave him to blackmail Lincoln, not
see him arrested. I don't think she wants Lincoln harmed."

"No, just punished." I stormed up to the carriage and
passed a penny lick cup to Gus. "I'm sorry it's a little melted."

"Was that Lady H you were talking to?" he asked.

"Yes. She ruined an otherwise pleasant morning."

"She's got a habit of that."

* * *

I FOUND myself at a loose end in the afternoon yet unable to
settle to anything. I wanted to voice my frustrations about
Lady Harcourt to Lincoln, but he and Seth were still out.
They were taking it in turns to watch Swinburn and his pack,
something that would be difficult to manage on their own.
Lincoln had refused Gus's help, saying he needed to be our
coachman for the day as well as assist with the cooking and
cleaning. We were starting to feel stretched too thin.

I wanted to help Cook in the kitchen, but he claimed
there was little to do since he planned on only a light meal in
such heat. So I patrolled the rooms and kept an eye on the
lawn for any armies that may suddenly appear. Alice and
Lady Vickers both napped. The house seemed too quiet
and empty.

The scrunch of wheels on the gravel drive had me
jumping off the sofa and running to the window, but it was
not an army's siege engine. The approaching brougham's
deep black paint swallowed the sunshine and my restless
mood. Then I saw the snake escutcheon on the side and

181

groaned. I wanted a visit from neither Lord nor Lady Gillingham now. He was never a welcome sight, and I wasn't sure what to say to her at the moment.

Their footman lowered the folding step and opened the door. His mistress took his hand and allowed him to assist her down. Harriet supported her round belly with her other hand and broke into a smile when she saw me through the window.

I couldn't pretend to be out now. I opened the front door and welcomed her inside. "Still no Doyle?" she asked. "Or Whistler?"

"I've allowed them more time off—"

"But the wedding is the day after tomorrow! Have you lost your mind?"

"We're coping well enough."

She clicked her tongue and appeared to be about to say something else, only to pause and clutch her pregnant belly.

"Are you all right?" I asked, taking her arm.

"I would like to sit down."

"Come into the parlor. The staircase is much too difficult in your condition." I steered her into the parlor and eased her onto the sofa. "Can I get you anything?"

"No, thank you. Come and sit with me." She patted the sofa beside her. "I feel quite all right now. I just have these pains every now and again."

"Have you spoken to the midwife about them?"

"I've decided not to engage a midwife. Not a human one, anyway." She bit her lip and a small crease formed between her eyebrows. "I'm worried what the baby will look like when it comes out, you see. Not because I care, but Gilly's right—we don't want to alarm anyone if it should be in beast form. So I've engaged one of my pack friends, only she's not always available when I need her. She's a little…"

"Unreliable?"

"Drunk."

"Oh. What about someone from Swinburn's pack? Surely the women from both packs have given birth before. Who helps them?"

"Midwives help those in Swinburn's pack, and family members assist those in Gawler's—I mean mine. They can't afford midwives. Apparently the babies are always born looking human, but I won't take that risk, and Gilly certainly won't." She rubbed her belly. "So you see, I may be all alone for the birth."

"You won't be alone. I'm sure your pack mate will sober up long enough to assist. And your husband will be there."

"Gilly! Lord, no. I don't want him in the house at all when my time comes. He'll just be a bore and get in the way, demanding this and that, and probably offending my pack mate, too. She's got quite a temper and it wouldn't surprise me if she struck him to shut him up. He can come across as quite offensive to some, you know."

"Yes," I said wryly. "I know."

She sighed and gave me a small smile. "I feel better already for having seen you, Charlie. You always manage to cheer me up. I was growing quite lonely at home. Not being able to run with my pack is awfully frustrating."

"You'll run with them again soon. Did you manage to get word to them about laying low for a while?"

She nodded as she plucked off her gloves. "Thank you for the warning. Tell me, have you thought any more about Sir Ignatius's motive for shooting Gawler?"

Is that why she was really here? To gather information to pass on to Swinburn? She had a nerve, if that were the case. "No."

"I'm sure you have more important things on your mind at the moment." She set her gloves on the table then got to her feet. "I need to take a turn around the room."

"I'll walk with you."

"No, stay there. I'll just toddle at my own speed." She ambled toward the window, her pace slow and awkward. "I feel like a waddling duck."

"You are getting quite big now."

"I think my time is very near. I may not even make it to the wedding." She smiled and walked back to me. Instead of sitting, she stood behind the sofa. Her cool hands settled on my shoulders and gently massaged. "In case I don't, tell me your plans. What does your dress look like?"

I eased into her hands, enjoying the sensation on my neck. I hadn't realized how stiff I was until now. The conversation with Lady Harcourt this morning had left me tense.

I described my gown to Harriet as she continued to massage. She wanted all the details, down to every last bead, and then asked me to describe the table setting and menu. I didn't mind. It wasn't a secret and it did seem as though she might not make it to the wedding.

She suddenly pulled her hands away and sucked in a breath. "Ooh, that was a big kick."

"Are you all right?" I said, turning to her. "Come and sit down. I should be massaging your shoulders, not the other way around."

"I think I should go home." She breathed deeply and blew it out slowly. "Will you help me back to my carriage?"

I assisted her outside and the footman had to almost lift her into the cabin. She waved at me through the window and I waved back as the coach drove off. A figure further along the drive had to step aside to let it pass, then he continued toward the house. I knew before I saw his face that it was Seth.

"Bloody hell, it's hot today," he said when he reached me. He removed his hat and jacket before he was even through the front door. He hung both up then proceeded to remove his waistcoat and tie too. "What was Harriet doing here?"

"Looking for company." I frowned. "It was a little odd. She seemed uncomfortable, and even a little restless. She should have been at home, not out making calls. What was even odder was that she took a walk around the room when she clearly wanted to sit down."

"That is odd." He undid the button at his collar.

I stared at his nimble fingers. Something bothered me. Something about Harriet's visit and her behavior, but I couldn't put my finger on it.

"Charlie? Does my masculinity distract you?"

"Hmmm?"

Seth opened his shirt wider. He'd undone the top three buttons. "My chest? Does it distract you?"

I laughed. "Good lord, no."

He rolled his eyes. "Thank you for bringing me back down to earth with a thud."

"Sorry, Seth, but I didn't even notice your chest. Go and show it to someone who is not in love with her fiancé."

He cast a longing gaze at the stairs.

"I was actually distracted by Harriet," I said. "Or, rather, her actions."

"Any action in particular?"

"She massaged my shoulders."

He frowned. "Why did she do that? Did you complain of soreness?"

"No. She simply took it upon herself to massage me. Then we got talking about wedding plans, then after a few minutes she left in a hurry."

"Perhaps she likes your neck." He pulled a face. "That even sounds ridiculous." He shrugged. "Pregnancy is turning her a little mad. Or perhaps Gillingham is. Now *that* I can believe."

I stared at the triangle of bare skin at Seth's chest. He

wore a silver chain around his neck with a small pendant. I gasped. My hands flew to my throat and the back of my neck. I thrust two fingers down my bodice as far as I could reach and patted my chest.

"Charlie?" Seth hedged. "Are you all right?"

"My orb necklace! It's gone. Harriet stole my imp!"

CHAPTER 12

"Are you sure you were wearing it?" Seth asked.

"Yes!" I picked up my skirts and marched toward the service area at the back of the house. "Gus! Gus!"

He appeared in the doorway, wringing his hands in his apron. "What's all this yelling then?"

"I need a coachman. I'm paying Harriet a call."

"I'll drive you," Seth said, buttoning up his shirt again.

"Weren't she just here?" Gus asked.

Cook appeared beside him, wielding a spatula. "Why you be undressed?" he asked, pointing the spatula at Seth.

"It's bloody hot out there and I walked all the way from the west end of the heath," Seth said. "And to answer your question, Gus, we're going to visit Harriet because she stole Charlie's orb."

Both Gus and Cook swore. Neither apologized for their language, and I was beyond caring. I was furious. Harriet was going to get a piece of my mind. I would tell her exactly what I thought of her betrayal, and then tell her not to show her face at our wedding. She had lost the right to be my friend when she chose to take Swinburn's side.

* * *

"She's not at home!" Lord Gillingham's bellow must have been heard three houses away because a neighbor's footman peeked out the front door. "How many times do I have to tell you?"

"I don't believe you," I snapped. "She's in here. She was feeling poorly when she left Lichfield."

"Poorly?" he murmured, all bluster gone. "And you just let her go?"

"I didn't have a choice! She simply up and left. Are you sure she hasn't come home?"

"Damned sure."

"She stole my necklace."

He snorted. "Why would she do that? She has a dozen necklaces. Diamonds, rubies—"

"My imp necklace! She took it from me!"

"Don't be absurd. Why would she steal it?"

"To give it to Swinburn." I suddenly realized I'd come to the wrong house.

I turned to go, but Gillingham caught my arm. Out of the corner of my eye, I saw Seth stand up on the driver's perch.

"Let me go," I growled.

"You stupid brat," Gillingham sneered. "My wife wouldn't do such a thing. Retract your accusation."

"Let me go or I'll strike you again."

His fingers loosened enough for me to wrench free. I marched down the steps and didn't give him a second glance. "Seth, take me to Swinburn's house."

"We should go home and tell Lincoln—"

"Lincoln isn't at home. He's out paying calls on goodness knows who."

Seth's lips clamped shut and he did not meet my gaze. I suspected he knew precisely who Lincoln was visiting. I wondered if he chose not to tell me or Lincoln ordered his silence.

"Drive fast," I said. "Or I'll climb up there and take the reins myself."

He drove as quickly as the traffic allowed. It wasn't quick enough for my temper, and by the time we reached Queen's Gate, I was fuming. I hammered Swinburn's door until the footman opened it. I pushed past him, catching him unawares.

"Miss!" he cried.

I rounded on him. "Do *not* try to tell me Sir Ignaitus is out. If he is not at home, then I will see Lady Gillingham alone. I *know* she's here."

The butler emerged from an adjoining room and sent the footman upstairs. "Will you wait in the drawing room, miss?"

I allowed him to lead me into the drawing room, but regretted it as I sat on a chair. There was only one exit and my street rat instincts recoiled. In a few moments, I'd be trapped in here with two inhuman creatures with uncommon strength. The old Charlie would not have made such a mistake. This Charlie had become too trusting and soft of late.

"I'll return to the hall," I told the butler.

He stepped aside for me but the exit became blocked anyway as Harriet entered ahead of Swinburn. She stretched both hands toward me and lifted her brows.

"Charlie, what a surprise," she said. "What are you doing here?"

"You know why I'm here. You stole my necklace!"

"Whatever are you talking about?" She winked at me. With her back to Swinburn, he would not have seen.

"What the devil are you accusing her of?" Swinburn demanded.

"She knows," I said through clenched teeth. "Give me back my necklace, Harriet."

"Don't be silly, Charlie. I haven't stolen anything from you. Why would I? Gilly gives me everything my heart desires. Particularly now." She rubbed her belly and smiled dreamily. "He's a very agreeable husband lately."

"Stop it, Harriet! Stop playing the fool. I know you removed it from my neck when you massaged me." I stepped closer, crushing my skirt against her stiffer one. "Give. It. Back."

Swinburn thrust his arm between us. "Calm down, Miss Holloway. This behavior is uncalled for."

I poked my finger at him, just shy of stabbing him in the chest. "You know what my necklace does, what it contains. Lady Ballantine informed you after seeing it on the Isle of Wight."

Swinburn batted my finger away. "Don't point at me, young lady."

Harriet touched my shoulder. "Why would I steal your necklace when we are friends?"

"To ingratiate yourself here," I said. "Firstly you deliberately provoke Gawler into confronting Swinburn then you rush here ahead of him to warn Swinburn. You two struck an agreement that would see you take over the pack. That has been your aim all along, hasn't it? And now, to prove your loyalty, Harriet, you took my orb and gave it to him!"

"Charlie, don't work yourself up like this. It's not good for you. It's not good for me either, or the baby."

"Did you ask her to steal it for you?" I spat at Swinburn. "Or did she take it of her own volition?"

"You're mad," he said.

"Charlie, stop this." Harriet took my hand and tried to steer me away.

I jerked free. "Give it back *now* or I'll call the constables."

"Charlie!"

"Enough!" Swinburn bellowed. "You've insulted my guest and therefore me."

"I quite agree." Harriet stepped aside. "You should leave, Charlie."

"No," Swinburn growled. "Not until she calms down. I won't risk her going to the police. I don't need that man Full-bright sniffing around here any more than he already is."

"He's sniffing because you murdered Gawler!" I shouted.

He put up a finger. "Quiet."

I was getting nowhere. I would have to confront Harriet on her own. As to getting my orb back from Swinburn, I'd have to come up with another solution. He wouldn't simply hand it back.

Until then, I needed to be careful. The imp inside the amber orb had saved me on more than one occasion. I felt vulnerable without it, particularly in Swinburn's house.

I glanced toward the door and picked up my skirts. I pushed past Harriet, but Swinburn blocked my path. "I said," he growled, "you are not leaving until you've calmed down."

I screwed my hands into my skirt, bunching the fabric. "You can't keep me here!"

"Sir Ignatius has a point, Charlie. You are somewhat impulsive and we can't risk you going to the police. Why not stay and have some tea."

"This is abduction!"

"You came here of your own accord." Swinburn strode to the door. "Come, Harriet. We'll leave her to stew in her own filthy temper for a little while. Jenkin will watch her."

"Jenkin is the footman," Harriet said stiffly. "And a shape changer. Don't try to get past him or he'll be forced to hurt you."

"Harriet! You're really going to comply with this? Lincoln will be furious."

"Do stop relying on him to rescue you, Charlie. You have the skills to rescue yourself."

I bristled. I never relied on Lincoln to rescue me. Did I?

"I have to return home now," she went on, "but Sir Ignatius will see that you're set free *after* you calm down so it's in your best interests to sit and have tea."

Swinburn opened the door and slipped out with Harriet. The footman took their place, closed the door and guarded it. He stood straight, his hands by his sides, seemingly not looking at me. But his eyes followed me as I paced the floor.

I could not believe it! Swinburn had a nerve keeping me here against my will. Seth would grow suspicious, for one thing, particularly after he saw Harriet leave. It was a deliberately provocative move, but I couldn't think why he'd do it. To show us he would not be manipulated? To prove that Harriet was loyal to him and not us?

Or to keep me distracted from something he was about to do?

I studied the footman, not caring that he noticed. He was young, tall and solid. He'd be difficult to beat in a fight. In his wolf form, he'd be impossible.

"You belong to Swinburn's pack, do you not?" I asked.

He nodded.

"Then you will know that your fellow pack mate, Nigel Franklin, suffered terrible injuries two months ago. Injuries inflicted by his deceased victim whom *I* summoned from his grave."

Jenkin's gaze met mine.

"Yes, I am that necromancer," I went on.

"Are you threatening me, miss?" he intoned. He was quite a pleasant looking fellow, and I regretted that he would bear the brunt of my anger and not Swinburn.

"Yes."

He swallowed but did not move.

"I don't want to hurt you, Jenkin, but you will get hurt if you don't release me. You see, I can summon the dead from anywhere. I don't need to be in a cemetery or mortuary, I simply need to know their name. And I know a lot of names. So please, step aside."

He shifted his stance, but remained by the door.

"Come now, Jenkin. I don't wish to have an army of dead marching through the streets of London, but that's what will happen. They will come from the cemeteries and besiege this house. Not only will they frighten innocent people along the way, but they will bring attention to your master. I'm quite sure he won't want that."

His gaze flickered. He licked his lips. "I'll check with Sir Ignatius."

"No. You will step aside and let me walk out. You may tell him I had calmed down and promised not to tell the police. There, will that suffice?"

"*Will* you tell the constables, miss?"

I simply smiled, but it was hard and cold.

He edged back to the door until his back was against it. "I don't know…" He licked his lips again. "My instructions are to keep you here."

"Brompton is the closest cemetery. I know five deceased buried there. I also believe Mr. Gawler's body was taken to Bow Cemetery. It would take him only an hour to walk here."

Jenkin suddenly looked quite hot.

"His full name is Jonathon Michael Gawler, by the way," I said, plucking a middle name out of thin air. "Did you meet him when he came here? Did you see how angry he was? I'm sure he's even angrier now that he's dead. Murder victims usually are."

He flinched at every word, as if each one pricked him. "I don't know… Let me just ask…"

"Jonathon Michael Gawler," I intoned in my best eerie sounding voice.

"Don't, miss!"

"Jonathon Michael Gawler, I summon your spirit here to me."

"Miss Holloway, please, stop at once!"

"Come, Jonathon Michael Gawler. I have need of you." No spirit appeared, since I'd used an incorrect name, but Jenkin didn't know that.

He fumbled with the handle and pushed open the door. "Go," he whispered, checking the vicinity. "I'll tell Sir Ignatius that you tricked me and slipped away. For God's sake, let Gawler rest in peace before he hurts someone!"

I thanked him and hurried out, quietly shutting the front door behind me. I ran down the front steps and straight for the carriage. "Go, Seth!"

"What the devil?" he said, sitting up. "Why are you running?"

"Just go! Make haste!"

I climbed into the carriage without lowering the step and was thrown onto the seat as we took off. Seth seemed to have taken my request for haste to heart. We sped all the way home, ducking in and out of traffic with such abandon that I slid from one end of the leather seat to the other before I could grasp the strap.

Seth drove straight to the coach house behind Lichfield where Gus and Cook joined us. Between us, we quickly had the horses unharnessed and settled in the stables.

"There be tea for you," Cook said as we crossed the court-yard cobbles to the house. "And almond cake."

"Lovely," I said. "I need tea after that drive."

"You asked me to go fast," Seth protested. "Why, may I ask? What happened in Swinburn's house?"

"You visited Swinburn?" Gus demanded. "Without Fitzroy?"

"I am capable of taking care of myself," I said hotly.

No one commented.

"Don't tell him," I added. "He'll only worry and there's nothing to worry about." It was probably best not to tell them that Swinburn had kept me prisoner. It had come to naught anyway, and they'd only get angry. Getting angry with Swinburn at the moment was proving to be a futile endeavor.

"So why did we need to leave in a hurry?" Seth asked.

"I simply don't like that man and there was no reason to remain behind after Harriet left."

He pushed open the service door and allowed me to enter ahead of him. "I spoke to her as she left. She told me not to worry and that you were having a civil conversation with Swinburn."

"She smiled at you, didn't she?" Gus asked with a chuckle.

"I don't fall for smiles," Seth shot back. "She seemed genuinely unconcerned for your safety, Charlie."

"You shouldn't trust her," I said, taking a seat at the kitchen table. "She has double crossed us. I think."

Cook poured the tea and sliced the cake. We sat at the large central table, surrounded by warmth and the delicious scents of the kitchen. It reminded me of my early days at Lichfield, when I'd taken over duties as a maid and before we got proper servants. We'd been a small, intimate family then. We still were, but it wasn't the same when the household was filled with servants. I must remember to give them all a day off once or twice a week so we could continue these cozy afternoons.

"So you retrieved the imp?" Seth asked. "You stole it back, didn't you? Is that why we had to leave quickly?"

"The imp is still lost."

Seth lowered his cup. Gus swore under his breath.

"It be *your* imp, Charlie," Cook said. "They can't use it against you. It be at your command."

"True, but I can't use it unless I have it."

"How will you get it back?" Gus asked.

"I don't yet know. But I suspect Swinburn has it, not Harriet. She gave it to him to prove her loyalty."

"She betrayed us," Seth grumbled, incredulous. "Sweet little Harriet."

"She's not so sweet anymore," I said. "Ever since discovering she's a shape shifter she has taken control of her life. I applaud it in the situation with her husband, but this...this turn worries me."

Seth rubbed his chin in thought. "We'll have to break into Swinburn's house to retrieve it."

"No," Gus said. "Fitzroy won't like it."

"Aye," Cook added. "He won't agree."

Gus settled back in the chair. "If you didn't steal back the imp necklace, why'd you stay in Swinburn's house after Lady Gilly left?"

"I was talking to the footman," I said.

"Why?" Seth asked.

"To learn more about our enemy. He's a shape changer in Swinburn's pack."

"I thought only toffs ran in his pack," Gus said.

"So did I, but it seems there is at least one who isn't a toff. Perhaps the pack contains any shifters who don't reside in the slums."

"What did you learn from him?" Seth asked, reaching for a second piece of cake.

"That there's at least one member of Swinburn's pack who is a good man. He expressed concern for the general public getting caught up in the latest murders." It wasn't quite the truth, but the sentiment was real enough. Jenkin had been genuinely worried about Gawler's body rising and harming people on his way to rescue me. "It gives me hope there are others in the pack who think the same."

Gus also reached for another piece of cake. "It don't seem like you got much out of staying, Charlie. You should have left with Lady Gillingham."

I smiled sweetly. "Yes, I should have. Now, when Lincoln gets back—"

"I am back." He strode through the door, jacket in hand and tie loosened. He'd tied his hair back but it was damp at the hairline.

"You look hot," I said. "Sit down and I'll fetch you a drink of water."

He hesitated and for a moment I thought he'd argue with me, but he dutifully sat. I fetched a cup and filled it from the jug we stored in the larder during hot weather. I took my time, hoping my delay would cause him to forget to ask me what I'd been about to say before he walked in. I had been about to remind the others not to tell Lincoln where I went today, or about the stolen necklace.

It was a foolhardy idea. Lincoln didn't forget anything.

"There," I said cheerfully, handing him the cup.

He took it but simply stared at it and didn't drink. I touched his cheek and he glanced at me.

"Lincoln?" I asked. "What's wrong? You look troubled."

"How can you tell?" Seth muttered.

"Lincoln?" I prompted.

"I've just come from Julia's house," he said, shooting a glance at Seth.

"And?" Seth asked when Lincoln did not go on.

"And she's dead. She killed herself."

CHAPTER 13

I plopped down on the chair and gawped at Lincoln. He kept his gaze on Seth.

"How?" Cook asked at the same time Gus said, "What happened?"

"According to witnesses, she threw herself into the path of a fast moving omnibus on Oxford Street."

I picked up my teacup but set it down again. Lady Harcourt, dead. I couldn't fathom it. "We only saw her this morning," I murmured. "We argued but she didn't seem any different. Certainly not like someone who would take her own life."

"She was a fighter," Seth agreed. "She pulled herself up from nothing and made herself into the person she always dreamed of being. I can't believe she'd do this. She wouldn't just give up."

"It must have been an accident," I said. "Perhaps someone bumped her in the hustle and bustle. It's a busy street for pedestrians and coaches alike."

"She *threw* herself," Gus said. "That ain't an accident."

"Or she was pushed." My pronouncement was followed

by a deafening silence. "I could summon her spirit to make sure."

"No," Lincoln said. "I, for one, think suicide is the more likely explanation."

Alice and Lady Vickers entered and asked why we looked so glum. We told her, and they both sat heavily.

"We argued with her," Alice muttered. "Do you think...?"

"No," I said, taking her hand. "I've argued with her many times, as have others, and she has always fought back."

"She did greet us in the most waspish manner. You're right. We can't take blame for her state of mind."

"It's more likely to have been building over time," Lady Vickers said, accepting a cup of tea from Cook. "Ever since the newspapers revealed her past at the Alhambra, she's been sliding into social oblivion. The gossips have been relentless, the invitations have dried up, and she's become an outcast wherever she goes. Many have delighted in her downfall. I thought they were vicious toward me, but I've managed to regain some measure of what I lost. She could not and never would."

"Because she wasn't born privileged," Seth said with a shake of his head. "God, I hate them all. And you want me to marry into that, Mother. I won't."

She wisely said nothing.

"Swinburn was her only hope for a secure future," Alice said with a pained look at me. "She believed marriage to him would win back some of the regard she lost."

"And then we told her Swinburn is using her." I groaned and buried my head in my hands. "That he'll use her then discard her when he has what he wants. Perhaps it *is* my fault."

A chorus of denials followed, but it was Lincoln's quietly insistent voice that cut through them all. "You are not to blame, Charlie." His warm lips caressed my forehead. "Everything that happened to her she has brought on herself. She chose to be cruel to you and others, and now she chose to end her life. She could have trodden a different path many times, but she did not. I won't mourn her. You shouldn't either."

"Nor me," Seth said.

"Good riddance, I say." Lady Vickers shrugged and picked up her teacup. "I don't care if that makes me sound horrid. I won't speak nicely of her simply because she's dead."

"Do you think Swinburn got what he wanted from her and did set her aside?" Alice asked no one in particular. "Do you think that's what drove her to suicide?"

It was entirely possible, even likely, and I pinned my hopes on that being the case. As much as I loathed her, it made my stomach churn to think my words had caused her such despair that she felt the need to end her life.

A pounding on the front door echoed through the house. My heart tripped.

Alice gasped. "The army!"

"Stay here," Seth said as he, Lincoln and Gus rushed out of the kitchen.

Alice and I followed, neither of us prepared to take orders until we knew what we were up against. We raced through the passageway and emerged into the entrance hall as Lincoln opened the door.

Andrew Buchanan stumbled inside, his fist raised to strike the door again. All three men could have caught him but none did. He stumbled to the floor and lay sprawled on the tiles, moaning.

Seth nudged Buchanan in the ribs with his boot. "Get up."

Buchanan rolled over onto his back and winced. His eyes were swollen and his nose red. His sweaty hair stuck to his forehead and he reeked of gin.

"Fuck you, Vickers, you cock sucking— Ow!"

Gus leveled his boot over Buchanan's face. "There are ladies present. Talk like that again and I'll smash that pretty nose of yours."

"Slum scum." Buchanan chortled. "That rhymes."

"What do you want?" Lincoln snapped.

Buchanan put his hand up but no one went to his aid so he rocked and rolled himself into a sitting position. He swayed and belched. "I want a drink."

"You've had enough." Lincoln put out his hand and after staring at it for several heartbeats, Buchanan took it. Lincoln hauled him up and only let go when Buchanan appeared steady on his feet.

"Julia's dead." Buchanan's voice sounded raw, scratchy. His face crumpled but a deep breath helped him regain composure.

"We know," Seth said. "We also know how it happened."

"Do you? Do you really?" Buchanan sneered. "Then perhaps you can enlighten me, Vickers, because I don't *know* anything."

"She...fell and an omnibus struck her."

"She didn't fall, she deliberately stepped into its path." Buchanan sniffed then wiped the back of his ungloved hand across his nose. It came away covered in snot. "She killed herself and I want to know why."

"We don't have the answer," I said. "We're as much in the dark as you are."

"Oh, I doubt that, little miss sweetness."

"Don't," Lincoln warned.

"And you! You're the worst." He shoved Lincoln's shoulders with both hands. Lincoln didn't budge, but he didn't raise a hand to ward him off either. "What did she see in you? Charlotte, answer me that? Help me understand. What do women see in him?"

"Don't punish yourself like this," Alice said more gently

201

than he deserved. "She's gone. There's no point going over well-traveled roads now."

Buchanan wagged a finger in Seth's general direction. "If she pined for *you*, I could understand. You're so god damned beautiful that *I'm* half in love with you." He patted Seth's cheek and gave him a slick smile.

Seth smacked his hand away. "If anyone needs me, I'll be around."

"Don't run away, dear Vickers. I'm just getting to the good part. The part where I blame you all for Julia's death."

Seth stopped and glanced over his shoulder, not at Buchanan, but at me.

"Not you." Buchanan touched Alice's face in the same way he'd touched Seth's. "I don't blame you, you divine creature."

Seth grabbed him by the jacket lapels and punched him in the face. Then he held out his hand to Alice. She took it and they left together without a backward glance.

Lincoln held the door open wide. "Get out."

Buchanan didn't look like he was going anywhere soon. He writhed on the floor, clutching his nose and pulling his knees up to his chest. "I'm bleeding!"

Gus shook his head. "If I have to clean blood off that floor, I'll punch you too." He strode off toward the service area.

Buchanan pulled out a woman's lace handkerchief from his jacket pocket, setting off another bout of sobbing. "They let me keep this."

"Who did?" Lincoln asked.

"The mortuary people. I had to identify her body. It was horrible." He sobbed and more tears and bloodied snot oozed from his orifices. "My beautiful Julia…ruined. I refuse to remember her as that bloody mess laid out on a cold table. She'll be forever lovely to me." He curled up into a ball and cried.

I sighed. "What shall we do with him?"

"The hack is still here," Lincoln said, signaling for the driver to wait. "Get up, Buchanan."

"Not until you admit you killed Julia." Buchanan swiped the handkerchief across his nose, smearing blood up his cheek. "She wouldn't have taken her life if you hadn't expelled her from the committee."

"She betrayed the committee," Lincoln said flatly. "She deserved expulsion."

Buchanan lurched onto all fours then pulled himself to his feet. "You could have treated her with kindness, considering your history together! But kindness isn't in your repertoire, is it? Only coldness and cruelty."

I stood in front of him, hands bunched into fists at my sides. "How dare you accuse Lincoln of cruelty toward her? *You* informed the newspapers of her past. *You* threatened to reveal your secret liaisons. *You* provoked her and manipulated her—"

"I *loved* her!" More tears streamed down his cheeks, and blood and snot bubbled from his nose. "No one else loved her but me. I only ever had her best interests at heart."

"You had *your* interests at heart. You couldn't accept her rejection so you tried to force her back into your arms by making her unhappy and desperate. How *loving* of you."

He folded in on himself and sobbed. I'd never seen a grown man cry so hard, and for a moment, I was fascinated by it and a little heart sick. Then I blinked and shrugged it off.

"Go home, Andrew," I said more gently. "Help your brother with the funeral arrangements. She would have wanted that."

Lincoln tried to walk him out the door but Buchanan's legs wouldn't cooperate so he tossed him over his shoulder instead.

Buchanan twisted to see me as Lincoln carried him down the front steps. "Summon her for me, Charlotte," he wailed. "Call her spirit so I may speak to her one last time."

"No."

His sobs could be heard even as the coach drove away.

Lincoln laid a hand on the back of my neck as I shut the front door. "I feel a little sorry for him," I said. "He did love her in his strange way."

"He doesn't deserve your sympathy." His fingers skimmed my neck at my hairline. "Where's your necklace?"

"My room," I said without missing a beat. "It doesn't go with this outfit so I took it off." I needed to stop talking or he'd detect my lie. Perhaps he did already.

"You should wear it always until the threat from the army is over."

I headed up the stairs to my room and shoved the guilt from my heart. I didn't regret lying to him. He had enough to worry about, and adding me to the list would only end up with him forbidding me to leave the house. I didn't want to argue with him this close to the wedding.

* * *

THE FOLLOWING MORNING, twenty-four hours before I walked down the aisle, my nerves finally set in. It began with the delivery of my gown. The dressmaker brought it herself and insisted I try it on one last time now that the final adjustments had been made. It was too tight.

Lady Vickers went into a flap that brought the rest of the household to my door in a panic. Seth barged in without knocking, catching me half out of the gown.

"Charlie—! Er, my apologies." He backed out of the door, knocking into Lincoln.

"Get out! Get out!" Lady Vickers screeched. "The groom

can't see the bride in her dress before the wedding!" She shut the door on them and collapsed against it. "That was close."

"Come and sit down," I scolded her. "You're making everyone nervous."

"That's because I am nervous." She did not sit but paced the room, vigorously fanning herself. "There's so much to do. And with no servants..." She stopped pacing and placed her hand to her chest. "I cannot breathe."

Alice helped her to sit at my dressing table then rubbed her back. "Count to three then take a deep breath."

Lady Vickers did as advised. She coughed through the breath. "I need a glass of sherry."

"It's far too early for sherry," Alice said with a laugh.

"Wine then."

Alice smiled at me and gave a little shrug.

The dressmaker sat on the bed with the gown so I went to work on Lady Vickers. I took her hand in both of mine and leveled my gaze with hers. "Everything will be all right. We'll finish setting the dining table soon then give the drawing room a quick dust. Cook has altered the menu to include simpler dishes that can be prepared ahead. He'll decorate the cake this afternoon. There's nothing more to do. There. Better now?"

"No. Yes." She sighed. "We haven't had time for that talk yet, Charlie."

I tried very hard to contain my smile. "The talk can wait."

"Wait! Wait for when? The moment he carries you into his bed?" She pinched the bridge of her nose and groaned. "I've failed in my duties as your..." A wave of her hand encompassed the unconventional nature of our relationship.

I caught Alice pressing her lips together very hard out of the corner of my eye. I leaned toward Lady Vickers and whispered in her ear so the dressmaker couldn't hear. "I know what goes on between a husband and wife in bed."

She did not reel back in shock like I thought she would. "Seeing the whores do it is not the same as a loving couple," she whispered back.

She had a point. "Lincoln can teach me."

She flapped her fan in front of her reddening face again. "Yes. Well. There is that. But still, if you have a moment today, I'd like to have a quiet conversation."

"I'll be sure to find the time."

The dressmaker was a fast worker and when I tried on the gown again, it fitted perfectly.

With that settled, we made our way to the dining room. Seth brought in a delivery of roses and assisted his mother to arrange them in the vases down the center of the table. Gus joined us and asked for Lady Vickers' assistance in the kitchen.

"Of course," she said, handing the rest of the flowers to Seth.

"Wait," he said. "Why is she needed in the kitchen?"

"Don't know." Gus wiped his flour-covered hands down the front of his apron.

"Do not drop any of that flour in here," Alice scolded him.

He put up his hands in surrender. "Cook wants her," he told Seth.

Seth grunted. "He does, does he?"

"Don't make a scene," his mother said cheerfully.

"Why not?" He pointed a pale pink rose at her. "Once upon a time, you wouldn't set a toe in the kitchen, and now you can't stay out of it."

"I am merely assisting Cook at this busy time."

"I can assist him. What does he want done?" he asked Gus.

"Don't be petty," his mother said. "He asked for me so I will go. Come along, Gus."

Seth darted in front of her, blocking her path. I set down

the cutlery I'd been laying out and exchanged a worried glance with Alice.

"Enough, Mother," Seth growled. "Stop this at once."

"Stop what?"

"Whatever it is you're doing with Cook. It can't go on."

"Seth, dear, Cook and I are friends, that's all."

He snorted. "Friends. That's what you used to say about the footman. Then you ran off and married him."

I thought she'd grow angry with him but her features softened. "It's true that George was not unlike Cook. Companionable, competent, honest and highly amusing. Do you recall the old rumors about the queen and her servant, Mr. Brown? It's like that between Cook and me."

"You are not the queen!"

"Weren't they lovers?" Gus asked.

Seth shot him a murderous glare. "Don't you dare marry Cook, Mother, or I won't be able to look either of you in the eye again." He folded his arms, an immovable wall blocking his mother's exit.

She patted his cheek. "That would be unbearable."

He arched a brow. "So you agree?"

"It's only fair that if I give him up, you must promise to do something for me."

He lowered his arms. "I suspect I'm not going to like this."

"Find yourself a suitable wife, one with a fortune and good breeding, and I will end any liaison I've been having with Cook."

"Ah, yes, because heiresses of noble birth grow on trees."

"There are a number in my circle, but you've refused to consider them."

"That's because I've met them. Vacuous little misses, all of them."

"So?" She lifted one shoulder. "That is my condition. Now, move aside, please. Cook needs me."

He hesitated then sighed and stepped out of her way. She lifted her chin and strode past him. Gus followed, smirking. Seth glanced in Alice's direction, but she was too busy fussing with a napkin to notice, so he left too.

"That was an odd conversation," I said attempting a laugh.

She sat down on one of the chairs and yawned. "Hmmm."

"Go and rest for a little while, Alice. I can manage on my own."

"I think I will. Keep an eye on the front lawn."

"Everything will be fine. Go."

She left, passing Lincoln striding in. He came straight up to me and hooked me around the waist, trapping me against his body. He kissed me fiercely, passionately, and did not stop until I pulled away.

"Lincoln?" I asked, half laughing, half eyeing him carefully.

My laughter died at the darkness swirling in his eyes. "Let's get married now."

"Now! Lincoln, it's all set for tomorrow." I indicated the table. "Everyone's gone to so much effort."

"The guests can still come for the breakfast. I want the ceremony now, today."

"They want to share the whole occasion with us, not just the food." I cupped his face with both my hands and stroked his cheeks with my thumbs. The darkness in his eyes didn't dissipate until he closed them and took my hands in his. "Why the hurry?" I asked, unease tightening my chest.

"Why the delay?" he murmured against my wrist. "I just want to marry you, Charlie. I only care about signing the papers to make you my wife. Why not today?"

"Lincoln, something's troubling you."

He opened his eyes and his gaze met mine. There was an earnestness there, and longing, but concern too.

A chill skittered across my skin. "Lincoln, tell me what's

happened. Is it the army?" I looked past him. "Has someone from Wonderland arrived?"

He shook his head and took my hand. "Come with me."

We got only as far as the hall table in the entrance where the post sat unopened on top of two newspapers. He handed one of the papers to me. It wasn't *The Star*, but a more respected daily. He did not need to point to the offending article.

It was about Gawler's attack on "an upstanding respected member of society" and his subsequent death at the hands of a "brave gentleman." It went on to say that Gawler was a werewolf and had acted alone. That was something, at least. The public would consider the threat ended if they thought him the only one of his kind.

I continued to read but stopped when I saw Lincoln's name in the same sentence as "harboring and protecting the murderer".

I felt sick. My head spun and I reached for him. I needed his solidness, his balance. I needed this to go away, to be over.

He pulled me to his chest and circled both arms around me. "It'll be all right. No harm will come to you."

"It's not me I'm worried about!" I cried.

"Nothing will happen to me. I'll engage the best lawyer and order a retraction."

"It's not these reports that concern me. It's how Mr. Yallop and his parliamentary cronies will react upon reading them."

"They can't do anything without proof."

"They'll find proof if the public demands it. You know that, Lincoln. I know you do. You're simply trying to make me feel better."

He pushed the hair back from my forehead and stroked my face down to my chin. He forced me to look at him.

"Whatever happens to me, stay here. Let the lawyer find a legal solution to the problem. Do not engage Swinburn. Is that understood? Stay at Lichfield. You're protected here. They won't find anything against me, and these accusations will come to nothing. Promise me, Charlie."

"I promise," I lied. If he thought I'd do nothing, he was sorely mistaken. "You're right, and I'm sure Fullbright won't act without evidence. You're the Prince of Wales's son, after all."

Yet that piece of information could not be used to keep him safe. We both knew it, yet neither of us mentioned it. It was easier to allow the other to think we remained positive. But I knew he was worried too. He wouldn't have urged me to marry him today if he thought everything would end well.

He kissed me lightly on the lips but broke away at the sound of wheels on the drive. He went to open the front door, but I caught his arm and held him back.

"No! Escape out the back way."

He shook his head. "If it's the police, I'll face them. If I don't, I become a fugitive."

"I'll go with you," I said in a rush.

He gave me a sad smile then gently pushed me aside and opened the door. I peered past him and my heart sank. Two constables sat on the rumble seat at the back, and another sat beside the driver. A fourth stepped out from the cabin, followed by Detective Inspector Fullbright and Mr. Yallop.

Mr. Yallop nodded at Lincoln. "Arrest him."

I stood in front of Lincoln and stamped my hands on my hips. The constables stopped advancing, unsure what to do with me. "You have no evidence against him," I said. "This is outrageous."

Mr. Yallop smiled. "We will have evidence when we find the records I know you're keeping from us."

"You've searched the entire house and found nothing!"

"We searched the house, but not the garden. Men, take him."

"I'll come willingly," Lincoln said.

I spun around to face him. "No, Lincoln! Don't go with them. They'll lie and make up evidence against you. If you go, you won't come home!"

"Charlie," he purred. "I love you."

My face crumpled. Tears pooled in my eyes. "Don't go with them," I begged. "Please, Lincoln. You can still escape. I know you can."

He kissed my forehead, his warm lips lingering.

"It's not wise to run," Inspector Fullbright said. "If you don't come with us, sir, you look guilty."

"Yes," Mr. Yallop said with a lazy drawl. "And a man guilty of conspiring to murder pays for his crime with ten years' hard labor."

CHAPTER 14

hey drove Lincoln away, leaving three of the constables to search the outhouses and garden. I followed them. When they reached the walled garden, I held my breath and not simply because the files were buried in the ground, but because of the manure we'd spread over the entire plot to cover the freshly turned earth.

They left empty-handed in the afternoon.

"Sit, Charlie," Cook said when I joined him and the others in the kitchen. "Eat." He put a plate of cheese and ham on the table in front of me.

I pushed it away. "I'm not hungry."

"Did they find anything?" Alice asked. She looked exhausted, her face drawn and pale.

"No."

"Thank God," Lady Vickers said, taking a seat beside me. "So now what do we do?"

"We wait," Gus said. "Like Fitzroy wants us to do."

"I'll visit his lawyer," Seth announced. "If he doesn't feel comfortable handling this then he can put us on to someone who will."

"I suspect Lincoln has already set that in motion," I said. "But go anyway. Thank you, Seth."

"I'm happy to do something. I *need* to do something." He kicked the table leg. "This situation is untenable."

"It ain't right," Gus said with a shake of his head. "How can they say he conspired to murder? He's bloody saved the people of this city more times than I can count. We should tell 'em about all these times, about Frankenstein and the general."

"They won't believe us," I said. "And they can accuse him of conspiring because he won't hand over the files they suspect—they *know*—we're harboring."

Seth paced the kitchen floor, circling the table. "God damned Swinburn. I'll bloody kill him."

"Don't do anything rash," his mother said. "Start with the lawyer and leave the killing to when all else fails."

"What if we do hand over the files?" Alice asked. "Will they release him then?"

"Possibly," Seth said, looking at me.

I shook my head. "Lincoln doesn't want them to have the files. He promised many people that he'd keep their records safe and he would hate for his word to be broken."

"Not even to save his life?" Seth threw his hands in the air. "Who cares about his word now?"

I rubbed my forehead. "We'll keep that in our corner if the lawyer fails. For now, we'll keep the files hidden and dig them up only if necessary."

"We know some of the people in those files," Gus said. "I can warn them."

"Good idea. Send a telegram to Frakingham House too."

Cook took up his piping bag and squirted an icing rosette onto the edge of the cake. It was almost finished, and what a magnificent piece of art it turned out to be. He'd sculpted a tiny sugar butterfly at the front, sitting on a rose. Only that morning he'd told me the butterfly symbolized me, free and happy. I'd asked him if that meant the rose represented Lincoln and he dared me to tell Lincoln he was a rose. In the middle of the cake, beneath an arch, stood a couple staring into one another's eyes.

I dashed away my tears. "Don't bother with the cake," I told him. "There can't be a wedding tomorrow with Lincoln in jail."

Seth placed a hand on my shoulder. "We'll free him."

"Perhaps," I whispered through my tight throat. "But not in time."

I WOULD NOT STAY at Lichfield and wait for a miracle to occur. I *could* not. After Gus dashed off messages to those recorded in the files whose addresses we remembered, he drove me to Buckingham Palace. I was prepared to beg, bribe or wait all day for an audience with one of the royal family but I was granted access to the queen immediately. I suspected that privilege arose because she wanted to ask me to summon her late husband. I was wrong.

"You lied to me, Miss Holloway." The queen sat at her desk in an office I had not yet been into. It was vast and somewhat empty, with chairs placed along the wall. A footman picked one up and went to place it by the desk but the queen waved him away. "She won't be staying."

I straightened from my curtsey and clasped my shaking hands in front of me. "Lied, Your Majesty? In what way?"

She lifted a finger and the footman left. I was alone with the queen. What could she say that required no witnesses?

But I knew the answer to that.

"You are not a medium," she said. "You are something...perverted."

Well, that was a new name for me. "I believe necromancer is the word you're searching for, ma'am."

Her small, hard eyes glittered beneath the puffy flesh of her lids. "You are an *abomination*."

I'd been called that before, by the man I'd called Father, no less. The word had been like a spike through my heart then. But not anymore. "No, I am not. This is how God made me. I didn't choose to be a necromancer, not like some people choose to be cruel or break laws. It is how I was born. Do you think God's creation an abomination?"

Her jowls shook as she worked up a response. Finally, she spat it out. "You duped me!"

"No, ma'am, I have never duped you. Yes, I lied about being a medium but that's because I've discovered calling myself a necromancer either frightens people or disgusts them. Neither reaction gladdens me. But I have never duped you."

"You told me you summoned my dear Albert's ghost."

"I did summon him."

"You're a necromancer, not a medium! If you summoned him, why could I not see him? Well?"

I drew in a breath and wished I had a chair to sit on. I wanted to be lower, on her level. It felt odd to be higher. "A medium can only talk to spirits that have not crossed to their afterlife. They cannot call the spirit back from there. A necromancer can, if the full name of the deceased is known."

"A lie. Necromancers *raise* the dead, Miss Holloway. You must think me naive to pretend otherwise."

"Ma'am, you are partly correct. Necromancers *are* capable of directing a spirit into a dead body and controlling that body, but it's quite possible simply to summon ghosts and not take that extra step. That's what I did in the case of your late husband."

She fidgeted with the rings on her left hand and did not meet my gaze. Her lack of response bolstered my confidence.

"Did His Royal Highness The Prince Consort not prove that it was he in the room with us?" I asked gently. "I seem to recall he said something that only you and he could know as proof."

She continued to twist one of her rings, a large sapphire with a thick gold band.

"Ma'am, who told you that I'm a necromancer?"

"That is private information."

"If it was Sir Ignatius Swinburn, I must warn you that he doesn't like me or Lincoln. He'll do and say anything to have the Ministry of Curiosities shut down."

"Why?"

"Because the ministry monitors supernaturals and their activity. We keep them in check and ensure they do no harm. And he's a werewolf."

"You've claimed that before, but it's proven false. He shot a werewolf only recently and he's not likely to kill one of his own, is he?"

It was a difficult argument to counter so I moved on to the reason for my visit. "Ma'am, Lincoln has been arrested for conspiring to commit murder. He's not guilty. You know he's not guilty."

"How dare you presume to know my mind?" Her eyes flashed, her jowls firmed. "Leave, Miss Holloway, or I shall have you thrown out."

"Ma'am, please. We're due to be wed tomorrow."

"So?"

"He isn't guilty!"

"Then it will be proved in court and he'll be set free."

"Will he?" I growled, charging forward. "Will he really be freed? Or will Swinburn use you like he has used everyone else to ensure Lincoln is executed?"

She rang a little bell on her desk and one of the doors opened. "Miss Holloway's audience has ended," she told the two footmen who entered. "Please see that she leaves the premises safely."

I slapped both hands down on the desk. "Don't do this, ma'am!" One of the footmen grabbed my right arm and the other my left. They pulled me away from the desk. My heels dragged across the floor, rumpling the rug. "I'll do whatever you want!" I called out. "I'll summon your husband's ghost! Don't you want to speak to him again? I'm sure he'd like to see you. Ma'am, please, help us!"

Another footman shut the door and I was unceremoniously pushed in the opposite direction. I tried to walk but the footmen were rough and tall and my feet hardly touched the floor. Others escorted us through the palace. It would seem I was to be thrown out after all.

"What's this?" came a familiar voice. We'd just entered a long room whose only purpose seemed to be to house statues and paintings. The Prince of Wales approached from the door at the opposite end. "I heard there's been a security breach."

"Your Royal Highness," I said, trying to sound rational and not at all mad or desperate. "Please, ask them to unhand me."

"Miss Holloway? Men, halt this instant."

The footmen stopped, clearly unsure whether to continue carrying out their queen's orders or their prince's."

"I won't do anything rash," I assured them. "No one is in danger from me."

"Of course not," the prince said. "It's absurd to even suggest it." He waved the footmen away. They bowed and moved out of earshot, but did not leave altogether. "What's the meaning of all this?" The prince glanced back the way I'd come. "Have you been speaking to Her Majesty?"

"I appealed to her on Lincoln's behalf. He has been arrested."

"What the devil for?"

I told him about Fullbright and Yallop, and about the files and Lincoln's refusal to give them up. "Even if he did give them up, I'm sure Mr. Yallop would find a way to keep him in jail. He seems determined to ruin Lincoln and close the ministry."

"This is a result of the newspaper articles." It was a statement, not a question, but I nodded anyway. "I'm not surprised that parliament worked swiftly on this. The public was afraid after the Ripper murders, and not everyone believes Gawler was the sole monster responsible this time. There was talk of rioting if the police didn't focus their full attention on keeping the East End safe. Something had to be done, or at least seen to be done, for the sake of peace."

"Yes, but it's not fair to blame Lincoln! *He's* the one who keeps the city safe from monsters."

"Clearly they have their reasons. Miss Holloway, there's no need to fret. A parliamentary select committee has a lot of power, but this Mr. Yallop won't be an unreasonable fellow. When he sees the good the ministry do, he'll let Fitzroy go."

"No, he won't. He is under Swinburn's influence, and Swinburn wants to see the ministry gone, and Lincoln with it."

He clicked his tongue. "Stop this constant blaming of Swinburn! I've told you before, he's a good man and a good friend. He has the realm's best interests at heart."

"He has his own best interests at heart, and you are deliberately turning the other cheek so that you don't see it."

He bristled. "I beg your pardon."

"Why did I think coming here would be a good idea?" I asked the chandelier dangling above me. "Why did I think one of you would listen? I didn't really expect your mother to care, sir, since she doesn't know. But you…you ought to care. He is your son, after all."

He glanced toward the nearest footman, standing as still as one of the many statues. "Don't," he said without moving his lips. "That *cannot* become known. Imagine the scandal! His mother was a gypsy woman, for God's sake. The damage done to my reputation would be irreparable, and then there's the queen's censure to contend with. If you dare tell anyone, Miss Holloway, I'll deny it most vehemently."

My heart sank with each word. Without the prince's influence, what chance did Lincoln have? Yallop and the members of parliament wanted to blame someone for allowing a murderous werewolf to roam our streets, and they'd made Lincoln their scapegoat, thanks to Swinburn. If one of the most powerful men in the realm refused to help, what hope was there? My chest hurt and my eyes burned with my tears. I wanted to scratch the face of the man standing in front of me and show the world that he was just a man, that he bled too, and ought to be held accountable for his mistakes as the rest of us were. The royal family didn't deserve to have their scandals buried. Not when revealing their scandals could save the life of a man.

"You are a disappointment, sir. I cannot believe Lincoln is your son. He is brave, honest and does *not* turn a blind eye to injustice. He owns up to his mistakes and makes amends for them. In short, he is a better man than you. Good day, sir."

I marched away from him as quickly as I could without breaking into a run. I expected him to stop me, or order one of his men to, but he did not. Whether he watched me go, I couldn't say. I didn't dare look back. My heart pounded furiously in my chest, and I feared it would smash every piece of my fragile body until there was nothing left but shards on the palace carpet. The footmen flanking me had to increase their pace to keep up, and I almost broke into a run when I spotted the exit. I lifted my skirts and raced down the front steps and into the safety of the Lichfield coach.

"Home, Charlie?" Gus asked.

I was furious and frustrated, and I needed to release my emotions on someone deserving, not my friends. "Take me to the Gillinghams' house. I'm going to speak to Harriet."

* * *

IT WAS unfortunate that Lord Gillingham was at home. I would have preferred to talk to Harriet alone. With him there, I might not even get to see Harriet at all.

"You will not speak to her," he told me. The footman had fetched Gillingham instead of his wife, even though I'd asked for her. "She wants nothing to do with you."

"Why?" I asked. My temper was very close to fraying, but I must not lose it with this man in his house. His servants would obey him and my efforts would be thwarted. I couldn't bear another failure after the palace.

"Because you are too closely associated with Fitzroy and the ministry, and my family must be kept as far from the scandal as possible. My wife's safety is utmost at this delicate time."

"You are closely associated with Lincoln and the ministry too," I shot back.

"I will distance myself from Lichfield Towers for as long as required."

"As much as I rejoice at your absence, I must speak to her now. Harriet!" My shout echoed off the papered walls and rose up to the high ceiling.

Gillingham signaled for his footman. "See that Miss Holloway leaves immediately."

The footman opened the door for me but a word from Harriet, standing at the top of the staircase, had him closing it again. He looked to her for further instruction, not his master.

"Gilly, that's no way to treat our guest and my friend," Harriet scolded. "Come and sit with me, Charlie," she said sweetly, holding out her hand.

Gillingham sucked air between his teeth, but he did not contradict his wife. I picked up my skirts and, keeping a wary eye on him, joined her on the staircase. With one hand supporting her belly, she led me to a cozy sitting room and we sat together on the sofa. Her husband followed and shut the door upon her request. No servants joined us.

I suddenly regretted my haste in coming here alone. I should have asked Gus to escort me inside or waited for Seth to return home. The woman beside me may be heavy with child, but she was still a werewolf who'd thrown her allegiance in with Swinburn. I could not trust her.

"Are you aware that Lincoln was arrested?" I began.

She gasped. "Arrested!"

Gillingham had been standing by the door but he now sat on an armchair. "This is in response to the newspapers that linked his name to the ministry," he said.

"And the parliamentary select committee's investigation," I said. "Mr. Yallop wants to shut us down, and he knows that achieving that requires removing Lincoln."

"It will come to nothing." He thrust out his lower lip as if that were the end of the discussion.

I ignored him. Despite his position in society, he could affect nothing. It had taken me until now to realize it, but he was useless, his influence non-existent. I turned to Harriet.

"You must convince Swinburn to end his campaign against Lincoln," I urged her.

"Swinburn!" she said, blinking her wide blue eyes at me. "You think him behind this?"

"I know him to be behind it. You know it too."

"She knows no such thing!" Gillingham bellowed.

She put up her hand to silence him, but did not bother to look at him. "You are probably right, Charlie. But I have no influence with Swinburn." She laid a hand over mine.

I pulled away. "Don't play me for a fool. You've switched allegiance to him."

She cocked her head to the side. "I did play the role superbly, but I thought you knew it was just an act. You must! I am your friend, and a friend to the ministry. Oh, please say you believe me, Charlie. I'll be devastated to lose your friendship, particularly now."

"You stole my imp necklace! If it were all an act, why not ask me to give it to you? Why go to such lengths?"

"Would you have given it to me? Of course not. You would never have handed it over. Charlie, listen to me. Sir Ignatius would only believe I was on his side if I proved my loyalty to him. He asked me to bring him the orb with the imp inside it, so I did. Now he confides in me as much as he confides in Lord Ballantine, perhaps even more, since Ballantine and he fell out over the incident with Leonora and Prince Eddy. Truly, Charlie, I thought you came to realize it was all a ruse when I winked at you after you confronted me in his house. Did you not see the wink?"

"Did you not hear the anger in my voice?"

"I thought it all an act." She laughed nervously. "You're a wonderful actress, after all, having pretended to be a boy all those years. I thought you were pretending, and that it worked. He believed your performance, and mine." She pouted. "I thought we made an excellent team, and now you tell me you doubt my loyalty to you. Oh, Charlie, the loss of your friendship leaves me bereft. My heart is broken and will not be put together until you say you trust me again."

She was convincing, and yet the kernel of doubt was lodged too deeply and I could not pluck it out. "You are now the leader of the East End pack thanks to Swinburn's machinations."

"That was never my aim."

"He guessed you would be chosen. You and he concocted the plan to remove Gawler together."

"No!"

"How dare you accuse my wife of being complicit in murder!"

"You've become powerful since Gawler's death," I forged on. "Thanks to Swinburn and your newfound loyalty to him."

"Loyalty that I only set out to prove to him at your insistence."

"It was *your* idea to spy on him by getting close to him."

She blinked tear-filled eyes. "Charlie, don't say such things. It was never my intention to become leader of the East End pack. I only ever wanted to help the ministry bring him to justice." She clutched my hand between hers and held it against her chest. "Please tell me you believe me."

I swallowed. I knew I ought to tell her I believed her...yet I could not.

"I think you should leave, Miss Holloway," Gillingham said, rising. "You're upsetting my wife."

"Sit down, Gilly," Harriet snapped.

He sat.

"Listen, Charlie." Harriet shifted closer to me. "Let me prove my loyalty to you by offering up some information."

Is that how she'd approached Swinburn? "Go on."

"I know you think me just a silly girl, merely a pretty face with no thoughts of her own."

"No," I said most emphatically. "I don't think that."

"Some do." Her gaze slid to her husband then back to me. "But I have eyes and ears and I use them to learn. Swinburn's pack mates are unhappy over Gawler's death. They see it as betrayal of our kind, of putting our entire species in danger by handing the body over to science. They think the disagreement between them should have been settled in the traditional pack way, with a fight in our beast form."

"Don't use that word," her husband muttered.

"There now, Charlie. Isn't that a useful piece of information?" she asked.

"Not particularly," I said. "It's not going to get Lincoln out of jail." I pressed my fingers to my forehead and rubbed the ache blooming there. "We're supposed to be married tomorrow."

"I know." Her brow crumpled. "You poor thing."

"If you are truly loyal to us," I said, "you will use your influence with Swinburn and ask him to see that Lincoln is released. It's his bloody fault the parliamentary committee was set up in the first place."

"I'm not convinced he was responsible," she said carefully.

"He is! He must be."

"It was set up because of the public outcry over the attacks and the revelation that the ministry exists to stop that sort of thing from happening."

"And who told Mr. Salter from *The Star* about werewolves and the ministry in the first place?"

"Swinburn," Gillingham said, stamping his hand on the chair arm. "Assuredly, it was Swinburn."

"No, it was not." Harriet turned toward him, her eyes narrowed to slits. "Stop this charade, Gilly. It's pathetic. I know it was you."

His jaw dropped and he spluttered words of denial but they did not form a full sentence. She let him ramble on, her glare unwavering, until he finally drifted to a stop. He closed his mouth and his audible gulp filled the silence.

"Go on, Harriet," I said darkly.

"I was looking through the correspondence on my husband's desk the other day," she said.

"You what?" he exploded. "Why?"

"Because it's time you treated me as your equal in all affairs that affect us as a family. Your business is my business, Gilly. Anyway, that is by the by. I was looking through your correspondence and discovered a letter from Mr. Salter thanking you for the information and asking for further details."

"*You* were his source?" I said to Gillingham.

He shot to his feet. "I don't have to listen to this!"

"You do if you want to keep my condition a secret," his wife said. "Believe me, I have no qualms in telling the world what I am. It might even go some way to proving that not all werewolves are dangerous. I have considered it, Gilly, and I will do it if you don't do as I say. Now, sit and listen. You planted the idea in Mr. Salter's head that a werewolf was responsible for those murders in the Old Nichol, then you gave him Gawler's name."

"My God," I whispered. "That's awful. Why would you do such a thing?"

His throat worked but he simply stared at his wife. The freckles on his cheeks darkened against his pale skin.

"Because he wanted to stop me running with Gawler and his pack," Harriet said. "He assumed if Gawler was arrested for murder, the pack would disband, or stop running until the dust settled."

"I did it for you, my love," he whispered. "For you and our child, to keep you both safe."

"From what?" she shouted. "We are only in danger from the authorities now thanks to you!"

"Anything could have happened during a run. It's the East End, for God's sake! Those people could have turned on you. They are scum, Harriet. They have no morals, no conscience. I hate to think what they might have done."

"You stupid fool. They are good people. Better than you, by far."

He leapt off his chair and lunged toward her. He grasped her shoulders. "Harriet, please, I did what I did for you."

She shoved him away and he fell onto the rug. He scooted back until he hit a table.

"Did you tell them about Lincoln, too?" I asked. "About the ministry?"

"No!" he cried. "I did not mention the ministry, Fitzroy or Lichfield. My aim was only ever to keep Harriet and our baby safe, not close the ministry. Be sure to tell Fitzroy that, Charlotte."

I appealed to Harriet. She lifted one shoulder. "There was no evidence in the correspondence that he informed Mr. Salter about the ministry. I sent him a message to ask him, and he wrote back that he will not reveal his sources."

"It's not me," Gillingham said weakly.

His wife lifted her finger in dismissal, as if she were addressing one of the servants. "So you see, Charlie, at least some of this situation is not Swinburn's fault. The original newspaper reports certainly aren't."

"The murders themselves are, possibly," I told her. "And he most likely told Salter and Yallop about the ministry. That is my concern now. Harriet, please just talk to him. Try to convince him that Lincoln and the ministry are not his enemy."

"I'll try, but the problem is that he wants power, and the ministry will thwart him at every turn."

"Because we don't want power to fall into the hands of a corrupt, amoral murderer. Swinburn is not a good man, and you know it. Is that the sort of fellow you want your child near?"

Her shoulders sagged and she linked her hands over her bulging belly.

"Why not petition Julia instead of my wife," Gillingham said, once again taking his chair. "She is Swinburn's fiancée, for God's sake. Surely she has some influence."

"She won't help Lincoln," Harriet said. "He threw her off the committee, after all. Anyway, I don't think she has much influence with Sir Ignatius. In my discussions with him, he doesn't seem particularly fond of her. Their arrangement benefited him, but now that she has passed on all the information she could about Lincoln and the ministry, I wouldn't be surprised if he ended it. God help us all when he does. She'll become even more desperate."

"She's dead," I said.

They both stared at me. "No, she isn't." Harriet laughed nervously. "I saw her two days ago. She was looking as healthy and lovely as always."

"She killed herself."

Gillingham spluttered a laugh, but it died when I did not join in. I told them the little I knew of the situation, which seemed woefully inadequate considering how well acquainted Lady Harcourt and I were.

"Poor Julia," Gillingham murmured. "We didn't get on but...to take her own life..."

"She must have been very unhappy," Harriet said. "To be honest, I didn't think she and Sir Ignatius a good match. I wonder if something happened there." She frowned and absently stroked her belly.

"Things were not going her way of late," I said.

"Yes, but..." Harriet shook her head. "Are you sure she wasn't pushed?"

What an odd thing for her to conclude. To think it an accident, yes, but she was implying Lady Harcourt was murdered. "By whom?" I asked.

"By someone who wanted to get rid of her, of course."

"Like Swinburn," Lord Gillingham suggested. When we

both gave him incredulous looks, he added, "You did just say he wanted to be rid of her."

"I don't know for certain. It was merely a thought, idle gossip." His wife sighed. "Poor Andrew. He'll be devastated."

"He is."

Harriet looked to her husband. "You ought to visit him and pass on our condolences."

"Me?" He sniffed. "No, thank you. He's a revolting person. Anyway, I can't stand being near grieving people. Send him a note, my dear."

"You write one, Gilly." She winced and cupped her belly. "I can't sit at a desk right now."

"Are you all right, my dear?" He crouched before her, his hands resting on her knees. He was the picture of a loving, considerate husband.

"Thank you, yes. You are a dear man for asking." She touched his cheek. "I forgive you for going to Mr. Salter, Gilly. I understand you only wanted to protect me, and Wolfie too, of course." Her lips pinched. "But don't try to manipulate me again. Is that understood?"

He nodded quickly. "You are my entire world, Harriet. You and our child." He drew her hand to his lips and kissed it. Her faced softened and she smiled at him.

I couldn't stomach any more and got up to leave.

"I'm sure Lincoln will be home in time for the wedding," Harriet said after I bade her goodbye. "The police surely cannot hold him for long."

"Get his lawyer onto it," Gillingham said.

"We have," I told them. "But I'm not sure he can do much. At this stage, it's doubtful that Lincoln and I will marry tomorrow."

"Oh, Charlie, I am sorry," Harriet said. "All the preparations have come to nothing. At least you can save the gown for when he does get out."

"*If* he gets out," her husband added.

"Gilly!"

I bade them good day after extracting a promise from Harriet that she would get my necklace back. I left wondering if her promises were now worth anything.

I asked Gus to take me home, and instead of sitting inside the coach, I sat beside him on the driver's perch. Being inside meant being alone, and I didn't want to be alone. I wanted to engage in conversation so my thoughts didn't wander in a hopeless direction.

Yet even conversation with Gus turned to the wedding. Neither of us could come up with a way in which Lincoln would be freed in time to marry me. Every method would take too long. Every *legal* method.

* * *

GUS SLOWED the horses when he spotted the two coaches parked at Lichfield's steps. "Who's here?" he asked, squinting against the sunshine.

The front door burst open and Alice and Lady Vickers met us on the drive. Lady Vickers flapped her fan at her throat, her bosom heaving. "They're back!" she gasped out.

"Who?" I followed Alice's gaze toward the walled garden.

Oh God no.

I lifted my skirts and jumped down from the driver's platform. I spotted Seth up ahead, standing in the entrance to the garden, his arms crossed.

"They brought shovels," Alice said, striding alongside me. "And more men."

"I thought they gave up," I said.

"It seems they didn't."

Seth looked over his shoulder as he heard us approach.

He shook his head in warning. "Don't say anything," he whispered.

"Is that Miss Holloway?" asked Detective Inspector Fullbright from inside the garden.

He was joined by a smiling Mr. Yallop. "Excellent timing," Mr. Yallop said. "We were just leaving."

"What are you doing?" I asked.

"Looking for these." Mr. Yallop indicated the constable wheeling a wheelbarrow between garden beds. It was filled with the hessian sacks we'd buried the files in.

I froze. Even my heart ground to a halt. "What...?" was all I managed to say.

"It's the evidence that will convict your fiancé and close down the ministry."

CHAPTER 15

Seth blocked the exit and inspected the hessian bags in the wheelbarrow. He would have opened one if Mr. Yallop hadn't slapped his hand away. "We've never seen this before," Seth told him.

Mr. Yallop merely smiled that sickly smile.

The detective ordered his man to load the evidence onto the carriage.

"Evidence?" Seth said, all innocence. "Evidence of what?"

"My guess is those are the files Mr. Fitzroy refused to hand over," Fullbright said. "They'll prove he has been withholding information about potential murderers from us."

"You planted them here!"

"Nice pun." Mr. Yallop chuckled.

"Nobody planted anything, sir," the detective said to Seth. "I became suspicious after my constables reported this entire walled garden had been covered with manure when the rest of the garden had not. It's too hot to be spreading manure. I'm a gardener in my spare time, and I only spread manure in spring. Early summer is not the best time."

"What do the files prove?" I asked. "How can they convict Lincoln of conspiracy to murder?"

"The thing is, Miss Holloway," Mr. Yallop said, "Mr. Fitzroy's refusal to hand them over didn't look good. But you are correct, it's not enough to convict him. I suspect proving that he was involved with Mr. Gawler and the murders will be, however."

"Lincoln had nothing to do with them! He was trying to find out who caused the deaths, just as you were."

"Mr. Yallop, sir," the detective warned. "Don't divulge too much."

"There's no harm in telling them that you spoke with Mr. Gawler's friends and neighbors, Fullbright. They all mentioned how Mr. Fitzroy called upon Gawler several times, both before and after the murders. Snippets of their conversations were overheard."

"Sir," Inspector Fullbright hissed.

"They spoke about the murders in an attempt to find out who did them," I cried, "not because they were colluding."

"Fitzroy defended Gawler," Mr. Yallop said.

The inspector shook his head and stormed off toward the carriages.

"That doesn't make him guilty," Seth growled.

"Doesn't it?" Mr. Yallop walked off too, the other constables in his wake.

"Mr. Yallop, please!" Alice called after him. "You can't do this. Lincoln and Charlie are getting married tomorrow."

"It will have to be put off until after the trial." Mr. Yallop stopped and looked at me. All supercilious smiles had vanished, and he seemed in earnest. "If I were you, Miss Holloway, I'd call off the wedding indefinitely. You should distance yourself from him. Being closely associated with Fitzroy now will not work in your favor."

I felt sick. I slumped against the brick wall and closed my

eyes. My dream of marrying now lay in ruins. But worse, Lincoln's freedom and life were at risk.

I'd never thought it would come to this. He was so competent, so self-assured, that he almost seemed above the law, or perhaps outside it, somehow. He'd not always followed a straight and narrow path to get results, yet none of that had ever got him into trouble before. Not on this magnitude.

It was being the leader of the Ministry of Curiosities that had brought about his downfall, the very essence of his identity—indeed, the reason for his existence at all. How cruelly ironic.

Alice and Seth flanked me as we headed back to the house. Mr. Yallop had driven off in one coach while Inspector Fullbright oversaw the loading of the files into the other.

"By the way," he said. "You were acquainted with the late Lady Harcourt, so I was told."

"Yes," Seth said. "And?"

"I feel obligated to tell you that she may not have taken her own life as first thought. A witness has come forward claiming he saw someone push her."

"Push her!" I said. "Who?"

"A man, according to the witness, but he could give no description. The suspect wore a hooded cloak."

"In the middle of summer?"

"Is Scotland Yard investigating?" Seth asked.

"Of course," the detective said, "but I'm afraid that unless another witness comes forward with a description of the hooded man, it will likely come to nothing. I simply wanted you to know that she did not take her own life. I hope it's some comfort to you in your time of loss."

Neither Seth nor I spoke. I felt somewhat guilty that we were not mourning her, and perhaps he felt the same. "That's very kind of you, Inspector," Alice said. "We appreciate you telling us. Have you told her family?"

"Lord Harcourt and Mr. Buchanan have been informed." He climbed onto the coachman's perch beside the driver and touched the brim of his hat to bid us good day.

"Who would do such a thing?" Alice asked as we walked up the front steps to where Lady Vickers stood waiting.

"Swinburn," both Seth and I said together.

Harriet's words echoed in my head—Swinburn was done with Lady Harcourt and wanted to be rid of her. I suspected she grew angry with him for ending their engagement. Perhaps she railed at him and threatened him. He wouldn't like that. He wouldn't like it at all.

"Come inside, you poor pet," Lady Vickers cooed at me. "Come and sit down. Cook will bring you something to eat."

Cook was one step ahead of her. He held a plate loaded with cream puffs. He knew I adored them, and I accepted one for his sake. He looked as worried as the rest but seeing me eat seemed to bolster his spirits a little.

No one spoke until Gus joined us and Seth informed him of what had happened. He swore under his breath. "This ain't right," he said. "What'll we do?"

"The lawyer is looking into it," Seth said.

"Does he think there's a chance Lincoln can be freed?" I asked.

"Not in time for the wedding."

"Forget the wedding. I mean at all?"

"It's too early to say." He tore a strip off his cream puff but didn't eat it.

"Go on," I said. "What aren't you telling me?"

"Nothing."

"Seth," his mother snapped. "She's not a child. Stop trying to shield her and tell her what you told us."

He gave me a sheepish look. "The lawyer said he doesn't

like the involvement of Mr. Yallop. He has a reputation for bulldoggish behavior and getting the results he wants, not necessarily the right results."

"You mean he's a bloody liar," Gus spat.

"A manipulator of the truth."

"Same thing."

"Apparently Yallop is the man that parliament puts in charge of the committees where they want a certain result."

"So someone is manipulating the select committee," I said with a sigh.

"It may not be someone. It may be a number of parliamentarians. The government want to move swiftly against the ministry—and Lincoln, since they believe he is connected to Gawler. It's in their best interests to quash the public's fear and look as though they're working decisively against undesirable elements."

"Supernaturals."

Seth nodded.

I told them how Gillingham was Mr. Salter's original source about werewolves in general, and Mr. Gawler in particular, but not the source for information about the ministry or Lincoln. "That, at least, wasn't Gillingham's doing."

"Are you sure he didn't lie?" Lady Vickers asked.

I nodded. "Gillingham's been a committee member for a long time. He could have caused problems before this, but he hasn't. He supports the ministry's main purpose—to act as custodians of information about supernaturals in order to control them."

"And that's precisely the reason Swinburn wants to get rid of us," Seth said. "He doesn't want us to have that control over him. My money's still on him for dropping the ministry in the dung heap."

I looked out the window at the drive, quiet and empty.

"The police have the files now, and those files contain his name as well as those in his pack." The files did not contain mine. Lincoln never included my information, for fear someone would get hold of it and use me for their nefarious purposes. That was a relief, at least.

"Speaking of Swinburn, you won't believe what the inspector just told us about Lady Harcourt's death." Seth informed his mother, Cook and Gus of Lady Harcourt's suspected murder. After their shocked exclamations, the conversation naturally turned to suspects. Chief among them was Swinburn.

I did not pay much attention to the theories. My mind kept returning to Lincoln and my growing sense of hopelessness. Why hadn't we removed the files from the estate? Or spread manure elsewhere in the garden? It seemed like such an obvious thing to do now, yet at the time we thought we were clever by burying the records. Even the best lawyer in the city couldn't free him now that the files had come to light. They were evidence of Lincoln's involvement with the ministry, and Mr. Yallop was intent on aligning the ministry with the werewolf murders. It was grossly unfair.

I had to free him before he went to trial, and the only way to do that was to somehow use my necromancy. Tomorrow I would visit him and tell him my plan. He wouldn't like it, but that wouldn't stop me.

"You look exhausted, Charlie." Alice stood beside me. I hadn't seen her approach, so lost in my thoughts was I.

"As do you," I said. "Perhaps we both need an early night."

I retired to my room after dinner but did not lie down. I picked up my wedding gown and placed it against me. It was beautiful, the silk soft to touch. It was a shame to leave it behind, but I could only take the essentials with me.

I packed a small bag and put on the plainest dress I owned, then checked the corridor before heading to

Lincoln's room. I quietly closed his door and placed the lamp on the desk. Would he need any personal papers? I eyed the painting, behind which lay the safe. I couldn't carry much on my own, so I left everything that wasn't absolutely essential. With Lincoln's formidable memory, we wouldn't need papers so I decided to leave everything but a few personal items. The only item I removed from the safe was money.

I wrote a letter to Cook, Seth and Gus, giving them the safe's code and instructing them to destroy the letter after reading it. The final lines proved almost impossible to write. Tears streamed down my cheeks and dripped onto the paper, smearing the ink. My hand shook.

I wrote, "I love you all. You are my world but Lincoln is my universe and I must be with him, no matter what. We will meet again one day, my dearest friends. I promise."

I set the letter aside to leave on my dressing table in the morning where they would find it when they came looking for me. My heart burned with a fiery ache as I pictured it being read. An ache that I doubted would ever leave.

With my tears still flowing, I collected some essential clothes from Lincoln's bedroom. Later, after I could be sure the household was asleep, I'd take what I could from the pantry. We might need food for a few days.

God, it was so hard. My body felt heavy, as if a great weight pushed down on me from above. I sat on Lincoln's bed and stared through watery eyes at the pillow. His head should be there now, and tomorrow night, mine should be next to it.

I lay down, wanting to be as close to him as possible. His scent was on the pillow. I curled up and closed my eyes, imagining his body behind me, holding me, protecting me. I could almost feel him there.

Almost.

Tomorrow night, I would lie with him like this. But not here at Lichfield. Never at Lichfield.

* * *

WAN light edged the curtains when I awoke. But that's not what woke me.

"Charlie!" Gus's shout boomed from outside Lincoln's rooms.

I'd fallen asleep on his bed, my arms around the pillow. I got up and straightened my dress then went to grab my bag. No, not yet. I'd intended to sneak out before the household woke up but that wouldn't be possible now. I'd have to find time after breakfast. Until then, I would act normally. The last thing I needed was someone to realize my plan and stop me from rescuing Lincoln.

"Charlie! Where the bleeding hell are you?"

I opened the door and slipped out to the corridor. "I'm here. Gus, what's wrong?"

His rough features lightened. "Thank God! When I saw your bed hadn't been slept in, I thought you'd gone out there."

"Out where? Gus, what is it?"

"I need to show you." He took my hand and led me back into Lincoln's sitting room. Luckily I'd left my bag in the bedroom.

"Why are you up so early?" I asked, trotting behind him.

"Keeping watch. Seth and Cook are awake, Alice too. They're arming themselves."

"Arming themselves!" Oh God, no. Not now. Please, not now.

He stopped by the window and edged the curtain aside. I gasped. A line of about one hundred soldiers ranged across our front lawn dressed in red and white regimentals. Each carried a sword strapped to his hip. Behind them stood a line of archers, bows in hand. And still another dozen or so pushed an enormous catapult into place near the orchard. And then there was the battering ram on the drive, ready to be slammed into our front door. A man on horseback barked orders as he rode back and forth in front of the troops. When he turned to look at the house, I recognized him as the commander of the army who'd attacked the school at Inglemere Castle.

His gaze suddenly lifted to our window. I released the curtain and stepped back.

"They've surrounded the house," Gus said.

"You said Alice is awake?"

He nodded.

Then they must have used a portal device and spell to get here, as the rabbit had done. *Damnation.*

I peeked out again and wished I hadn't. The catapult was being loaded with a boulder as large as me. Lichfield wasn't a fortified castle like Inglemere. A weapon that size would do considerable damage. The battering ram could easily break through the front door, too.

"What do we do?" Gus sounded scared. He'd never sounded scared before, no matter what he faced.

I pitched backward against the desk. I clutched the edge with both hands and tried to think of a solution. Gus waited for instructions. Without Lincoln to guide us, he put me in the position of leader. He and the others were depending on me.

But I wasn't Lincoln. I didn't have his quick wits and intense focus. And I had no clue how to fight an entire army.

"I don't know, Gus. I honestly don't know."

ootsteps pounded along the corridor. Gus pulled out a pistol where it had been tucked into the waistband of his trousers. He stood in front of me. I wasn't even armed with a knife.

"It's just me," came Seth's voice.

Gus stood aside but he didn't put away his gun. Seth held one too. His face was pale but set like a stone and his eyes gleamed like gems in the poor light. "Everyone is armed," he said. "Even my mother. We're ready."

"No," I murmured. "We are not ready. We're very far from being ready. We can't fight an army."

"We have guns, they have swords and arrows."

"And siege machines, and they greatly outnumber us."

He threw a hand in the air. "Are you giving up, Charlie? Just like that?"

I folded my arms over my chest and fought back tears. Part of me wanted to give up. With Lincoln gone, there seemed no point in fighting anyway. Without him, Lichfield was empty. My life was empty.

But Lincoln wasn't gone. He was in jail, and I was his only hope of getting out.

"If we had the imp, it could attack," Gus said, peering out of the window again. He swore and let the curtain go. "We have to warn the others to stay away from the front of the house."

Seth followed him but stopped. "Come on, Charlie. It's not safe in here. The kitchen is at the back of the house. We'll make that our base."

"The imp," I echoed, eyeing the safe.

"Charlie?"

"I'll follow in a moment. I have an idea."

* * *

"LET ME GO!" Alice's panicked voice came from the service area.

I broke into a run and burst into the kitchen. "Alice!"

She struggled against Seth and Gus who held her back. "She wants to give herself up," Seth said.

"I have to!" she cried, trying to wrench free of his grip and failing. "We can't beat an entire army! Be reasonable. This is the only way to make them leave. Let me go before they let one of those boulders loose."

"No," Seth growled.

"Lady V." Alice appealed to Seth's mother who was watching Cook load a pistol. "You understand. I must give myself up or we'll all die!"

Lady Vickers turned a deathly white face and wild eyes to Alice. She wore a shawl around her nightgown and her hair hung in tangles down her back. She looked like a madwoman escaped from the attic. "I do understand," she said. Upon her son's protest, she put up her hand. "But you are not going out there. You are to remain here at all costs. Is that clear?"

"No!"

Cook finished loading the weapon and handed it to Lady Vickers. She aimed it at Alice's foot. "I will shoot you if necessary."

Alice stopped struggling. Seth and Gus slowly released her.

"Now," Lady Vickers said crisply, "where should I stand to get the best shot at one of those soldiers?"

"You're not shooting at them, you're staying here as the last line of defense," Seth told her. "With Alice."

Alice plopped down on a chair and buried her head in her hands. "This is all my fault," she groaned.

"No," I said, stroking her hair. "You were a child when you came here. Whatever happened in Wonderland that led to you being sent here is not your fault. Now, arm yourself. I have a plan to get out of this before a shot is fired."

Lady Vickers expelled a loud breath. She held up the pistol. "Thank God for that! I have no idea how to use this thing."

Seth pushed it away. "First lesson: aim it at the enemy, not your only child."

"What be your plan, Charlie?" Cook asked.

I opened my mouth to speak when a resounding crash boomed through the house above us. Glass shattered. Bricks and wood splintered. Pots rattled and crockery fell off the hutch, smashing onto the floor.

Lady Vickers screamed. A gun went off and she screamed again.

Everyone dropped to the floor, hands over heads, as plaster drifted down from the ceiling and formed little white piles of powder on the flagstones. The house fell silent except for the tinkling of the chandelier in the entrance hall.

"Reload!" came a distant shout.

Seth crawled over to his mother and took away her pistol.

"You can have a knife instead." He got to his feet, a pistol in each hand. "It'll take them a few minutes to reload the catapult," he said. "Charlie, tell us your plan before they destroy Lichfield."

I got to my feet and refused the weapon he offered me. "There's no time to discuss it. Come with me and follow along. You too, Alice."

"No," he said. "She stays here."

"The plan won't work without her."

He looked set for an argument but Alice marched between us and out the kitchen door. I raced after her, Seth and Gus on my heels. I was grateful that Cook remained behind with Lady Vickers. She seemed to need comforting, and it was wise to have someone with a level head to look after the house and her in case I failed. Failure was an extremely likely possibility.

I caught a glimpse of the clock on the table as we gathered in the entrance hall. I should have been getting married in three hours. It seemed like a fantasy now.

"Alice, stay here until I call you," I said. "Seth, Gus, put down your weapons." I pushed open the door before either man could protest.

I put up my hands in surrender. Beside me, Seth and Gus did the same. We looked out to the soldiers swarming our lawn, spreading as far as the eye could see to left and right. The catapult was already loaded, a team of men drawing back a boulder ready to release it.

"Stop!" I cried. "I'll give you Alice!"

"Charlie," Seth hissed. "What are you doing?"

"Trust me, Seth. Please."

The leader on the horse put up a hand to halt his men. The team stopped but did not disarm their catapult.

"Where is she?" the commander demanded. He was not terribly old but he had the weathered features of an experienced soldier and the bearing of a man used to command. His stature, sitting erect on the biggest horse, was impressive. Where his men wore red jackets with white breeches, his uniform was entirely black. The gold buttons and watch added a handsome elegance.

"She's inside," I called back. "She will only go with you if you stop laying seige to the house."

"Naturally," the commander said.

"And on one other condition."

I felt the gazes of both Seth and Gus on me.

"And that is?" the commander shouted.

"That you help us capture her enemy in this realm first."

Beside me, Seth grunted. "I like your thinking, but they'll never agree to it."

The commander leaned on the saddle pommel and shifted his weight. "Why would I do that? We outnumber you." He indicated his army behind him. "We can just take her."

"You could try," I said. "But she'll kill herself before she lets you. She's inside now, holding a gun to her temple. If you refuse my request and storm the house, she'll fire it."

He cocked his head to the side. "Gun?"

One of other riders came up to him and said something. He was considerably younger than the commander. He spoke in tones that didn't carry to us, but whatever he said held the commander's attention. When he finished speaking, they both looked at us.

"Well?" I asked. "Will you help us in exchange for Alice?"

The commander shifted his weight forward again and I realized he did that when he was thinking. The advisor beside him said something. He looked to be in earnest.

The commander nodded. "Miss Alice will be returning to Wonderland to stand trial," he called out to us. "If she is found guilty, she will die anyway. Here or there, it matters not."

"Jesus," Gus muttered.

"I don't believe you," I said. "You would not be negotiating with me if it didn't matter. You would have taken her before now, dead or alive. But I suspect you don't want to deny your queen a trial."

The distance between us was great, but I could just make out the commander's grunt. The advisor nodded sagely. My hunch was correct then—Alice was worth more to them alive than dead. She was, after all, the queen's niece, and the Queen of Hearts wanted her to face trial in Wonderland.

At the advisor's prompting, the commander nodded. "We agree! But I want to see Miss Alice first."

"No!" Seth shouted back.

"I am here," came Alice's voice behind us. She held a pistol to her head.

The commander straightened. The advisor closed his eyes in relief. Then he opened them and wheeled his horse back to the line of soldiers. He ordered them to stand down, to lower their weapons. They obeyed him and the commander did not seem to care that his underling was barking orders at his men.

"What now?" Seth asked me.

"Now we approach," I said. "Carefully. Alice, take my hand. We'll go together."

"I don't like this," Seth said.

"We ain't got no choice," Gus told him.

"Charlie," whispered Cook from the doorway. "Want me to ride to Marchbank?"

"The Gillinghams' first," I said. "Tell Harriet to meet us at Swinburn's house. Then inform Lord Marchbank."

Alice's hand touched mine. I held it firmly and gave her a

grim smile. I wanted to reassure her, tell her it would be all right, and that I knew what I was doing.

But I couldn't offer her false hope. I did not know if my plan would work. The more I thought about it, the more I doubted that we could pull it off. So many things could go wrong.

We walked together to stand before the commander. Seth and Gus stood behind us. The commander's steely gaze flicked over them then me and settled on Alice.

He bowed his head. "Miss Alice."

She clutched me tighter. "Who are you?"

"Loren Ironside, General of the Wonderland Army. We have met but you were too young to remember."

"Clearly."

He grunted, as if her off-handed comment amused him. She hadn't meant to be funny.

The advisor returned. He too bowed his head. "Princess —" At a sharp glare from General Ironside, the advisor coughed. "Miss Alice. It's a pleasure to see you again."

"We've met too, I suppose," she said. "When I was young and living in Wonderland."

"I was ten when you...left, and I remember you well. Markell Ironside, at your service."

I glanced between the two men and saw the resemblance. Both had clear, clever green eyes and dark hair, although the general's was tinged with gray. Where the general had probably been handsome when he was the advisor's age, the burdens of battle had settled into the tired grooves across his forehead and hardened the set of his mouth.

"Father and son?" Alice asked.

"Guilty," Markell Ironside said with a quirk of his lips.

The general grunted again and I still could not decipher what it meant. He was harder to read than Lincoln.

"Tell me, sirs, what is all this about?" Alice asked. "Why am I under arrest for treason?"

"There'll be time to discuss it later." The general wheeled his horse around. "Get on the cart. All of you. Take us to your enemy so we can vanquish them and go home."

"Not vanquish," I said. "We need him alive."

"Forgive him for being terse," the advisor whispered. "He's feeling his age."

Under different circumstances I would have liked him.

"This is not a joke," Seth snapped. He muttered something very rude under his breath.

Gus jabbed him in his ribs with his elbow.

"Mr. Ironside?" I asked as he led us to a nearby cart. "You called Alice a princess just now."

"It's Sir Markell," said the cart driver. He glanced at Alice and dipped his head, although he kept his gaze on her. She nodded at him and he blushed.

"Sir Markell?" I prompted.

"She is the queen's niece," the advisor said. "Hence she is a princess. She has been stripped of that title, however, by order of Her Majesty."

"Why does the queen think she committed treason? Alice came here as a little girl. She's done nothing wrong in your realm."

He leaned on the pommel in the same way his father did. "It will all become clear in the trial."

"But how can she prepare a defense if she doesn't know the charge?"

"Enough questions!" bellowed the general, rejoining us. "Sir Markell, stay at the back of the line."

The younger man rode off, but not before he took one last, long look at Alice.

Seth huffed out a breath. "Prick."

"Seth," I hissed. "Don't anger them."

"You!" The general pointed to me. "What is your name?"

"Charlie Holloway."

"You are a commander, Charlie Holloway. Your people follow you. Are you queen in this realm?"

Despite everything, I smiled. "No."

He grunted then signaled for the cart driver to walk on. We jerked forward and fell into a steady rhythm. It didn't take long before Lichfield was far behind us, and the trees lining the edge of Hampstead Heath gave way to houses. The gray pall of central London shrouded the city ahead. It would swallow us before long.

"It's quite a walk," I told the general, riding ahead of us, his back stiff and head high.

"My men are used to walking," he said without turning around.

"We must move quickly." The sun had beaten back the dawn but still hung low on the horizon. Thanks to the early hour and being a Saturday, few commuters were out. Even so, we caused a sensation on the streets and considerable chaos for the traffic. Drivers waved their fists and shouted for us to move, once they got over their initial shock.

"They'll think we're a circus troupe," Alice said. "I hope."

"Ain't like Barnum and Bailey's," Gus said. "Remember that, Seth?"

Seth didn't respond. He hunkered down, his knees drawn up, and glared at General Ironside's back. Seth was not a brooder, but these circumstances were far from normal. In Lincoln's absence, he must feel responsible for our safety.

"It'll be all right," I told him. "Alice will not return to Wonderland."

"Is that so?" he said darkly. "Then perhaps you can enlighten me. What happens after the army has destroyed Swinburn? How will you stop them taking Alice? Or killing us?"

"The imp."

"The imp that you do not have."

I was saved from answering by the general riding back to ask for directions. We spent the rest of the journey directing him in between silences as deep and dark as a pit.

The army was not silent, however. I could hear them marveling over some of our engineering feats, from the water pump to The Great Western Royal Hotel at Paddington Station. I could only guess what they'd make of a train if they saw one. They seemed somewhat primitive compared to us.

"How big is this village?" asked the cart driver. He tilted his head to peer up at the roofs of the townhouses near Regents Park and whistled.

"It's a city," I told him. "And you've only seen a small portion."

The sight of Kensington Palace had him almost running off the road, but a sharp word from his general returned his focus.

We arrived at Swinburn's house after an hour of brisk walking. It was still early for most of the upper classes but their servants were out and about.

"Just a circus troupe passing through," Gus told them cheerfully. He waved. One or two waved back, but most simply stared.

"Knock on that door there," I told the general when we arrived at Swinburn's house. "Ask for Sir Ignatius."

The general ordered one of his men to do it. Jenkin the footman opened the door on the third knock and gasped. He fell back a step and tried to shut the door, but the soldier wedged himself into the gap.

"Jenkin!" I called out. "Fetch Sir Ignatius immediately."

Jenkin disappeared. A moment later, Swinburn stood in the doorway, dressed in a well-tailored dove-gray suit.

"What is the meaning of this?" he demanded. "Who are you?"

"General Ironside of the Wonderland Army," the general said. "Is this him, Miss Alice?"

Swinburn squinted. "Miss Holloway? Is that you? What the devil is going on?"

I jumped down from the cart. One of the soldiers thrust his sword at my throat. The cold steel halted me in my tracks. Seth and Gus rose but I warned them not to make any rash moves.

"This army is from another realm and they will destroy you," I told Swinburn. "Unless you have Lincoln released from jail."

"His arrest is nothing to do with me! I can't get him released."

"It's everything to do with you. You are pulling Mr. Yallop's strings, just like you pulled Mr. Salter's and Lady Harcourt's."

"You're mad."

"You committed those murders in the Old Nichol, didn't you?"

He folded his arms over his chest. "And if I did?"

Someone to my left gasped. It was Lord Ballantine, standing on his doorstep. Three of his pack mates stood with him.

"Did you kill them?" Ballantine asked Swinburn.

Swinburn ignored him and studied the general. "Tell your friends to disperse, Miss Holloway. I don't want any trouble."

"Then come down here," the general commanded. "I will not see innocents suffer."

"Thank you," I said. "You're a good man. Only Swinburn here must be vanquished, and *only* after he releases my intended."

He grunted. "I do not have all day."

"Send Jenkin to Mr. Yallop's house," I ordered Swinburn. "Tell him to release Lincoln now. The army will remain here until I see him safe and well."

"Don't be absurd." Swinburn went to close the door. "I have no influence over Mr. Yallop or the police."

"Yallop owes you money."

He stilled. "That is irrelevant. I haven't spoken to him about the ministry."

"Perhaps not directly. Perhaps the Duke of Edinburgh did it for you."

"Be careful, Miss Holloway. I wouldn't suggest such a thing about a member of the royal family if I were you."

"Then how about another suggestion. Did you kill Lady Harcourt?"

"Pardon?"

"Did you kill her? She was no longer of use to you, was she? And you prefer not to be burdened with a wife."

Swinburn thrust out his chin. "I didn't kill her! What an absurd notion."

"You do not look unhappy about her death."

"No, you do not," said Ballantine approaching slowly and carefully. "You held a party last night after being informed of her death. I found it distasteful." Two of his pack mates nodded.

The muscles in Swinburn's jaw bunched, his lips flattened. "Stop it, Ballantine. She's trying to drive us apart when we must be united now."

Ballantine stopped advancing and lowered his head. "You're right. My apologies, sir."

Damnation. I almost isolated Swinburn. It would have made it easier to attack him, if necessary. With his pack on his side, they would get hurt if they tried to defend him.

"I am willing to take this all the way to the end, Swinburn," I said. "This army will not leave empty handed, and I am giving them you."

"Why?" Swinburn addressed the general. "What do you get out of this arrangement?"

"Someone we have spent years searching for." The general looked back at the cart.

Alice thrust the gun under her chin, daring him to take her.

The general muttered something under his breath and turned back to Swinburn.

"You have outwitted General Ironside," came Sir Markell's quiet voice as he rode up beside me. "I commend you. It's not easy to best him but you have managed it."

"Not yet," I said. "We seem to be at a standstill."

"What will break it?"

Death. I did not say it. Could not. Swinburn's blood was the only one I wanted on my hands, but I was afraid there would be much more.

"Do as she says or I will attack," the general demanded of Swinburn. "Send your letter. Release the one named Lincoln."

Swinburn crossed his arms and did not move.

"Do it!" Seth shouted. He too jumped down from the cart to stand beside me.

Sir Markell drew his sword and placed the point to Seth's throat. "No further."

Seth scowled at him.

"You harm a single one of my friends and I will pull this trigger," Alice cried. "I have nothing to live for anyway. My family abandoned me, no man will have a strange creature like me, and my future is unclear. So you see, I am standing on the edge and I will throw myself over it if I have to."

The general merely grunted without turning around. His son, however, approached the cart. "Please don't, Princess." He spoke quietly so that his father wouldn't have heard.

"Your parents would not want their hard work undone like this."

Alice lowered the weapon to her lap and stared wide-eyed at the advisor. He steered his horse away and returned to me.

"Will you send the letter?" I asked Swinburn.

"I will not," he said.

"Now what?" Seth muttered.

"We think of something, and think quickly," I whispered.

"You have tried and failed, Miss Holloway," Lord Ballantine said. "You don't really want to harm anyone. It's time for you to go. People are beginning to stare."

"I cannot go! Lincoln will be sent to jail if I fail. If you think I will just give up, you are sorely mistaken. Sir Ignatius!" I called to Swinburn. "Either you do as I say, or the army will kill your pack."

Swinburn didn't move. Out of the corner of my eye, I saw his pack huddle closer together.

"Ignatius!" Ballantine shouted. "Do as she says. What does it matter if he's released or not?"

Swinburn's lips curled up at the edges. "She won't give the order."

"She might not," the general said, "but I will."

"Change into your wolf forms," Swinburn ordered his pack. "Then attack them."

"We can't beat all of them!" Ballantine cried. "There are too many!"

Swinburn turned his icy glare onto him. "You're just like your father and grandfather. No wonder the leadership passed to me. You're spineless, as they were. I said," he roared, "change and attack!"

"Wait!" The shout came from behind me. Dozens of feet shuffled as the army parted to allow the newcomer through. "Wait! Nobody attack!"

"Harriet!" Relief flooded me at the sight of her.

She held her belly with both hands and puffed heavily. She looked hot and drained, her waddling gait awkward as she approached us.

"Seize her!" General Ironside commanded.

"No!" his son blurted out. "She's with child."

"Seize her *gently*."

Two soldiers gripped her arms. She did not struggle, thank God.

"Harriet, are you all right?" I asked.

"No," she snapped. "I am very far from all right. I am as large as a house, my knees ache, and I feel ugly. I was fast asleep when Lady Vickers demanded I come here. What is the meaning of this?"

"My mother?" Seth asked.

"I sent her back to Lichfield with the cook."

He nodded his thanks. "We're sorry you had to be dragged into this, but we need your help. Can you convince Swinburn to speak to Yallop and drop all charges against Fitzroy and the ministry? He might listen to you."

"I doubt it," she muttered.

"Just try!" I snapped. "Or are you on his side?"

She pouted. "Charlie, we went through this. I am your friend. You know that. Please say you do."

I turned my back on her.

"Sir Ignatius," she called out. "Come now, be reasonable. Charlie has the upper hand. They greatly outnumber you. Have Lincoln released and everything can be as it was before."

"Why would I?" he said. "Why should I?"

"Because your pack is in danger!" I cried. "What sort of leader lets them die because he's too proud to admit when he's beaten?"

"The sort of leader who will get a new pack."

Ballantine expelled a breath. His pack mates murmured among themselves, too far away for me to hear their words.

"You don't deserve them," Harriet said. "They would die for you—some already have. And yet you will toss them away. I knew you were a weak man when I met you. An upstart, that's all you are. A ridiculous little sailor who cares for no one but himself."

"Enough!" Swinburn bellowed. "Kill them all. I don't care."

He went to shut the door but Jenkin grabbed him and pulled him back outside. He threw Swinburn down the steps to the pavement. Swinburn groaned but lurched to his feet.

"You damned fool," he growled at the footman.

Harriet clapped her hands. "Well done, Jenkin. Now, I have a task for you."

The footman stood to attention. "Yes, ma'am?"

"There is a necklace in Sir Ignatius's possession that belongs to Miss Holloway. It's an amber orb pendant. Please fetch it."

Jenkin's gaze darted to his master.

Swinburn bared his teeth and emitted a low, animal growl. "You will no longer be welcome in my pack if you do."

"You will be welcome in mine," Harriet said. "I will also employ you. I can always do with a handsome shape shifting footman."

Jenkin disappeared into the house.

I glanced at Harriet over my shoulder. She smiled at me and I gave her a nod. It was all I could manage.

"You will not be safe anymore, Harriet," Swinburn snarled. "I will come for you and for your offspring."

Harriet's lips quivered, her chin wobbled. "Oh, Sir Ignatius, how could you say such a thing? Did you hear that, my lord?" She appealed to Ballantine. "He has no care for his own kind. No care at all. I can excuse his murder of Gawler by telling myself it was self-defense, but this threat is horrid. Simply horrid."

"He admitted to murdering those people in the East End too," I said, playing along. It would seem this fight wasn't going to be won with weapons or claws, but with words. "All because he wanted to put the blame on Gawler so he could remove him and become the leader of both packs."

Harriet gasped. "Ignatius, how *could* you."

"Not only that," I said, "but he has put all of you in danger by telling the newspapers and Mr. Yallop about the ministry. You are all named in our records, and those records are now in the possession of the police."

Ballantine dragged a hand over his mouth and jaw. "Why?" he growled at Swinburn. "Why did you do that?"

"I didn't inform the papers!" Swinburn cried. "Christ, man, she's lying. She's trying to turn you against me."

"Who else would have done it?" Seth snapped. "We know you used Julia to get as much information about us as you could, and then you killed her too."

"She killed herself!" Swinburn said.

"Not according to the police."

"Mr. Salter admits that you gave Gawler's name to him," Harriet said to Swinburn.

I frowned. Lord Gillingham had given Gawler's name to Salter. It would seem she was going to cast blame onto Swinburn to keep her husband's name out of it.

"You dog," Ballantine snarled.

The other pack members prowled toward Swinburn, their shoulders hunched forward, their attention on their prey. I'd seen packs of stray hungry dogs stalking rats in such a manner, their focus so intent that they didn't notice me.

Swinburn stumbled back into the iron railing behind him. "Come now," he said, his voice shaking. "Stop this. I am your leader."

"Gawler was one of us," Ballantine snapped.

"And a good man," Harriet agreed. "You've betrayed our kind, Ignatius. You ought to be ashamed of yourself."

"She's lying," Swinburn warned the advancing pack.

"I am not," she said crisply. "For goodness' sake, Sir Ignatius. Stop pretending. You do not care for your kind, or for your pack. You only care about yourself."

"How dare you!" Swinburn stepped forward and stabbed his finger in her direction.

"Seize him." The general's command was laconic in comparison to Swinburn's tirade. Yet his men obeyed him without question.

Two of them grabbed Swinburn but he easily shook them off. Another two joined their comrades, but he pushed them away with two pounding swipes of his arm. Then he got down on all fours and howled.

The four soldiers scrambled backward out of the way, but they weren't fast enough. Swinburn pounced, grabbing one of the soldiers and wrapping his big hands around the man's throat. The soldier's eyes bulged and his face turned purple. The other three soldiers went to rescue him, but Swinburn once again batted them away.

The general drew his sword.

"Change!" Swinburn shouted at his pack. "Now!"

"No!" Harriet cried. "Everyone, be calm! Please!"

But it was too late for calmness. One of the other shape shifters began to remove his clothing. The others followed Swinburn's lead and readied to pounce. It would seem they would still take his side, despite everything. It was pack law.

Soldiers crowded closer, their blades drawn. Their general barked orders, setting out a formation to surround the enemy. The poor soldier in Swinburn's grip lost consciousness and went limp, enraging his comrades.

I looked to Alice, trembling on the cart. Gus tried to

comfort her but he could do nothing if the general shifted his attention to her. And he would, as soon as Swinburn was dealt with.

"Seth, see to Alice," I said. "Don't let her surrender."

"What about you?" His voice cracked. He was not looking at me but at the advancing army, drawing closer to us with each step. Every soldier had his sword drawn. "I can't leave you."

"I can take care of myself. Alice can't."

"Jesus, Charlie…"

I shoved him in the shoulder but still he didn't move. He was torn.

The general raised his sword, ready to swipe it down and order the attack.

Seth swore. Then he grabbed the sword from the nearest soldier and surged forward so quickly that the soldiers didn't have time to react. The pack did not see him coming until too late.

"No!" I screamed. "We need him alive!"

Seth cut horizontally through the air and sliced Swinburn's head cleanly off. It rolled away.

The general lowered his weapon. The army stopped. The wolf pack stared at the body of their former leader, now lying on the pavement covered in blood.

And I watched the spirit of Sir Ignatius Swinburn rise. His ghost hovered above his body, a look of vile hatred cast in Seth's direction.

"Good lord," Harriet said. "Seth, I didn't know you had it in you."

He stood there, hands at his sides, blood dripping from the blade. He looked more terrible than I'd ever seen him. If I didn't know his past or situation, I would think him a powerful lord, confident in leadership, the world at his feet.

Part of me felt pride, yet I was disheartened too. Seth's soul wasn't as gentle and affable as I'd always thought it.

"I should have done that months ago," he said.

Ballantine stormed toward him but halted at a barked order from Harriet. "Sir Ignatius's time is over. He committed terrible crimes. He will be mourned in our way and then he'll be forgotten. Is that understood?"

Ballantine nodded. The other pack members followed suit.

Jenkin emerged from the house and shook his head at me. He was empty handed. I closed my eyes. Damn it. Damn it to hell.

"Charlie?" Seth said. "Charlie, don't say that was your only plan."

A lump formed in my throat. Lincoln was still in jail with no hope of release now that Swinburn was gone, and my bargain with the general had come to an end. I wanted to fold in on myself and cry a flood of tears.

Sir Markell Ironside held out his hand to Alice as if he were asking her to dance. "Come, Miss Alice. It's time to go home."

"No!" Seth shouted. "She's not yours! She doesn't belong with you, she belongs here!"

"With you?" Sir Markell shook his head. "This is not her home. You are not her people." He stretched his hand out further. "You know this, Miss Alice. Come home and answer the charges against you with your head high."

"You're leading her to certain death," Seth choked out.

Sir Markell ignored him. He only had eyes for Alice.

Seth's lips drew back and he surged forward.

The general flicked the point of his sword in my direction. Four of his men quickly drew their weapons on me and Seth halted. The color drained from his face, taking all his determination and anger with it. He threw down his weapon.

"Charlie!" Gus cried. "Don't move."

I put my hands in the air. "I'm sorry," I said to Alice.

She bit down on her quivering lower lip and nodded. "I know," she whispered.

She took Sir Markell's hand.

"Ha! Good!" said Swinburn's ghost. He smirked at me. "You lose, Miss Holloway. You lose everything."

Hot tears slid down my cheeks. He was right. I'd sold my friend to her enemy and I had not helped Lincoln's plight. I was a fool to think I could effect change, a naive, pathetic fool.

The general tugged on his gold watch chain. The device! It was the same one the rabbit had used to come and go from our realm even though Alice was awake. All it would take was one click on the watch's button while speaking the words of the spell, then they'd all be gone, Alice with them.

The general began the strange words that I'd heard the rabbit speak.

CHAPTER 17

"No!" Seth pushed toward the general. He even managed a few steps before one of the soldiers smashed his fist into Seth's face.

"Seth!" Alice cried as he fell back.

He regained his balance, and tried again. This time he struck the soldier first. Another two caught him. He could not get to the general in time to stop him speaking the spell. Not with so many against him.

But his actions had achieved one thing. It had bought me time. And in those few seconds, I'd realized something.

"Sir Ignatius Swinburn, I order you to tell me where you hid my necklace."

My command interrupted the general. He looked around, searching for the spirit perhaps. How long would it be before he resumed the incantation?

"Tell me!" I shouted.

The ghost swirled. It was neither human nor animal in shape, just gray and white streaks whipping about me. "In my pocket," whispered the breeze.

I dove for the body and rummaged through his jacket pockets. His blood smeared my hands, my dress. I didn't care.

"What is she doing?" Sir Markell asked.

I finally found it in the breast pocket. With shaking fingers, I clutched the orb. "I release you, imp!" I shouted. "Come out, imp!"

It did not come out. It had done this on the Isle of Wight too. I suspected it went into deep sleep between summons, or perhaps it was becoming ill.

"Markell!" the general shouted. "The prisoner!"

Alice had taken the moment's distraction to get out of Sir Markell's reach and scuttle to the other side of the cart. Gus pushed her behind him but he was unarmed. Sir Markell leapt from his horse onto the cart. He had not drawn his sword.

"You! Men!" the general shouted. "Stop Miss Holloway from whatever magic she is conjuring."

Three soldiers showed no fear in advancing on me. Two of them put away their swords, but the third did not.

I turned and ran up the steps toward Jenkin. His expression told me precisely the moment my life was in danger.

"Imp! Now!"

Light burst from the orb, forcing me to turn my face away. My attackers had to do the same. By the time they turned back, the imp had grown to its largest size, higher than the windows of the house. It wasn't a pretty creature with its wrinkled skin, oversized ears and lack of fur, but it was the best sight I'd ever seen.

Not so those who'd never seen it before. The soldiers fell back, stumbling down the stairs, horror imprinted on their faces. The shape shifters, including Harriet, retreated to Ballantine's house, and the army fell into disarray. Some at the back scurried off. Others simply stared up at the cat-like beast towering over them as if it were the devil incarnate.

The general barked orders at his men but they were largely ignored. Those who did draw their weapons were swiftly swiped by the imp's massive paw. They scattered like skittles along the street.

"Miss Alice!" Sir Markell cried. "For God's sake, run! Get away from here!"

Alice did not run. She had never seen my imp before, but she must have known it wouldn't attack her. Perhaps because neither Seth nor Gus looked worried. She did, however, clutch Gus tightly and stare with a mixture of horror and wonder at it.

The imp took a giant step forward. Neighbors who'd come out when the army arrived screamed and shut their doors. More of the army ran away up the street. Sir Markell returned to his horse, giving up on Alice.

"General, we have to go!" he shouted at his father.

"Not without Miss Alice." The general charged forward, the watch still clutched in his hand.

The movement caught the imp's attention and it went after him.

"Say the words!" Sir Markell cried.

"No!"

Damn him. Why was he so intent on retrieving Alice for his queen? Did he need to bring her to justice so badly that he was prepared to risk his own life and that of his son?

"Seth," I hissed. "The watch. You must get it."

"You want to keep them here?" He shook his head. "Charlie—"

I clicked my tongue in frustration and stormed down the steps. The imp leapt in front of the general and his horse reared. He caught hold of the reins in both hands, but dropped the watch.

"Father!" Sir Markell cried. His frightened horse wheeled about, ears flat, but he managed to control it. He drew his sword and aimed it at the imp. "Say the God damned words before it kills us all!"

"I can't," the general said. "I lost it."

His horse reared again. Its hooves came down, aiming straight for the watch lying on the road. If it broke, they would be stuck here.

I dove for the watch. Pain burned my hands and knees as I hit the ground. Several voices screamed my name. I looked up just in time to see hooves descending toward me. I closed my eyes and threw my arms over my head.

There was a thud, then another, and the squeal of a frightened horse.

I lowered my arms. The imp stood by me on all fours, panting heavily. It was growing weak. Two riderless horses took off down the street, reins dragging on the road.

"Father? Father? By the Gods, are you all right?" Sir Markell helped his father to sit up.

The general blinked dazedly at his son. Then he turned to stare at the imp. "What beast is that?" he murmured.

"It's her pet," Seth snarled. "And it's going to tear you apart if you don't leave."

"Not without Miss Alice," the general said.

I pulled out the piece of paper I'd tucked into my pocket after retrieving it from Lincoln's safe earlier. Then I chanted the written words, the same ones the general had begun moments ago, and clicked the watch button.

By the time Sir Markell and General Ironside realized what was happening, the final words left my lips. They vanished. Their horses disappeared and so did the army, the watch, and even the cart. Gus and Alice fell unceremoniously onto the ground, and the street became oddly quiet, like the morning after a fierce storm.

Seth rushed to Alice's aid and crouched before her. She

gave him a wobbly smile. He smiled back then pulled her into a fierce hug.

"Come here, Imp," I said, clutching the orb. "Sleep now."

Light flashed and when I opened my eyes, the imp had disappeared. The orb pulsed once and I could just make out the tiny creature settling inside it. I placed the necklace around my neck.

Harriet waddled over to me and drew me into a hug. I hesitated then hugged her back. "Oh, Charlie, you are so brave! That thing..." She touched the amber nestled against my chest. "Sir Ignatius described it to me, as it was described to him by Lady Ballantine, but I didn't believe him. It seemed much too fantastical to be real."

"I've seen a lot of things that seem too fantastic to be real, and yet they are. Are you all right, Harriet?"

She pressed her palm to her belly. Her features were pinched and her eyes huge in her pretty face. "I think I ought to go home. I feel...different. The baby seems to have moved lower and the most awful pain ripped through me just a few moments ago. Besides, Gilly will be frantic. I forbade him to come with me. There are some things a husband shouldn't know about his wife, and seeing me with my pack is one of them."

"Then go. We'll talk later."

It wasn't until after Lord Ballantine had assisted her into her coach that I realized she'd said "my pack". Her pack wasn't here; Swinburn's was. But he was gone, and Lord Ballantine was bowing to her as she drove off. It would seem the two packs might combine after all under the one leader.

I watched as her coach turned the corner, a peculiar thought taking root in my head.

"Is anyone going to hug me?" Gus asked.

I smiled and threw my arms around him. "You can get a hug from me any time you want."

He kissed the top of my head. "You all right, Charlie?"

"Fine. You?"

"Seems like I got through this fight unscathed."

"Miracles do happen."

He chuckled. "How long before the army comes back?"

That was a very good question. There was another good question, however—how were we going to explain the presence of an army, a giant hairless creature, and their subsequent disappearance?

Up and down the street, neighbors emerged from their homes, scratching their heads and shrugging at one another. Some pointed at us, or at Lord Ballantine. He ushered his pack inside his house and shut the door. Only Jenkin, Swinburn's footman, remained. He stood by the body of his dead employer and pack leader.

"The police will have to be notified," I said, joining him. "They are probably already on their way."

"I should put the head with the body," he said.

I glanced at it, some feet away, and shuddered. Those sightless eyes would haunt me for days.

Speaking of haunting... I could not see Swinburn's ghost. "Sir Ignatius Swinburn, are you here?" I tried to think of his middle name but couldn't remember it. If he had crossed, I'd need it to call him back.

But he hadn't crossed. His spirit rose up from the stairs leading down to the basement service area. Even in shades of gray, the slit at his throat was clearly visible, as was the blood, but I was rather glad the ghostly head was still in place on his neck. I half expected him to be carrying it under his arm like a hat. Another shudder wracked me.

"What is it?" Swinburn snapped.

"You haven't crossed," I said.

Gus, Seth and Alice gathered around me, following my

gaze toward the spirit. Jenkin backed up the stairs and disappeared inside, slamming the door shut.

The spirit pointed at Seth. "When my murderer is caught, I will cross."

I didn't look at Seth. I didn't want him knowing Swinburn remained here because of him. "I have some questions for you, Sir Ignatius, and you will answer them. That is a command."

The ghost shimmered. "Go on. I have nothing to hide now."

"Did you murder those people in the Old Nichol?"

"Yes," he said.

"So you could blame Gawler and have him arrested?"

"Arrested, tried for murder, and hanged." He spoke coolly, dispassionately. It was unthinkable that he didn't care for his fellow shape changer. I doubted he cared for anyone. "To answer your next question, Miss Holloway, I did it to take over his pack."

"Harriet took over his pack, not you."

"She would recognize me as the head of our kind and defer to me on important matters. Much like a lord and his king, or a minister to the prime minister."

So it did come down to power in the end. The descendent of sailors had set his sights high, and he'd almost reached the pinnacle.

"I didn't tell that reporter about Gawler, you know," he said. "Harriet had that wrong."

"I know." I didn't tell him her own husband had been Salter's source. "But you did tell him about Lincoln and the ministry."

"No." The spirit swept up to me and whooshed around my head. I managed to stay still, calm, despite wanting to duck out of the way. "I have never spoken to *The Star's* reporter or any newspaperman. The information about Fitzroy did not come from me."

I blinked. Blinked again. "Tell me the truth, Sir Ignatius," I commanded. "Did you tell anyone about the Ministry of Curiosities and Lincoln Fitzroy? Anyone at all?"

"No! My name is in your files, for God's sake! Fitzroy made a point of telling me so. I didn't like him or your damned ministry, but I'm not a fool, Miss Holloway. I know when to keep my mouth shut."

My chest tightened. My throat felt dry. If he hadn't told Mr. Yallop or Mr. Salter, who had?

"What is it, Charlie?" Seth asked, a hand on my lower back. "You look faint."

"It's already quite warm," Alice said.

I shook my head. "It's not that. Sir Ignatius," I said to the ghost. "The police informed us that Lady Harcourt was pushed into the path of the omnibus. She did not kill herself. Did you do it?"

"No! Are you mad?" he blurted out. "What if I'd been seen? I wouldn't risk it simply to get rid of her. Anyway, I quite liked her. I didn't want to marry her but I would have settled a sum on her when I broke off the engagement. I'm sure she would have seen the sense in that."

I doubted it but didn't say so. I was much too shocked by his revelations. If he hadn't killed her, who had? Most likely it was the same person who'd told the newspapers about the ministry and mobilized Yallop.

"You may go," I murmured. "I have no more questions for you."

The ghost crouched before his body on the pavement. The blood had begun to dry and an insect buzzed around the head. "I think I'll stay here a little longer. I want justice."

"You there!" someone shouted from up the street. "Halt!

All of you." Two constables hurried toward us, truncheons at the ready.

Seth greeted them. The use of his full title blew away their superior air and had them treating him with deference.

"We were told of a commotion here, sir," said one of the men, glancing at the body. "Did you see what happened?"

"In a way," Seth said. "We were strolling along and saw a mass of people gathered. It seemed to be some sort of protest against that man there." He pointed at Swinburn's body. "Next thing we knew, he'd fallen and the crowd dispersed."

Swinburn's ghost swirled round and round. "They won't believe that ridiculous story. Besides, there are witnesses up and down this street."

None of whom were close enough to identify Seth as the one wielding the blade. There'd been an entire army in the vicinity, obscuring their view.

One of the constables inspected the body. Finding the head missing, he scanned the vicinity and pulled a face when he spotted it. "What kind of weapon did that?"

"Good question," Seth said. "You should search for a sword, that would be my guess."

"Damned idiots!" Swinburn shouted in the constable's face.

We gave the constables our names then left them to clean up the mess. Swinburn's spirit followed me for a few feet then found he could not go any further. He was tied to this spot.

We caught a hackney back to Lichfield. By the time we reached the gate, we'd decided we probably should have gone straight to Scotland Yard. For one thing, we ought to notify Detective Inspector Fullbright of Swinburn's death. He would soon find out anyway, but somehow we had to make it sound as if we were innocent. I couldn't quite think clearly enough to make up a better story than the one Seth had given the constables. Perhaps later.

I also wanted to ask Fullbright where to find Lincoln. Hopefully he was still in a Scotland Yard holding cell and not already transferred to a prison.

The sight of the damaged house squeezed my heart. The catapult's boulder had torn off a corner of the top floor, leaving broken, jagged beams jutting into the sky. Bricks and other rubble lay scattered at the building's base, including the twisted remains of the attic desk and chair.

We picked our way through the mess and found ourselves enveloped in warm hugs from Cook and Lady Vickers. They directed us to the kitchen where Cook set out biscuits, sandwiches, cheese and whatever else he could find.

"These were supposed to be for my wedding," I said, plopping down on a chair.

"Aye," he said gently. "No need for them to go to waste."

I glanced at the clock. I ought to be getting married in less than thirty minutes. Tears welled but I didn't want the others to see them so I set about pouring the tea. Everyone ate except Alice. She simply stared into the teacup, her brow furrowed.

"What do we do now?" she asked. "We can't go on like this, waiting for the army to return at any moment. We just can't."

Seth touched her chin, forcing her to look at him. "We take it one day at a time." She shook her head and opened her mouth, but he put up a finger to stop her. "There'll be no more discussion of you going to Wonderland. Is that clear?"

She took a very long sip of her tea.

"Speaking of people not leaving," Lady Vickers said, her tone stern. "I discovered the letter you wrote, Charlie."

I groaned.

"What letter?" Gus asked.

"A farewell note," Cook said. "She be planning to break

Fitzroy out of prison using her necromancy and run away with him."

A total and profound silence filled the kitchen. I felt hard gazes on me but didn't dare meet them.

"And what then?" Seth snapped.

"And then we would keep running," I said. "For as long as necessary."

Gus shook his biscuit at me. "And what about us, eh? What were we s'posed to do? Just wait here?"

"You would go about your daily lives and deny any wrongdoing. The police would blame us since we'd run off. It was a neat solution to our predicament."

Seth suddenly stood and kicked over his chair. He stalked to the stove and stared down into the pot of simmering water.

I stood beside him and tucked my hands into the crook of his arm. I leaned against him, my head on his shoulder. "What else could I do, Seth? I love him. I'll do anything to be with him, go anywhere."

His muscles relaxed and his chest rose and fell with his deep sigh. He turned and drew me into a hug. "We're your family too," he murmured into my hair.

"Yes. You are. And I'm sorry. I'll try to think of another way."

"Bloody hell," Gus murmured in wonder.

"Should I be worried?" came a familiar voice. A voice that belonged to a man who should not be there.

I pulled away from Seth and stared dumbly at Lincoln, standing in the doorway. His hair hung loose to his shoulders, and his jaw was shadowed with stubble. But he was in every way the most wonderful sight in the world.

"I'm no expert on women's preparations," he said idly, "but shouldn't you be wearing your wedding gown by now?"

He opened his arms and I ran into them, trying very hard not to sob.

We held one another so tightly I could feel his heart hammering, feel his heat and hard muscles through our clothes. Then his lips were on my forehead, my cheeks, my eyelids, my mouth. His hands dug into my unbound hair, and he cradled my head to keep our mouths locked together. He needn't have worried about me pulling away. I wasn't going to. I was precisely where I always wanted to be.

After a long moment that seemed to go on forever, and yet not long enough, another set of arms came around us both from behind me. It was Seth.

Lincoln smiled against my mouth and we parted. He stroked my hair from my forehead. "So you missed me," he murmured, a smile toying with his lips.

"God, yes," Seth said. "You have no idea how much."

I laughed and kissed Lincoln again. We only separated when someone cleared his throat. Lincoln let me go and embraced Gus's big frame. They slapped one another on the back in a manly fashion before Cook demanded it was his turn. Lincoln finally called enough after he'd embraced everyone.

"We don't have time for this," he announced with a glance at the clock.

My heart clenched. "Did you escape? Are the police after you?"

"No." His mouth curved in that most deliciously wicked way of his. "But we're getting married in fifteen minutes, and it takes ten to drive to the church."

I stared at him, my mouth ajar. Then I tried to tug him toward the back door that led to the courtyard and outbuildings. "Then stop kissing me and move!"

"There's a carriage waiting out front. If some ride on the outside, we should all fit, despite an extra passenger."

"Who?" I asked.

"We can't just run out now!" Lady Vickers cried, picking up her skirts and rushing off. "We are not prepared!"

"Correct, madam," Lincoln said. "Gus, the rings."

Gus pushed past her. Seth followed. "I'll fetch you a clean shirt," he said over his shoulder. "You're not getting married in the one you wore in prison."

"At least I don't have blood on mine," Lincoln called after him. "Does someone care to explain why Seth has blood on him? And why part of the house is damaged?"

"I will later," I said.

Lady Vickers strode after her son only to return to us, her skirts lifted high above her ankles. "But the dress!" she cried. "And your hair, Charlie! You can't get married looking like a wild thing. And you, Lincoln, are no better."

"There's no time to change," he said, pulling me toward the door. "The vicar won't wait, and nor will I."

Fortunately the flowers had arrived so I was able to hold a nosegay of blush pink roses. I removed the blue ribbon holding the bunch together and handed it to Lincoln. He was still tying back his hair when Cook opened the front door and I caught a glimpse of the coach waiting for us. Two grooms and a driver dressed in crimson livery waited with it. One of the grooms opened the door and the Prince of Wales peered back at us from inside.

"Good morning, all," he said cheerfully. "Are you ready to get married, Miss Holloway?"

"I…I am, yes." I allowed the footman to assist me into the cabin and settled beside the prince. "Did you free Lincoln?"

Instead of answering, he gave orders to his men. "You two, wait here until I return. Fitzroy, you and your men can ride at the back or sit alongside the driver. The ladies can ride in here with me." The prince settled back with a sigh of satisfaction as we drove off. "Your words affected me, Miss

Holloway, more than I let on at the time. I spoke with the queen and we decided to speak to Mr. Yallop on your behalf. That was late yesterday afternoon. It took until this morning for the slow wheels of politics to move. So here we are, off to the church in time for your wedding."

"But the queen was so angry with me," I said. "I got the distinct impression she never wanted to see me again."

"She was upset, but once she calmed down, she saw your side of things. She's like that. It takes a number of years before one can learn her moods and how to navigate them." His mouth turned down and his heavy eyelids lowered. "Inspector Fullbright informed me this morning, when I collected Fitzroy, that he was about to head out to Sir Ignatius's residence. Reports of a disturbance had come through. Do you know anything about that?"

I exchanged a glance with Alice. "He's dead," I said. "His ghost admitted that he'd murdered those men in the Old Nichol. I'm sorry, sir, I know you don't want to hear it, but he duped you."

He grunted. "A man doesn't like admitting that he put his trust in the wrong fellow. According to Fullbright, Swinburn's name was in your records."

"As a werewolf, yes."

Another grunt. "The odd thing is, Miss Holloway, that he was the only living person mentioned in your ministry's files. All the others were deceased persons."

"That can't be—"

Alice kicked me and I swallowed the rest of my response. I tried to think how the names of every living supernatural except for Swinburn could have been removed from the files and came up blank. I'd remembered burying them complete.

Alice yawned then apologized to the prince. "I haven't been sleeping too well of late."

"Insomnia?" he asked.

"Mr. Fitzroy suffers from it too." She looked to me.

Ah yes, the night she couldn't sleep and had seen Lincoln crossing the lawn back to the house. He must have been coming from the walled garden after digging up some of the files and reburying them elsewhere. It was typical of him to be one step ahead of everyone else.

Thankfully supernaturals would now be safe from police scrutiny. I didn't want to face Mr. Langley's ire, for one, and Lincoln's disappointment in himself if their names had been revealed.

"Sir," I said, "your influence may be required again."

"This sounds ominous," he said.

"Some very strange things happened at Sir Ignatius's house this morning. It will take some convincing for Inspector Fullbright to make sense of it."

"Perhaps it can all be explained by the hallucinogenic fumes reported in that area."

I smiled and he smiled back.

The coach pulled up in front of the church and Seth wouldn't let me out until Gus and Lincoln were inside. He opened the door and assisted his mother and Alice from the coach, then politely inquired if his highness was staying.

The prince hesitated.

"Please do," I said. "You're most welcome."

"Perhaps at the back," he said, and got out.

When they were all inside, I took Seth's arm. He beamed at me. "You look happy and beautiful, Charlie, despite wearing your worst dress, as my mother would say."

"It's the very worst, " I said cheerfully. "But I don't care."

* * *

THE CEREMONY WENT by in a flash. One moment I was Miss Holloway and the next I was Mrs. Fitzroy. Lady Vickers was the first to congratulate me and call me by my new name. I almost burst out laughing. It would take some getting used to.

A frenzy of congratulations followed next, firstly from our closest friends from Lichfield. Leisl, Eva and David Cornell were also there, since they had not been aware of Lincoln's imprisonment. Lord and Lady Marchbank were not in attendance, and neither were Lord and Lady Gillingham. They didn't know that Lincoln was free. Lincoln asked the vicar if he could dash off a note to them immediately.

I looked around for the prince, but he had already left. Perhaps that was for the best. His past with Leisl had been shrouded in mystery, and he didn't like to be reminded of his night of passion with the pretty gypsy girl. At least he seemed to have come to terms with fathering Lincoln. Indeed, more than come to terms with it, if his efforts in getting him released were an indication. I'd say he was heartily proud of his son.

As was I. I clung to the arm of my new husband, not prepared to let him out of my sight all day. So when he started to discuss Swinburn as we emerged from the church, I rounded on him.

"You are *not* continuing the investigation today," I said, hand on hip.

"Seth told me what Swinburn's ghost told you," Lincoln said levelly. "We have to find out who is responsible for informing the newspapers and Yallop about the ministry. There's also the matter of Julia's death."

"I agree, but not today. Today you are mine. And there's no urgency now that the prince has spoken to Mr. Yallop and stopped the investigation."

"There is always Salter and *The Star*. We have to nip this in the bud before it rears its head again." When I hesitated, he added, "Come with me. I want your company anyway. Very much."

I narrowed my gaze. He was too charming. Lincoln was never charming. He also had a good point. The longer we let the real villain roam the streets, the longer he had a chance of causing us more problems.

"Besides, Gus has an errand to run for me," he said. "So the feast can't begin until he gets there."

I shot a glare at Gus. "What errand?"

"It's a good one!" Gus cried. "Promise, Charlie."

"Lincoln, I don't like surprises."

He took my hands in his and tugged me closer until our bodies pressed together. I tilted my head back to peer up at him. He smiled down at me and I fell into the deep, mesmerizing pools of his eyes. "You'll have to wait and see, Wife." He kissed me gently but with a longing that tugged at my insides, low down in my belly.

I sighed into him. "You're not playing fair."

His smile turned lazy and he leaned down to whisper. "You haven't played fair with me ever since I met you. Everything about you is perfect. I never stood a chance."

For someone who could be as blunt as a brick, he somehow managed to say all the right things.

"Gus'll be a good half hour at least, so we have time before we dine," he said, taking my hand. "We'll meet the others back at Lichfield." He gave orders for everyone to disperse and prepare for our return. David was the only one who grumbled at being ordered about, but the others complied cheerily.

Gus went in search of hackneys with a promise to send one our way. As I waited with Lincoln, and listened to the happy chatter of those around me, I realized he already had a plan.

"Seth told you everything that happened this morning?" I asked him.

"Yes." He put his arm around me. "Apparently you did exceptionally well. It seems I wasn't even required."

"I will always require you, Lincoln. Never think otherwise."

He blinked rapidly and tucked me against his side. His kiss lingered on the top of my head.

"Where are we going first?" I asked.

"Around the side of the church."

"There are only gravestones and trees there and no cabs."

"Also no witnesses. You're going to summon Julia's spirit."

She wasn't someone I expected to see on my wedding day, but if this matter was to be resolved, it was necessary. She was our only hope of finding out who pushed her. Once we learned that, the trail would hopefully lead us to the person who betrayed us.

Yet I hated to think what her answer would be. As much as I didn't quite believe Harriet was entirely innocent, the thought of her being a murderer and traitor sickened me.

"What's her middle name?" I asked as we stood in the graveyard, pretending to pay our respects to the deceased. No one was about but it was wise to be cautious. It was unnerving summoning a ghost at the best of times, but even more so in a holy place.

"Iris," Lincoln said. "Remember to use Buchanan not the Harcourt title."

"Julia Iris Buchanan," I intoned. "Come to me, the spirit of Julia Iris Buchanan."

A breeze ruffled my hair and brushed my skin. It was warm, not cool, and no ghost appeared. "Julia Iris Buchanan," I said again, then added, "Otherwise known as Lady Harcourt. I summon you here to speak with me."

Nothing happened. I tried again and was about to try

another time, when Lincoln told me to stop. "I expected you to fail," he said.

"Why? Does she have another name? Perhaps I should use her maiden name." What a scandal that would be if it turned out she'd never married Lord Harcourt after all.

"It won't make a difference. Her spirit can't be summoned because she's not dead."

CHAPTER 18

*L*uckily Lincoln held my hand as I stumbled through the graveyard back to the front of the church or I would have fallen. I hardly noticed where I stepped. My mind reeled with questions and theories, none of which made any sense.

The others had left and a hansom waited for us by the curb. Lincoln assisted me to the seat and closed the door in front of our knees. Lincoln gave the driver directions to Harcourt House through the ceiling hatch before changing his mind and giving him a different address. I didn't recognize it.

"How did you know she wasn't dead?" I asked as we drove off.

"I had a long time to contemplate it in my cell," he said. "There were too many things that didn't make sense, and I concluded that we were wrong. Swinburn wouldn't risk his life and reputation to bring about my downfall, and Julia wouldn't take her own life. She's not the type."

He wasn't the first to say it. I should have taken more notice of those who knew her well. "But...I don't understand.

Did she stage her own death? How, when her body was recovered and identified?"

"Identified by Buchanan. To be fair, I don't think he knew when he visited us after seeing the body in the mortuary. He thought she was dead. I asked Fullbright only last night about the injuries and he said the face was badly damaged. Buchanan identified the body based on clothing, rings and other personal items."

"Items that could easily be given to someone else." I shook my head slowly, barely able to comprehend the lengths she'd gone to. "She found someone of similar height and weight to herself, didn't she?"

"Most likely a whore. She dressed her in her own clothes and sent her on her way. She put on men's clothing and at the right moment, pushed the imposter in front of an omnibus."

I swallowed the bile rising up my throat. I knew the answer to my next question but asked it anyway. "Why?"

He squeezed my hand but offered no response.

"Where are we going?" I asked.

"Buchanan's residence. She'll need help now. She can't go home, she can't be seen by anyone who knows her, and he's the only one who'd help her."

It was true. He'd do anything for her; he was completely devoted, in his own perverse way.

Andrew Buchanan rented rooms in an uninspiring Bloomsbury house. The landlady led us up two flights of stairs. Buchanan opened the door on our knock and was clearly shocked to see us.

"Fitzroy! What the devil are you doing here?"

Lincoln thanked the landlady, dismissing her. He waited until her footsteps receded then muscled his way inside. Buchanan offered little resistance, although he tried.

"I say! What are you doing?"

Lincoln peeled off into the adjoining sitting room only to emerge moments later. He searched the rest of the lodgings, ignoring Buchanan's protests as he trailed behind.

I made myself comfortable in the sitting room. It was rather barren, with the barest of furniture and no pictures on the walls. No knick knacks made it a home. A box of unpacked books stood to one side, perhaps because there was no bookshelf to arrange them on. The window was open and the curtain drifted back and forth with the light breeze. Even so, the room was stifling.

Lincoln and Buchanan returned. Lincoln's expression was unreadable, and Buchanan's was anxious. At least he was sober, and there were no signs of mourning. When he'd come to Lichfield after learning of Lady Harcourt's death, he'd been inconsolable, and I'd predicted he'd be like that for weeks. The clear-eyed, clean-shaven man before us was out of character. I needed no more evidence that Lady Harcourt was alive, and not only did he know it, but he was helping her.

"What's the meaning of this?" he demanded.

"Just a visit," Lincoln said, his eyes hooded.

"We thought we should see how you were faring," I said. "You were in a bad way last time we met."

"Yes. Well. Thank you, I'm fine now. I am rather busy, though."

"Are you moving back into Harcourt House?" I indicated the box of books.

"No."

"Why not? Now that she's gone, it must belong to you and your brother in its entirety."

His lips stretched thin. "I can't face it yet. This place will do me nicely for now."

"Of course. Did you know that Lincoln and I got married this morning?" I held up my hand to show him the wedding ring. I hadn't even put gloves on before racing out of the house.

Slowly, slowly, he smiled. It wasn't cruel or disdainful, as I expected from him. It was victorious. "I'm pleased. Very, very pleased." He shook Lincoln's hand then kissed my cheek. "Congratulations. And here I thought you wouldn't get out of prison in time, Fitzroy."

"How did you know I was in prison?"

"Well." Buchanan affected a laugh. "I believe it was Lord Gillingham who told me."

"You're lying."

Buchanan's mouth shut with a clack of back teeth.

The front door opened and I shot to my feet, expecting Buchanan to warn Lady Harcourt to flee. But he did not. Perhaps because it wasn't her. Perhaps we'd been wrong and she wasn't hiding out here.

The throaty voice coming from the hallway put my doubts to rest. "I cannot believe it!" cried Lady Harcourt. "They let him go!" She appeared in the doorway, stopping dead when she spotted Lincoln.

It was one of those moments in which time freezes. No one and nothing moved, not a finger or an eyebrow. Even the breeze died.

Lady Harcourt did not try to run away, perhaps because she knew she could never outrun Lincoln.

"It seems congratulations are in order," I said when no one else tried to break the heavy silence. "You are not dead, Lincoln is free, and we are married. What a wonderful day this has turned out to be."

Her throat moved with her swallow and she reached out to grasp the door. It would seem our news had unbalanced her more than the sight of seeing us.

That was why Buchanan hadn't warned her—he wanted her to see that she'd failed and that Lincoln and I married after all, despite her machinations to keep us apart. He was always trying to win her back, always trying to force her to love him above any other, even now.

"Won't you congratulate them, dear Julia?" Buchanan drawled. "Show them you're pleased for them. Come now, water under the bridge and all that."

"Stop it," she snarled. "Stop this charade, Andrew. You are in as much trouble as I am."

"For what?" he blurted out.

"For harboring me. For not notifying the police that I was alive after I showed up here."

"True," Lincoln said. "But that is not a hanging offence. Murder is."

She swallowed again but she let go of the door. Buchanan promptly sat. "Don't tell anyone," he begged Lincoln. "Let her go. If she hangs, it will be on your conscience."

Lincoln didn't take his gaze off Lady Harcourt. If he'd heard Buchanan's plea, he showed no sign. She stared defiantly back, daring him to capture her.

"She committed murder just so she could stage her own death," I said to Buchanan. "An innocent woman—"

"Whores aren't innocent," Buchanan said. "Not even the ones of respectable birth and good breeding." He fluttered a hand in Lady Harcourt's direction.

She rounded on him. "Will you not stop? Can you not see it's over? Do you exist only to torture me?"

"A man must get his pleasures where he can."

She made a harsh sound low in her throat. "You were pathetic when I showed up on your doorstep. Pathetic and ridiculous. He fell all over me," she told us. "He was so happy to see me alive that he couldn't stop pawing me." She crossed the room to the window and slapped a hand on the sill. "He took me right here with the curtains open. Anyone could have seen. The neighbors..." She closed her eyes. "It was hideous and humiliating. I wished I really was dead."

Buchanan's chest heaved. His hands opened and closed at his sides and his face screwed up, as if he were trying hard not to cry or shout or both. She thrust out her chin, daring him to react.

With her sickening words ringing in my ears, I stood. "I'll ask the landlady to fetch the police."

Out of the corner of my eye I saw Buchanan rush toward me. I had only a moment to settle into a fighting stance, my fists up to defend myself. Lincoln was too far away to stop him.

But Buchanan hurtled past me, straight for Lady Harcourt. I realized what he was going to do in the moment before he did it. My reaction was too slow.

I watched in horror as he pushed her out the window then followed her through it. There was no scream or shout, merely a distant thud.

I covered my cry with both hands. My knees trembled and I had to sit again. Lincoln strode to the window and peered out.

"Are they...?" I murmured.

He nodded. "People are already milling. I have to see that the police are informed."

"Go. I'll be down in a moment."

He touched my shoulder as he passed. Someone in the distance gave a horrified cry and another shouted. Then everything went quiet, calm, and I suspected Lincoln had taken charge.

I wanted to join him but I waited for the drift of mist to coalesce in the sitting room. I wasn't all that surprised when two figures formed, one in the shape of Lady Harcourt and the other of Andrew Buchanan. They were inseparable even in death. How fitting.

"Well," she said, looking at him. "That's that." She touched the bloodied, damaged side of her face then stared at her hand.

The back of Buchanan's head had caved in, leaving his handsome face untouched. He smiled at her. "Forever together, as it should be. We are meant for one another, Julia. You know that. This proves it."

She simply lifted one shoulder, the movement as elegant in death as in life. If someone had just pushed me out the window, I would do more than shrug when confronting him.

"You goaded Mr. Buchanan," I told her. "You wanted to end it all, but you wanted him to end it for you, didn't you?"

She drifted to the window and peered down at the bodies. Or perhaps she was looking for Lincoln.

"He's quite the man," she said, confirming that he did indeed capture her interest.

Buchanan's spirit shimmered violently and he bit off a string of foul words. "Can you not forget him now? It's over!"

"Even if he never met me," I told her, "he wouldn't be with you."

"I thought sending him to prison would keep him from you." Her spirit deflated, although there was no breath within her to expel. "It was a foolish notion, borne of desperation. I admit that now."

"You told Mr. Salter about the ministry," I said. "You told him and other newspapermen about Lincoln being the leader, and you urged your parliamentary friends to set up a committee to investigate him."

"The newspapers, yes, but I have no political sway. I heard the Duke of Edinburgh boasting about it so I suggest you look there."

So he'd played a part after all. We could do nothing to bring him to justice, but at least his influence had been trounced by his brother's.

Her full lips curved seductively. "The possibility of losing Lincoln upset you, didn't it, Charlotte?"

I didn't answer. I simply sat with as serene an expression as I could muster through my anger. The last thing I wanted was to act exactly as she hoped. She would end her existence here without that satisfaction.

"I came up with the idea of landing Lincoln in trouble after reading the report about the attack in *The Star*," she went on. "It went a little too well. I wasn't expecting his arrest. I don't know who informed the reporter about werewolves, but I knew you would suspect Ignatius of the attacks. Horrid man."

Buchanan's spirit shimmered again. "If you disliked him enough to implicate him, why did you want to marry him?"

"Don't pretend stupidity, Andrew. You know why. I needed the security marriage to him would bring me. He would have released me before we walked down the aisle, you know. I admit to being a fool there. I gave him everything I knew about Lincoln and the ministry. I should have kept some in reserve." Her voice drifted away and her spirit thinned. She was about to cross.

"We could have been happy together," Buchanan whined.

She looked at him and her ghostly form strengthened.

"We could have run away together, gone where no one knew us," he said. "We could have made a fresh start." He swooped and circled her before settling once again. "But you wanted to stay so you could be near *him*."

She looked down at the scene below again. "It made me happy knowing his plan to marry Charlotte was thwarted. So very happy. He broke my heart so it was only fair that I played a hand in breaking his."

"Except you didn't." I flashed my ring at her and stood. "Now, if you don't mind, our guests are waiting."

Her spirit rushed forward and stopped in front of me. She

bared her teeth. It was rather a frightful sight, considering those on her left side were smashed or missing altogether. "I will haunt you, Charlotte! I will make your life miserable!"

"No, you won't. You can only haunt the place where you died." I indicated the sitting room. "I can't imagine Lincoln or I will ever have the need to come back here."

The spirit suddenly dispersed, emitting a chilling scream that rang in my ears and hung in the air long after she was gone. I looked out the window but couldn't see her there, either. I allowed myself a deep, slow breath of relief.

Buchanan swirled around, looking for her. He tried to leave the room but found he could only go out the window, down to his death, and back up again. Everything else was off limits. When he realized she was gone, he pleaded with me not to leave yet.

"What happens now?" He looked frightened and confused, almost childlike.

"You either cross over to your afterlife or stay and haunt here," I said. "It's your choice."

"There's no point staying here without her."

"Goodbye, Mr. Buchanan."

"Call me Andrew. We were friends, after all, weren't we, Charlie?"

I said nothing, just watched as his spirit dissolved. Then I went downstairs and joined Lincoln.

* * *

WE FOUND our guests in a genial mood sitting in the shade of an oak tree on the lawn. Leisl, Lady Vickers and the March-banks sat on dining chairs while the rest lounged on rugs. Even David smiled. Cook commanded the picnic basket while Seth topped up Eva's glass. She watched him through lowered lashes, a secret smile on her lips. Alice watched them both with a small frown. It would seem my friend was jealous of the attention Seth paid Eva. Good. Jealousy meant she cared about him. He would be pleased, and I half suspected he was flirting with Eva for that exact reason. I only hoped she didn't get the wrong end of the stick.

Our arrival was met with warm embraces and congratulatory cheers. Seth placed a glass in my hand and Cook produced dish after dish from the basket. Somehow he'd managed to cook pies, tarts and scones, roast beef and duck, and prepare the most mouth-watering desserts with no staff to help him.

"This is excellent," I told him. "You're a marvel."

He beamed and his entire head flushed red. "Best thing is, there be plenty more to take round to Mrs. Sullivan and her orphans later."

"You do think of everyone." I kissed his cheek and received another blush for my efforts. "Is the dining room damaged?" I asked, looking at the house.

"It wasn't hit but most of the glasses and crystal broke," Seth said as he eyed off a plate of scones. "It's a bit of a mess. We salvaged some chairs and other bits and pieces." He indicated the vases of roses and silver cutlery.

"Poor Lichfield," I said on a sigh. "We only just finished fixing the kitchen after General Eastbrooke's explosion, and now this."

Lincoln laid a hand on mine. "We'll set it to rights quickly. The damage doesn't look too extensive."

"At least the tower is intact," Gus said.

"Now," Lord Marchbank said, "I have to know what you two have been up to."

"Ewan, this is a celebration," his wife scolded.

"It's all right," I said. "I'd rather get it over with now so we can move on to happier things." I looked to Lincoln and he urged me to go on with a nod. "Lady Harcourt and Andrew

Buchanan are dead. He pushed her out a window then he followed her."

I expected a barrage of questions, but not the stunned silence. I gave a brief account of what happened and my conversation with the ghosts afterward.

"I know I ought to feel sympathy for them," Lady Marchbank said, "but I find I don't."

I suspected she was not alone in her feelings.

"I am glad they crossed over," Lady Vickers said. "Imagine how the new tenant would feel having the spirits of Lady Harcourt and Andrew Buchanan haunting the house."

"So that is the end of that," Seth said, leaning back on his hands. He looked to Alice but she didn't notice. Her tired gaze darted around the garden. The army's presence, only a few hours earlier, was evident in the divots made in the lawn from the boots and horses' hooves. She needed a distraction from that nightmare.

"Alice, I need you in the house," I said. "You too, Eva, if you wouldn't mind."

My room was at the opposite end of the house to the damage, fortunately. With Eva and Alice's help, I shucked out of my old dress and put on my wedding gown. "I was determined to wear this thing at some point," I told them with a laugh.

Alice did up the hooks and eyes at the back while Eva brushed out my hair. It was a bit of a mess after all the activity of the morning. It took some time for them both to arrange it with the string of pearls Lady Vickers had left on my bedside table. She also left a scented note saying she hoped I could make use of the loan. I certainly did. The effect was very becoming.

"I feel like a princess," I said, studying my reflection.

"You look lovely," Eva said, stepping back. "What a beautiful bride. Lincoln will be delighted to see you in the dress."

"I suspect Lincoln would rather see her out of it," Alice said with a wicked smile.

A hot flush heated my entire body, and I suddenly didn't know where to look.

"Speaking of which," Alice went on, "we've all made arrangements to stay with Mrs. Sullivan tonight so you'll have Lichfield to yourselves. She has room in that big old house if some of us share a bedroom."

I slipped on my heeled shoes and we headed back outside. Lincoln stood upon seeing me, an odd smile on his lips. It took me a moment to realize it was somewhere between a stunned smile and a happy one. I did a twirl upon Lady Vickers' command then found myself scooped up into Lincoln's arms. He kissed me more thoroughly than was acceptable in front of our guests, but nobody minded.

"Do you like the dress?" I asked.

"I do," he murmured. "But I like what's in the dress more."

I circled my arms around his neck and kissed him again until Lady Vickers declared enough was enough. "There'll be time for all of that later."

"Is the dress easy to get off?" Lincoln whispered in my ear as he set me on my feet.

"It could provide you with a challenge," I said.

"Good." He nuzzled my neck. "I like a challenge."

"I wish we had music for dancing," Lady Vickers said. "Why didn't we organize a quartet?"

"We could sing," Gus said. "I'm a good singer."

Seth snorted. "You sound like a strangled cat."

Gus threw a strawberry at him.

Lincoln suddenly turned in the direction of the front gate. His sister and mother did the same thing. A rider appeared a moment later. I recognized him as one of the Gillinghams' servants. He handed a message to Lincoln then rode off again.

"What does it say?" Lord Marchbank asked.

"It's from Harriet," Lincoln said, lowering the note so I could read it too.

"She's had the baby!" I told them.

"Isn't she only a few months along?" Lady Marchbank asked.

"Ah, I forgot to fill you in on that little piece of news, my dear," her husband said.

"She was near full term when she found out?"

"No, the gestation period of wolves is shorter, apparently."

David pulled a face. "Did she give birth to a wolf?"

"According to this," I said, "the baby looks normal. She and the baby are well but Lord Gillingham fainted."

That produced a round of chuckles.

"The letter also says that she encouraged Gillingham to tell Mr. Salter that he made up the story about werewolves and Gawler's involvement in the murders," Lincoln said. "A retraction will be printed in tomorrow's edition." He folded up the letter. "That should ease the public's fear."

"And be the final nail in the coffin of Mr. Yallop's select committee," Seth added.

"Once the palace exert some pressure in the same direction, I think Mr. Yallop will have no choice but to stop his investigation."

It was an immense relief and meant I could enjoy the rest of the afternoon. The only problem left to tackle now was what to do about the army. I was at a loss for suggestions, but I also didn't want to think too much about it. Not today. Today was for laughter and feasting, and enjoying Lincoln's company, and the heady anticipation of being alone with him tonight.

He excused himself and headed back to the house. I watched him go, admiring the shape of his body as it tapered from broad shoulders to narrow hips, and the way his trousers fit nicely.

Gus came to stretch out alongside me, leaning on his elbow. He nodded in the direction of Eva and Leisl, having a quietly earnest discussion. I wouldn't have thought much of it except they kept glancing in Seth's direction as he lay flat on his back near Alice, his eyes closed.

"They're arguing about him," Gus whispered.

"Why?" I asked.

He shrugged. "Do you see the way Alice is looking at him too?"

I studied Alice, sitting with her feet out to the side, leaning on her hand. She was looking at Seth, perhaps taking advantage of his eyes being closed to study him properly, but her features were unreadable. She looked away when Lady Vickers called her name then joined her with a smile. At least those two were getting along now.

Leisl nudged her daughter but Eva shook her head and spoke crossly. I was extremely curious and was trying to think of a way to get closer without making it too obvious that I was eavesdropping when Lady Marchbank interrupted me.

"Where will you go on your honeymoon, Charlie?" she asked.

"I don't know. I think Lincoln has something planned, but we can't go yet." I didn't dare glance in Alice's direction. "When things settle down."

"You must go," Leisl declared. "Alice has her destiny and it does not involve you or Lincoln."

"Destiny?" Alice echoed. "What do you mean?"

Seth sat up abruptly. "Who else does it involve? Me?"

"Not everything's about you." Gus threw another strawberry at him. Seth caught it and popped it in his mouth.

Leisl waved away their questions and claimed she could

see very little, although I could tell from Eva's face that she didn't believe her mother. Fortunately, further interrogation was headed off by Lady Marchbank.

"What's Lincoln holding?" she asked.

He strode across the lawn toward us carrying a basket considerably smaller than the picnic one.

"Is the cake in there?" I asked Cook.

"No, but thanks for the reminder." He got up and headed toward the house.

Beside me, Gus chuckled. "Is this the thing you were sent to fetch after the ceremony?" I asked him.

He smiled smugly and refused to answer.

Lincoln knelt before me and set the basket down on the rug. "My wedding gift to you, Charlie." He leaned across the basket and planted a light, airy kiss on my lips that promised more later.

"But you've given me so much already," I said. "The wedding dress, jewelry, all of this today and everything to come."

"Those weren't my wedding gift. This is. Open it."

What could he possibly give me that had to arrive in a basket? And why was the basket moving? It yapped.

I lifted the lid and a little brown ball of fur with long floppy ears and a white patch on its chest leapt up. "A puppy! Lincoln, you got me a puppy!" I gathered up the wriggling dog and snuggled him in my arms. I giggled as he licked my hand. "He's adorable."

"You mentioned wanting a dog."

"Oh, Lincoln, he's the sweetest thing. What's his name?"

"He doesn't have one yet."

I set the puppy in my lap but he wanted to explore so I let him go. We had to put away all of the leftover food but he seemed happy enough to wander around sniffing everything and everyone.

"Where did you find him?" I asked.

"An advertisement in the paper. I took a look at the litter last week and picked him out. It was the day I came home smelling like lavender."

"Why lavender?"

"I didn't want to smell like dog or you'd guess, so the owner gave me some lavender water to wash my hands in after handling the puppies. I didn't consider how it would seem to you until later. Then I worried you might think I'd been doing something else."

I smiled. "No, Lincoln. It never entered my head."

He settled behind me and I leaned against him, watching the puppy explore. Lincoln put his arm around me and murmured, "Happy, Mrs. Fitzroy?"

I tilted my head back to peer up at him. "Very. You?"

"Yes." He languidly stroked my chin with his thumb and held my gaze. "I never thought I would be this happy. Never allowed myself to even consider it. Never felt I deserved it," he added in a quieter tone.

I turned in his arms to look at him directly. "You deserve it more than anyone I know, Lincoln. And if anyone says otherwise, they'll have to answer to me."

He smiled as he touched my hair near my ear. "If you believe I'm a good person, Charlie, then I believe it too."

He kissed me, his lips pecking and teasing mine. It wasn't enough. I leaned into him and deepened the kiss, only breaking away when the puppy yapped at us.

A while later, when the sun lost some of its heat, we packed up our picnic and headed inside. The Marchbanks went home, the Cornells too, and Cook, Gus and Alice packed the leftovers, including slices of wedding cake, for Mrs. Sullivan and her orphan charges. Seth and Lincoln had quiet, serious words in the library. The snippets I caught mentioned the army and Wonderland. I didn't want to think about that now.

I went to my room to rest, only to find Lady Vickers there, waiting for me. She patted the bed beside her.

"We need to talk," she said crisply.

I groaned. "No, Lady V, please, spare me. I know you want to discuss marital relations, but I already know how everything works."

Her spine stiffened. "That wasn't what I was going to talk to you about."

"Oh." I sat beside her and she took my hand. "Is it about Seth and Alice?"

"It's about you, my dear." Her eyes filled with tears. "You're the closest thing I have to a daughter and I wanted you to know that I couldn't be prouder of you if you were."

I felt my own eyes well. "Thank you, Lady V, you're a wonderful mother figure. I'm very lucky to have you in my life." I drew her into a hug and kissed her cheek.

She hugged me back then pulled away. "Now," she said, "I've brought up some water and dropped in a few rose petals." She indicated the basin on the washstand. "You must prepare for your husband."

So it would seem we were having that discussion after all. Would it be rude if I ordered her out?

"I hope you're not too tired," she said. "From the way your husband looks at you, I suspect it's going to be a long night."

I was almost too shocked to ask, but I had to know. "How does he look at me?"

"Like a man who has desired you for a year and not acted on it."

I blinked at her. She smiled then signaled for me to turn around so she could undo the dress. "My wedding gift to you both is on your dressing table."

"Oh. Thank you. That's very kind."

The conversation I'd expected to happen never eventuated. Indeed, she departed after helping me out of the dress and I was left to my own devices. I laughed when I unwrapped her gift. For both of us indeed.

By the time I went downstairs, Lincoln was alone in the library, reading, the puppy asleep on the hearth rug. He'd shed his tie and waistcoat and sat in his shirt, the top buttons undone to reveal a spray of dark hair on his chest. I found it difficult to focus my attention anywhere else.

"Have they all gone?" I asked.

"Yes," he said, voice raspy.

"I thought I heard the carriage leave. What are you reading?"

He looked at the book as if surprised to see it in his hand. He shut it and set it down on the table. "I have no idea. I wasn't really reading."

I padded in my bare feet toward him, my hands clasped behind me. His Adam's apple bobbed with his swallow. "What were you doing if not reading?" I asked.

He gripped the chair arms. "Thinking."

"What about?"

"You."

I got within a foot of his outstretched legs and stopped. "What were you thinking about me?"

"That I can't wait to get you out of your wedding dress." His eyes turned smoky as his gaze dipped to my bare thighs. "But I see I'm too late."

I looked down at my new outfit, a short chemise that fell below my rear but not much further. "It's a gift from Lady V. Do you like it?"

A low growl rumbled from his chest. "Remind me to thank her."

I moved my shoulder, dislodging one of the chemise's thin straps. It fell down my arm, revealing the swell of my breast. "Apparently it's for both of us, but I don't think it'll fit you."

He stood slowly and prowled toward me, stopping so close I could almost taste him. "I think it looks better on you anyway."

He cupped my breast through the muslin and stroked his thumb across my nipple. We both moaned. Then he picked me up and carried me upstairs to our bedroom.

THE END

LOOK OUT FOR

The 10th Ministry of Curiosities Novel
by C.J. Archer

Seth, Gus, Alice and Eva have their own adventure in
Wonderland to resolve Alice's problem once and for all. But
with the evil queen intent on capturing her, Alice must rely
on her friends, both new and old, and follow her heart.
Meanwhile, back at Lichfield, see what Charlie and Lincoln
are up to.

Sign up to C.J.'s newsletter via her website
WWW.CJARCHER.COM to be notified when she releases
the next Ministry of Curiosities novel plus get exclusive
access to a Ministry of Curiosities / Freak House
cross-over story.

A MESSAGE FROM THE AUTHOR

I hope you enjoyed reading VOW OF DECEPTION as much as I enjoyed writing it. As an independent author, getting the word out about my book is vital to its success, so if you liked this book please consider telling your friends and writing a review at the store where you purchased it. If you would like to be contacted when I release a new book, subscribe to my newsletter at http://cjarcher.com/contact-cj/newsletter/. You will only be contacted when I have a new book out.

GET A FREE SHORT STORY

I wrote a short story featuring Lincoln Fitzroy that is set before THE LAST NECROMANCER. Titled STRANGE HORIZONS, it reveals how he learned where to look for Charlie during a visit to Paris. While the story can be read as a standalone, it contains spoilers from The 1st Freak House Trilogy, so I advise you to read that series first. The best part is, the short story is FREE, but only to my newsletter subscribers. So subscribe now via my website WWW.CJARCHER.COM if you haven't already.

ALSO BY C.J. ARCHER

ABOUT THE AUTHOR

C.J. Archer has loved history and books for as long as she can remember and feels fortunate that she found a way to combine the two. She spent her early childhood in the dramatic beauty of outback Queensland, Australia, but now lives in suburban Melbourne with her husband, two children and a mischievous black & white cat named Coco.

Subscribe to C.J.'s newsletter through her website to be notified when she releases a new book, as well as get access to exclusive content. She loves to hear from readers. You can contact her in one of these ways:

Website: www.cjarcher.com
Email: cj@cjarcher.com
Facebook: www.facebook.com/CJArcherAuthorPage
Twitter: @cj_archer
Instagram: @authorcjarcher

Printed in Great Britain
by Amazon